Five Tales
of
Tangled Lives
and
Lasting Ties

by S. N. Kashyap

Published by: Kashyap Creative LLC
ISBN: 978-1-967629-00-8

*This is a work of fiction.*
*Names, characters, places, and incidents are either the product of the author's imagination or used fictitiously. Any resemblance to actual persons, living or dead, events, or locales is purely coincidental.*

*To Amma and Appa,*
*who indulged every book*
*and gifted the freedom*
*to explore its world*
*to my heart's content.*

# Contents

# Czech, Please

## 70% and Falling

Drunk to the gills and merry without occasion, we entered the tented enclave in Letná Park. A generous tapas buffet awaited, presenting the unrefined palate with a dilemma of choices.

I gathered a delegation of the least threatening items on a plate, deliberately avoiding anything that returned my stare, and slid over to the beverage station.

Rooting around the oversized ice cooler, I unearthed Pilsners galore but none of the dark Czechvar lager I'd relished earlier. I chose a bottle of lime-flavored seltzer, consoling myself that I'd been looking for a mindful, healthy option all along.

The Brazilian "cohort" (the program's term for each academically knit group) was already there, bunched together, a sea of light skin and dark hair.

Male, with two stunning exceptions.

A blonde and her.

"*Desi?*" I whispered to Venky, who discreetly followed my gaze. He turned to me with a subtle nod.

"Go say hello," he urged.

I hesitated, giving my engineering brain an extra second to complete its analysis and present its findings.

*The skin color … seems off.*

*Desis* come in all complexions, but there are shades of brown that are immediately identifiable as non-*Desi*. Hers was chestnut with an olive sheen. She wore a black knee-length skirt and a white blouse—formal yet predictable. The blonde was in a loudly patterned dress—summery, quirky, and equally elegant.

*One appears to have stepped out of a LinkedIn profile, and the other from a French art film shoot.*

The women appeared to be friends, conversing animatedly. But they seemed alone, even among their fellow students.

*Brazilian bro culture … worse than American …,* I silently tut-tutted. As a fellow *Desi*, I empathized with her. *Been there, experienced that.*

"Go on," Venky smiled. "Hugh and I are right behind you."

I knew that if I didn't act, Venky would be launching into a sermon about "stepping out of my comfort zone."

*Uh.*

I hesitated, contemplating the ground, willing an escape hatch to appear.

*… maybe if I waited long enough.*

I sensed Venky shifting.

*Alright, alright. Here goes.*

I sighed in resignation, double-checked the level of my social battery (hovering around 70% but steadily depleting), and led the way.

"Hi, I am Srini." I extended my hand. Her sharp facial features seemed like they had been sketched in charcoal. A small wave of brown light rippled across her long, shiny black hair. I could not help but notice that the skin on her face, arms, and legs was flawless and glowing.

I wondered how much her skincare routine set her back each month.

"Meera," she shook my hand and broke the grip immediately. As if she had gripped a wet sock.

*Ugh ... palm must have been damp from holding the drink.*
*Or from the sheer terror of approaching strangers.*

Our eyes met.

Hers were hazel and brown, with a hint of wariness.

*Great—she thinks I am trying to hit on her.*

I turned to the blonde, subtly wiping my hand on the side of my jeans.

"Srini."

"Hi, I'm Paulina!" I detected a European accent. She gave my hand a firm shake and a radiant smile. Her dress's yellow and blue hues set off her hair and eyes.

*I like her. No judgment. No preconceived notions.*

"Very nice to meet you, Paulina."


The University of Pittsburgh's Executive MBA program included three week-long Leadership Summits where Prague, Sao Paulo, and Pittsburgh would take turns hosting students from the other cohorts. This was the first.

Hugh, the Czech ambassador assigned to the Americans, had led us on a picturesque city tour the previous hour. Of English and Czech heritage, he was raised in London and lived and worked in Prague.

For the past two hours, conversation and Czechvar had flowed freely inside the bus, which stopped at every landmark worth seeing or exploring on foot.


I introduced Hugh and Venky, heralding an exchange of handshakes and pleasantries.

"Ladies, Hugh suggests dinner at a rooftop restaurant. You are welcome to join us," Venky said, giving me an encouraging look.

"We're meeting in the lobby at 6:30 p.m. and walking over," I added meekly.

Meera looked at me and glanced uncertainly at the huddle of Brazilians conversing boisterously in Portuguese. One or two glanced in our direction, smiling.

"Everyone is welcome. There should be enough seating available," Hugh interjected helpfully, his British accent accentuating his charm.

"We would love to," Paulina smiled, pearly whites and blue eyes shining.

"Great, we'll see you later," Hugh smiled back.

I glanced at Meera. Her face was set, carefully devoid of expression.

# Rooftop Restaurant

Within the first hour of the mixer, I was swept into the "speed-dating" event (as the program staff referred to it) involving most of the Prague and São Paulo students. Among other things, I learned that Paulina was single and worked as a German expatriate in São Paulo. Meera did not divulge personal details, at least not to me.

A strange mood appeared to envelop the gathering—an alchemy of nostalgia, midlife crises, and alcohol. Most of us in our mid-40s carried mental burdens in the form of professional and personal responsibilities, instilling a defensive mindset of risk avoidance. The Prague Leadership Summit offered a sanctioned route to a bygone era of fraternity and frivolity.

And everyone seemed determined to make the most of it.

The mixer ended.
Venky took a cab to the airport to receive his wife, Alexa.
The Czechs left for their local domiciles.

In motley, multinational masses, the rest of us staggered our heady way over yards of cobblestones to the Hilton Prague Old Town.

I hurried to my room and lay prone on the bed, hoping to catch a quick nap.

Sleep escaped me, however.

My mind kept returning to Meera.

I was no stranger to women's aloofness, which was standard protocol with me, but hers stuck.

*Like the first time I'd met Karina.*

*Deja vu.*

I forced myself off the sheets to answer the light tapping at the door.

It was Venky and Alexa.

Alexa flung her arms out and gave me a tight hug. She and Venky had developed a deep loyalty and affection for me for unfathomable reasons—a fiercely mutual feeling.

"I've missed you, buddy! How've you been?" Alexa's riot of red curls twinkled in concert with her light-brown eyes. "And how're the kids?"

"All well, Alexa. They are at Karina's. Hope you had a comfortable journey … and … welcome to Prague!" I replied, groggy but pleased. Alexa could put a smile on anyone's face, especially mine.

"Want to go hang out at the bar?"

"Yeah, dude … I am way wired."

The Hilton lobby oozed timeless elegance, with the neutral wall color accentuating the rich burgundy and gold furnishings.

I signed the check, grabbed two bottles of Czechvar, gingerly picked up a glass of red wine from the counter with my other hand, and headed to the cozy lounge where Alexa and Venky were sprawled on plush chairs.

"Nusdravi," Alexa said, holding the glass aloft.

"Nusdravi," I handed Venky a bottle and raised mine.

"Nusdravi," Venky echoed.

We clinked drinks.

"Someone's checking us out," Alexa leaned forward, whispering conspiratorially.

I slowly followed the barely perceptible flick of her glance to the far side of the lobby. Meera and Paulina were gazing in our direction. Meera looked away immediately. Paulina waved, smiling radiantly.

"Come make new friends, Alexa," I drained my beer.

Introductions were dispensed with. Alexa made small talk, trading compliments about dresses. Venky nudged me, discreetly tapping a finger on his watch. It was now close to 6:30 pm, and the American contingent was starting to emerge from the twin elevators and congregate at the front door.

"Coming?" I asked Paulina.

*She is easier to talk to, anyway.*

"Oh," Paulina began uncertainly. "Meera and I are waiting for our group. We have a lax attitude about time back home in Brazil." She laughed apologetically, her Deutsch punctuality discipline seemingly at odds with her loyalty to her adopted country of residence and employment.

Meera nodded and flashed a tentative smile at me.

The hint of friendliness momentarily left me nonplussed.

I smiled back.

Alexa's heart-shaped face was in my peripheral vision, dimples deepened in amusement.

"Oh, no worries," Venky interjected smoothly, "We will save you a couple of tables … take your time."

Perched atop a historic building, the Astrum Terrace sported a gorgeous rooftop ambiance. Open-air seating surrounded by glass railings provided an unobstructed view of Prague's architecture. As dusk faded into night, the setting was illuminated by the soft glow of string lights overhead and twinkling city lights below.

I sat across from Alexa and Venky, conversing in a low voice.

"So," Alexa looked up, her eyes telegraphing mischief. "You kind of malfunctioned back there—when Meera smiled at you."

"Brain reboots occasionally due to lack of sleep," I laughed lightly.

"Cute, though," Alexa teased. "And I have to say—you both make quite the striking couple."

"Eh?" I gaped awkwardly.

"Visually, you know?" Alexa added soothingly.

"Uh … ok," I laughed sheepishly.

"She looks fantastic. Especially in red … I can never pull that off," Alexa sighed. She cast her eyes around. "Everyone looks great—you're a good-looking bunch."

"We aim to please," Venky bowed smilingly.

Scott joined our table—straight-laced, with short-cropped hair, a square chin, and a gruff voice that befitted his military background.

"Ugh, Corporate Finance midterm grades are out," he grunted.

"Yeah," I smiled.

"Dang Professor Saltzman. Couldn't he have waited a few more days? You crack it?"

"Nah, that would be Venky. Dude got a perfect."

"What? How?" Alexa exclaimed, the surprise in her voice evident.

"My wife, everyone …," Venky said in mock exasperation. "Oh, ye of little faith …"

"Sorry, babe, but come on, everyone knows Srini is at the top of your class."

Alexa's foot nudged mine under the table. I looked up and caught a flash of red on the right. I turned my head towards the stairwell, which was disgorging the Brazilians, led by

Meera and Paulina. They made their way to the two remaining empty tables. I tried not to glance at them during dinner, which went by swiftly, especially after Hugh joined us.

I stood up, raising my drink. I was feeling heady. And happy.

"To Alexa and Venky, my friends for life. Happy Anniversary, lovebirds!"

There was a chorus of greetings. A toast was raised around our table.

Hugh's drunken baritone started to render the Beatles' "When I'm Sixty-Four."

The mood was infectious.

Most gathered around the abashed couple and joined in the chorus.


"Let's get a group pic," Alexa suggested.

"On it," Hugh stepped to the front.

The rest of us huddled behind the celebrated couple.

I found myself flanked by Paulina and Meera.

"Ready?" Hugh raised his phone.

I instinctively extended my arms towards the small of their backs.

Paulina threw her arm around my shoulder.

Meera flinched as if I'd offered a live tarantula for inspection.

Mortified, I pulled my hands in.

"Sorry," I silently mouthed, catching her eye.

She did not react, her expression guarded.

"Cheese!" Hugh demanded our attention and gaze.


"Dude, what was that?" Alexa laughed, squinting at the photo on Hugh's phone after we returned to the table.

I peered over her shoulder.

Meera was frozen mid-recoil, leaning away from me.

Alexa sniffed. "You smell fine—was it something you said?"

I explained. "... I didn't even touch her."

"Don't worry," Alexa consoled. "She just needs to get to know you."

"Plenty of opportunities this week," Venky added sagely.

We bid goodbye to Hugh.

Tribal lines were established once more.

We regrouped and left for our hotel with our respective cohorts.

# Day 1 of Class

I slept in fits and starts. My mind appeared bent on not letting my biological clock reset.

I was glad to have breakfast with an equally bleary-eyed Venky in companionable silence and trudge to class in the hotel's Emerald conference room.

"Welcome to Business Negotiations," intoned Professor Whitman as I took large sips of black coffee to chase down the painful doses of information he was dispensing.

The lecture mercifully concluded with a fictional case study involving a mid-sized "boutique" consulting firm negotiating the terms of its acquisition by a large multinational corporation.

We were divided into nine groups for a class exercise, with three from each cohort. We gathered to review the case study details and strategize on negotiating positions. Our group represented the acquirer's executive team, while an opposing group represented the acquiree's.

Venky looked at the financials and scoffed, "This is a no-brainer." He had uncovered a critical flaw in the cash-flow numbers that favored us.

We strutted to the table where the other team waited to begin negotiations. Holding the case description handout open to the financial page, Paulina looked at us quizzically.

The rest of her team, including Meera, shook heads and shrugged shoulders to various degrees.

"You guys notice?" Venky asked.

"Yeah," Paulina nodded, waving the papers in her hand resignedly.

"And?"

"You win."

Meera caught my eye and gave a wry smile that was half amused and exasperated. I wasn't entirely sure if I was an accomplice or a bystander who had wandered into her field of vision.

The afternoon session of the class was sparsely attended— only a handful were present from the Brazilian and Czech cohorts. The EMBA staff was making a spectacle of meticulously recording attendance, and the word was that missing classes got you a bad grade. None of us were in the program for academic honors, but most of our American employers pegged our tuition reimbursement to our grades.

The professor mercifully dimmed the lights and showed a video of a complex business negotiation, occasionally pausing to highlight a point or two.

*Now, this stuff does not suck at all.*

I was paying rapt attention, taking notes.

The class concluded with the professor bidding us a good evening and reminding us that we had a written paper due at the end of the next day.

As Venky and I were gathering our stuff, Meera walked in. She looked around and came up to us.

"Hey," she tentatively addressed Venky.

"Hey," Venky responded.

"I went to check on Paulina and missed the afternoon class."

"Oh … everything ok?"

"She will be fine … just jetlagged."

"Ok."

"What did I miss?"

"He showed us a video, kept a running commentary, and assigned us homework."

"Oh? Can you share your notes with me?"

"Ask Srini," Venky laughed. "He is the note-taker. I try to keep it all in my head, but nothing went in today."

Meera turned to me, deliberately making eye contact and arching an eyebrow.

A smile played on her lips.

*Here we go again.*

*An attractive woman, willing class notes off me.*

*A time-honored tradition dating back to engineering grad school days.*

*Most memorably, Karina in Calc 780.*

*Then again, that's how she began talking to me.*

"Sure," I shrugged, opening my laptop and punching some keys. "It should be in the printer in the lobby."

"Thanks, Srini," she squeezed my arm and hurried away.

Her pronunciation of the sibilance in my name was perfect.

*Mysterious.*

I gave Venky a small smile.

"Sucker," he said.

We both laughed.


Venky and I left the classroom and entered the lobby. Hugh was seated by a window and waved us over.

"Not me, buddy. I'm going to my room for a nap." Venky waved back and headed to the elevators.

Before I reached Hugh, Meera emerged from the hotel's business center carrying a sheaf of papers. A broad smile lit up her face.

"Srini, I truly appreciate you giving me your notes," she began, her voice echoing with gratitude. "They are so detailed and organized that I can easily catch up and complete the assignment."

"Oh, you're very welcome."
"Do you mind if I share these with Paulina?"
"Not at all."

I joined Hugh with a bounce in my step, oddly pleased that my interaction with Meera had involved exchanging words rather than deciphering body language and inscrutable expressions.

# Club Roxy

"Got your dancing shoes on?" Alexa asked, eyes sparkling in anticipation.
"All of mine are," I joked, "and mostly left-footed."
"You know that's not true!"

On many Fridays, Alexa and Venky had taken me out after a full day of classes. Although the venues varied, the routine was always the same: drinks, dinner, and dancing.

Together, Alexa and Venky embodied poetry on the floor. They found their mutual passion in a Social Dancing class in college. Over the years, they had honed their skills by training and competing in semi-professional circuits in Pittsburgh. With their chemistry and impeccable sense of rhythm, they were at ease with any groove a DJ would likely spin on a given evening.

Alexa and Venky always encouraged me to join them and gave me more than a few pointers. Although I was not in their league, I could now hold my own.

Scott met us in the lobby. "We leaving or what?"
"Waiting for someone," Alexa turned to him with a wink.
"Oh, stop it," I groaned.
"They'll catch up—let's head out," Venky urged.
We stepped outside and hailed a couple of cabs, which deposited us outside the garishly lit entrance of Club Roxy.

Alexa walked in unchallenged while the rest of us were halted by a stubborn bouncer who pressed us for a cover charge as it was "ladies' night." We fumbled around, but none of us had the local currency. Finally, Scott forked over a couple of twenty-dollar bills, which seemed to do the trick.

The multi-colored dance floor was a sea of exuberant bodies swaying to a vibrant beat. The neon-bathed bar area at one end was abuzz with activity, the two bartenders busily mixing cocktails and raking in tips. The elevated DJ booth at the other end was dominated by giant, visibly pulsating sound speakers.

Alexa left her purse with Venky and immediately rushed to the floor. Scott snagged us a high-top while I went to get drinks for everyone.

The Mojito, the daily special, was exceptionally mixed. The sugar, alcohol, and ambiance created a heady mixture.

Occasionally, Alexa emerged to sip her drink. Although her forehead had a faint sheen of sweat, her radiant smile and glowing face signaled her upbeat mood, which was infectious.

Despite my jet-lagged insomnia, I felt oddly energized.

The DJ put on a slow number.

"That's me," Venky said, vanishing into the sea of humanity.

"One more?" I asked, nodding at Scott's empty glass.

"Sure, man," he replied.

I had just ordered our drinks when I felt a tap on my shoulder.

I turned.

It was Paulina.

Meera was standing behind her.

I was inexplicably glad to see them.

"Hey, you made it!" It was a lame thing to say, but the ladies did not seem to care, as their shining eyes and eager nods indicated.

"So, Srini. You are married?" Paulina asked.

We were huddled around our table, sipping drinks.

"Haven't been for years," I shook my head.

"Oh," she frowned. "But you wear a ring?"

"Out of habit," I said, subconsciously spinning the golden band around my finger.

Meera, who was chatting with Scott, glanced in our direction.

Paulina and I chatted about our families—mine in the USA and India, and hers in Germany. Although she had been with someone for about a decade, she had never married. The relationship did not survive her move to Brazil—she was being fast-tracked as a Marketing Executive for a global retail company.

"I am sorry to hear that," I commiserated.

"Oh, it is in the past," she shrugged laconically. "So, I am trying to date now. I do not seem to be very good at it."

"There is someone for everyone … you will find yours, I'm sure."

"What about you?"

"Karina was my first … and only love," I smiled. "Life sort of steamrolled our romance … and our marriage."

"Aww."

"No regrets now," I shrugged. "We are on good terms."

I noticed Meera looking intently at me.

As if she'd been following the dialogue.


"Dude, why aren't you dancing?" Alexa grabbed my arm from behind, pulling me towards the dance floor. "Oh, hi Paulina! Hi Meera!"

"Hi!"

"Come on, all of you … the DJ is insane!"

"Shots first. I just ordered a round," Venky said.

A waiter appeared with shot glasses and a bottle of liqueur.

"Oof … what the heck is this? Tastes like medicine!" Alexa complained.

"A Czech specialty, Becherovka."

"Ok, ok, let's go! Scott, come on—you must join us this time," Alexa urged.

The next hour was a blur of movement and fun.

"You can dance!" Paulina exclaimed.

I shrugged. "If you can call this dancing ... but no one knows me here, and I'm not hurting myself."

Meera joined her in laughter, and I felt strangely triumphant, as if I'd cracked a cryptic crossword clue.

"I think we're all going to get along well, Srini."

I was charmed by Paulina's disarming words.

"I feel the same way, Paulina."

I smiled at Meera, and she returned it.

*Huh.*

*Guess I've been upgraded from "anonymous" to "tolerable."*

# Day 2 of Class

Professor Whitman kicked off our second team exercise in negotiation—an American multinational suing a Chinese company for stealing their design of an airport inter-terminal people-mover. The Chinese side maintained that the timeline was too short for plagiarism, while the plaintiff argued that the prowess of Chinese manufacturing made IP theft entirely probable.

Once again, we were organized into teams. This time, Meera and I were on the same one.

As our team lead, we nominated Jack, a seasoned executive with experience outsourcing manufacturing to China. At a complete loss, the opposing team left their fate in the hands of Sam, a corporate lawyer who relished a good debate. Jack furiously lobbied facts and figures at Sam, who doggedly countered that businesses always learned from competitors, and the current matter was one of negligent imitation, not criminal plagiarism.

An hour crawled by.

Professor Whitman was making rounds and came to "observe" our teams. On cue, we all made vague comments to convince him of our academic diligence.

Another excruciating hour passed. By now, our exercise had devolved into an exchange of opinions between Jack and Sam.

Meera sidled up beside me.

"*Aiyyo!*" The cry of lament, so widely used among Tamilians, and although now in the Oxford English Dictionary, was utterly incongruous in the current setting.

I turned sharply, nearly giving myself whiplash.

"Careful," Meera said, extending a hand and stopping my swinging elbow.

"S-sorry," I stuttered, then recovered.

"*Shemma kadi,*" she said, eyebrows raised, eyes widened. She shook her head imperceptibly.

Her feelings about the onerous session mirrored mine. "Indeed," I agreed.

Finally, it was time to break for lunch.

Professor Whitman appreciated everyone's effort. However, since none of the teams was close to concluding the exercise, he canceled the afternoon lecture. We had until the next day to complete negotiations and submit a one-page summary of the settlement points.

Meera and I found a place to sit down with our plates.

I was utterly befuddled.

"How do you know Chennai Tamil?" I finally blurted out.

"Grew up there," she said matter-of-factly.

"For real?"

"My dad was a Catholic missionary. He worked with the Santhome Church. We moved when he was posted to Brazil. Now he works for the big guy."

"Who?"

"The Pope. At the Vatican."

"And mom?"

"*Amma* stayed back in Brazil for my sake. She didn't want to uproot me again. She jokes that she will always love one and only one Italian, not the entire nation."

Comprehension dawned on me.

*That explains her eyes and complexion.*

She seemed to read my mind and laughed.

"I have to give you credit, Srini. Usually, *Desis* are more curious about my background," she added playfully. "It's rare to meet one who respects personal boundaries."

I winced inwardly, recalling my foible at the rooftop restaurant.

As I groped for the appropriate response, she mercifully continued, "My mom is Telugu but was born and raised in Chennai. In college, she fell hard for this holy man who showed up on campus for a debate on Theology she had organized."

"Quite a story," I marveled.

"Yeah, it was quite the scandal within her family, which is very conservative."

"So … do you speak Telugu at all?"

"Yeah, I was with my mother's parents in Chennai until about six. My dad's work took him around the globe, and my mom decided I needed a stable home. My grandparents insisted that I speak to them only in Telugu."

"So … Telugu at home, Tamil outside. My situation was the inverse of yours," I laughed. "I grew up in Hyderabad."

"*Avunaa?*"

"*Avunu.*"


We resumed our academic exercise during the afternoon session.

Professor Whitman was nowhere to be seen. Word spread that he was napping in his room, and the other teams quickly concluded their negotiations.

But Jack and Sam were getting warmed up for the second act.

Not wanting to abandon our team leads, the rest of us stayed put.

But we altered our seating arrangement. While Jack and Sam sat across from each other deep in debate, the team members intermingled and started sidebar conversations in smaller groups of twos and threes.

Meera and I chatted about our childhood in India, switching between Tamil and Telugu at will.

The following two hours went by … fast.


# Bombay Bar


Jack sent a group email with bullet points summarizing the negotiations. Our team gathered around him at the hotel bar to express appreciation by buying him drinks.

As a team, we decided to have a contest to determine who would convert Jack's notes into a two-page summary.

A hilarious elimination game of rock-paper-scissors ensued, and everyone tried their best to lose.

I "won."


Paulina approached us from the other end of the bar, drink in hand.

"My third," she sighed. "What a day."

"Brutal."

"I am so done with this course. It gets over tomorrow morning, right?"

"Yeah, just the final exam left."

"What?"

Meera kept a straight face, while Paulina's was a carousel of alternating expressions—shock, dismay, and apprehension.

Finally, I had to laugh.

"That … was bad," she punched me lightly on my shoulder, otherwise looking immensely relieved.

"Sorry. Now you are ready for the real bad news. We start the Innovation course in the afternoon, and there is a reading assignment on Design Thinking. Rumor is there will be a pop quiz."

"Oh, I am familiar with the topic. The quiz does not worry me," Paulina waved airily, then made a face. "Hopefully, the class is not as painful."

"I heard it is quite fun."

"Geek," Paulina teased.

"As charged," I laughed, half-raising my hands in mock surrender.

"A cool geek," Meera smiled.

"I'll take that," I raised my drink.

*Cool geek, huh?*

*Against all odds, and perhaps against her better judgment, is Meera starting to warm up to me?*

*Or is this a long con to keep my meticulously detailed notes flowing?*

"Any plans tonight?" Paulina asked.

"Nope. Alexa's flight home is this evening, and Venky is dropping her at the airport. Thought I'd hang around with Scott here, then catch up on sleep."

"That sounds lame. My team talked about this place called The Bombay Bar. Come hang out. Bring Scott," Paulina said.

"Oh?" I was intrigued by the name.

"Yeah, a restaurant on the lower level, but the main level is supposed to be very cozy. Not like that Roxy place. Good for sitting down for conversations, but also has a dance floor for you to show off on."

I laughed. "It does sound pleasant."

"Join us. We plan to get there by 7."

"Which means 8," Meera added with a smile.

"Okay," I conceded, surprised by a surge of anticipation.

*Sleep-deprived, emotionally stunted, and yet willingly agreeing to a social plan instead of feigning an ailment?*

*Something's definitely wrong with me.*

I went to the lobby to meet Alexa and Venky for dinner and bid her a safe journey.

The concierge gave me directions to The Bombay Bar. The walking route was complicated, but he also gave me a mnemonic to remember each turn.

Scott was in the lobby at precisely 7:15 p.m.

The Autumn evening air was crisp and redolent with the smell of roasted chestnuts hawked by street vendors.

Every dining establishment was bursting with patrons.

We arrived at the Bombay Bar around 7:45 p.m. The venue, hidden from the main road, exuded an inviting, homey feel. On the left, we passed a modest-sized hall and made our way to the back room, which had a few scattered wooden tables and chairs. None were occupied.

"Cozy indeed," Scott remarked drily.

"Beer?" I asked, heading to the bar in the rear left corner.

Scott gave a thumbs-up.

By the time I drained my second drink, Scott was halfway through his fourth. He became increasingly loquacious about his Navy days, returning from service, marrying his high school sweetheart, and single-handedly raising his two boys as a widower.

I took a long sip, feeling a surge of gratitude for Karina's presence in my life.

*Even after remarrying, she remains my best friend.*
*A wonderful co-parent.*
*And my life coach.*

Scott went to order a round of shots while I indulged in people-watching.

Unlike at the Roxy, the DJ played a mellow mix of R&B, Motown, and Rock—the Classics—my kind of music.

My gaze was dragged to the front door, which opened, ushering in a gust of breeze along with Paulina and Meera. I stood up and waved, catching Paulina's eye. She nodded and whispered in Meera's ear.

They both turned towards me, their radiant smiles cutting through the lively ambiance.

Paulina wore a short, silver dress that sparkled under the coruscating lights. A stylish belt hugged her waist. Meera wore a demure black and blue dress.

The front door swung inward again, and people from all three cohorts, including Venky, started tumbling in.

Clearly, the group exercises in class had succeeded in fostering new friendships.

Paulina pointed at me, and they all made their way to the back room.

Soon, every sitting area and standing room was occupied. Shots after shots were ordered and consumed. The regular patrons, perhaps sensing our mutual camaraderie or likely put off by our rising raucousness, slowly vacated the premises. But our dollars seemed more than welcome, with the bartenders and the DJ turning their full attention to us and exhorting us to raise a glass … and shake a leg.

Venky seemed distracted by a text about Alexa's flight, which had been delayed.

"She has a tight connection in Frankfurt," he explained. "I'm heading back to the hotel—I may have to book her a different flight if she misses hers."

"Need help?"

"Nah … you guys stay and enjoy your time. I'll be back."

"Yup … keep me posted."

Venky left.

"Your friend ditched you?" Meera slid into the chair Venky had just vacated.

"Ha, ha … only temporarily, I assure you. At least, I hope so," I laughed. "Brazilians doing ok?"

"Planning to go barhopping. Want to join in?"

"Nah, Venky might be back," I said. "But thanks for asking."

"Honestly, Paulina and I would like to hang out here. We really like this place."

"Your company will be very welcome," Scott said, sounding slightly slurred.

"There she is," Meera waved, catching Paulina's eye as she emerged from the restroom across from the bar.

Paulina weaved her way to our table.

"What are we doing?" she asked Meera.

"Hang out with Srini and Scott?"

"Sure," Paulina exclaimed, "they are playing my favorite songs. I want to dance some more."

"Go on then. Both of you," I urged, extending my hand. "Your handbags are safe with me."

"Thanks, Srini. We did not think this through," Paulina giggled.

"I was hoping you'd join us," Meera turned to me with a mock pout.

"Then you don't know me at all," I smiled. "Take Scott. The man is primed."

"Scott?" Paulina raised her eyebrows.

"Your wish is my command," Scott announced gallantly. He downed his shot of Becherovka, and they left.

After about half an hour, Paulina and Meera emerged from the crowd and made a beeline for me.

"Srini, Paulina wants to return to the hotel. Can you walk us back, if you don't mind?" Meera asked. Paulina was behind her, swaying slightly on her feet and breathing heavily. Her eyes were heavy-lidded.

"What happened?" I was concerned.

"She is not sober, and I cannot follow what she is saying. But something seems to have upset her," Meera replied.

"Okay," I said, getting up and giving the place a quick scan to make sure Scott was in safe hands.

We let ourselves out through the side door.

I had no trouble recalling the cues I had memorized. Meera and I took turns holding Paulina's arm and steering her.

The cool evening air cleared Paulina's head, and we rapidly reached our hotel.

"Thank you, Srini. You are a gentleman," Meera said as the elevator doors closed and bore its occupants upward.

## Day 3 of Class

The first half of Day 3 was sparsely attended. Most teams had submitted their final reports and taken the morning off. Many had succumbed to the revelries of the previous evening, if not the jet lag.

The professor was nowhere to be seen.

Still, the EMBA admins busily marked attendance … or the lack thereof.

I opened my laptop and started on the final report. Jack's notes were so thorough that I only had to alter the prose.

I finished the first draft and decided to take a bio-break.

I ran into Meera.

"Morning," I greeted.

"Morning, sorry I am late," she apologized.

"No worries. Hardly anyone in class. I am working on our report."

"I wanted to help and would have come earlier, but …," she hesitated.

"Paulina?" I asked, somewhat unnecessarily.

"Well, yes … and no."

"Huh?"

She hesitated for a moment. "Hey, what is with your friend Scott?" she blurted, somewhat belligerently.

"Wha—what?"

"He was dancing with Paulina last night and doing something weird," Meera said.

*Scott? The man could not offend anyone, even if he wanted to.*

I must have looked mortified as she hesitated.

"Paulina says he hooked his thumbs over her belt on either side of her waist," her tone was edged with discomfort.

"… and pulled her close, holding her tight … um … and … forcing their hips together."

"Wait, what?" I blinked, at a loss for words.

"She admits it might have been accidental—like maybe he … or she … or both lost balance," Meera added quickly, her brows knit with concern. "But it was awkward, and long enough, she felt uncomfortable."

"Wow …," I exhaled slowly, unsure how to respond. "That's definitely … not great."

Meera nodded sharply. "Yeah. She doesn't want to make a big deal out of it, but she's not sure what to think … or do."

I rubbed my chin.

"Scott—well, he's probably never danced with anyone except his late wife. I'm sure it wasn't on purpose."

"Maybe," Meera admitted, though her expression remained skeptical. "But still, Srini, he should've been more aware."

"You're right," I agreed firmly. "I'll talk to Scott. He should know how he came across. And please tell Paulina that I'll vouch for him. I don't think he meant to cross a line."

"I will," she promised. Her tension seemed to ease, and she smiled tentatively. "Now, let's take care of that report."

The mood lightened somewhat over the following hour, during which we edited the report and reminisced about other scenes from Bombay Bar.

Finally, the document was emailed to the professor, and the Negotiations class was done.

Our conversations continued over lunch.

Without the long lines, we quickly grabbed our Italian fare.

We had just finished our meal when familiar faces appeared at the venue.

Meera excused herself to talk to Paulina.

Scott and Venky joined me, and I filled them in on what I had learned from Meera.

Looking equally horrified and contrite, Scott immediately hastened toward Paulina. They must have worked it out, as I soon saw them laughing.

A few minutes later, Scott, Meera, and Paulina walked over.

Scott took our teasing in stride. "Alright, alright, I admit it. I was awkward out there," he chuckled, rubbing the back of his neck. "But hey, I don't get out much."

Venky clapped him on the back. "Just maybe keep your hands to yourself next time."

Scott grinned sheepishly. "Lesson learned. Never dancing again without adult supervision."

"You sound like Srini," Venky laughed. "Alexa and I have to drag him onto the floor each time."

"My self-appointed dance coaches," I said.

"More—we're his social coaches," Venky clarified. "Commissioned by his ex-wife and best friend, Karina."

"A sort of pet project?" Paulina teased.

"A pity project," I smiled.

"Like a reality show where they transform a socially inept man before time runs out?" Meera joined in. She was clearly enjoying the back-and-forth.

"Except there's no prize money," Venky snorted. "But, got to give him credit. Dude's come a long way in the past few months. Now he makes eye contact with humans just as well as with books."

Venky's good-natured ribbing drew chuckles all around, though mine masked deeper feelings.

*Karina had always been the one woman with whom I could be myself. I'd missed that ease.*

*Even with Alexa, it took several months.*

*And now ... within days ... it feels like I'm experiencing it again. Especially with Meera.*

*Unsettling.*

"Wait, can we go back to Scott?" I pushed my thoughts aside and sighed dramatically. "When did I become the punchline?"

The table erupted in laughter.

I wondered if I imagined the hint of affection in Meera's.

# Double Trouble

The second half of Day 3 of class was off to a riveting start. We began the course on Design Thinking, and the charismatic professor's lecture on innovation, liberally sprinkled with case studies, was utterly captivating.

"I know you are exhausted, Srini, but you must check out Double Trouble on a Thursday evening," Hugh urged after the day's lessons concluded.

I had decided to take a nap, but Hugh was insistent.

"Plus, there may be a midget show," he added.

"What?" I was not sure I had heard him right. Hugh's straight face was as British as his accent.

"He's kidding. Apparently, it was a thing until a few years ago, but no longer," Venky laughed.

"Dancing on tables is still permitted, though you can find a quiet place to relax and watch the rituals," Hugh grinned. "Everyone is going," he added as if it were an academic footnote.

"Including someone in particular?" A knowing smile played on Venky's lips.

Hugh gave an exaggerated shrug and a grin. "Maybe."

"Wait, what am I missing?" As usual, I need to be clued into the social goings-on.

"Hugh needs wingmen," Venky replied mysteriously. "Come on, Srini, you don't want to miss out. And you can always catch up on sleep later, right?"

"Your Bohemian attitude towards sleep will ruin your health, man," I laughed.

I gave in—Venky had never steered me wrong.

I was also somewhat curious about what the boys were cooking.

As soon as we walked in, the smell of weed hit us, followed by the noise of patrons urging each other to climb on top of sturdy wooden tables. Those who made the ascent were generously rewarded with shots of Becherovka.

Paulina and Meera were enthusiastic participants and instant hits with the crowd.

Hugh secured a booth in the back, where it was relatively quiet.

"This place claims to serve the strongest beer in the world? Gotta have that," Scott cocked an eyebrow.

"What's Hugh's big mystery?" I asked Venky after we placed our orders.

"Let's just say he is interested in the company we keep," he replied. Seeing my puzzled expression, he added, "Follow the man's glazed eyes."

"Like a love-sick puppy," Scott grinned.

"Oh, shush," Hugh smiled, his gaze fixed on Paulina, who, along with a few Brazilians, had started an impromptu samba class.

Before long, Hugh joined his fellow Czechs to encourage local patrons to hit the dance floor and take photos.

We watched the happenings from the sidelines, occasionally chuckling at the antics.

The strongest beer in the world arrived in a golden goblet. Thick and dark brown, it tasted like sweet table wine with a hint of hops. I did not like it much, but its high alcohol content was undeniable. I hadn't eaten, and it went straight to my head.

I was feeling heady, and the second-hand-smoke-laden atmosphere was not helping.

Venky and I decided to step out.

"How're you holding up?" Venky asked, lighting a cigarette. His voice had traces of concern and curiosity.

"Not sure if it is the drink or the air, but I seem to have brain fog." I took a couple of drags from him.

"You and Meera seem to be getting along."

"Huh? Yeah. As friends," I said, maybe somewhat defensively. "You know I appreciate you and Alexa's ongoing mission to fix me up with someone, but as I've assured you—repeatedly—I'm not looking."

"Okay, okay," he nodded reassuringly, holding his hands up in mock surrender. "It's just that you seem to light up whenever she comes around."

I opened my mouth to argue, but at that moment, Hugh emerged and walked over. He produced a joint and started smoking.

"Want a hit?" he asked.

*What the heck, a couple of puffs won't matter.*

*They did.*

My mind started snapping back and forth, from place to place, from past to present. I would vividly converse on a specific topic with Hugh and Venky, and then my head would be flooded with memories from recent and distant pasts.

*Interesting.*

Curiously, I was also overwhelmed with deep affection for the new acquaintances I had made over the week.

"I think I am going back in," I announced.

"Have fun, man. I'll get you back home."

*In Venky, I trust.*

I have no memory of the rest of the evening or how I got back to my hotel bed. Pleasant echoes of laughter and lively banter filled my foggy mind, and I slept soundly that night.

*Finally.*

# Day 4 of Class

I woke up profoundly refreshed on the morning of Day 4 of class.

The professor kept a fast-paced narration of real-life case studies of disruptive innovations in the steel industry. He had a knack for storytelling, and his systematic treatment of how micro-mills ultimately upended the vertically integrated colossuses of the steel industry was both chastening and engaging.

I was paying rapt attention and, for once, rued the onset of the lunch hour.

I sat back in deep thought, reflecting on the lecture while everyone around me filed toward the exit.

A tap on my shoulder snapped me out of my reverie.

It was Paulina.

"Lunch?"

"Oh, yes," I closed my laptop and followed her.

"Can we sit somewhere and talk privately?"

"Sure."

We carried our plates to an empty conference room.

"What's up?" I asked, tucking into a massive salad.

"Hugh," she started uncertainly.

"Hugh?"

"Yeah, did you not notice us last night?"

"Uh," I stammered. "Truthfully, I do not remember much of what happened," I added abashedly.

"Oh? Do you not remember leading everyone on your version of Samba?" she giggled. "*Sambar* Samba, Meera called it."

"Huh?"

"Oh, it will be so much fun when you see the pictures."

"Pictures?" I was mortified.

"Indeed. It was some evening. Meera was so tired she decided to sleep in—attendance be damned."

"So … what about Hugh?" I asked.

"Nothing, nothing," she waved the topic away. "Let's get back to class."

I received a text message from Karina and spent the rest of the day in class in a quiet daze. I vaguely recall being organized into groups and given a real-life problem to solve using Design Thinking—something about stopping the snowline in the Chilean Andes from receding.

I barely contributed, my thoughts drifting to Karina. *I'd invited her as my +1 out of habit.*
*I never thought she'd show.*
*But she always seems to know when and where to appear.*
*She's the one who encouraged me to join the EMBA program.*
*Nay, insisted.*
*To step out of my comfort zone and broaden my intellectual and social horizons.*
*Oh, how I'd grumbled.*
*Even argued.*
*Resisted like our housecat during bath time.*
*But—she was right.*
*The program opens my eyes to a new world each day.*
*Of academia.*
*And beyond.*
*Still, everything's been moving a little too fast lately.*
*Her presence will steady me.*
*As it always does.*

## Life Coach

That evening, the EMBA staff organized a lavish event—a formal dinner hosted within the ancient stone walls of an underground restaurant in the basement of a historic church. The place settings were exquisite, and the space was bathed in the warm glow of strung lights and candles. The mood and ambiance were meticulously designed for an evening of companionship and connection.

Everyone was dressed to the hilt, including the Brazilian and American cohorts, who wore the formal attire we were instructed to bring along. Many attendees were accompanied by their significant others.

I looked around, appreciating the casual elegance with which my classmates carried off their tailored suits and fashionable dresses. I was used to seeing them in collegiate wear—jeans, sweatshirts, and sneakers.

As the wine flowed freely, I introduced everyone to Karina, who had arrived by cab from the Airport Ritz-Carlton, where she was staying.

Poised and polished as ever, Karina was at ease in our midst—discussing football with Scott, charming Hugh with her dry wit, and exchanging laughs with Paulina and Meera.

Everyone rapidly warmed up to her long-limbed elegance and grace.

"Why didn't you tell us she was coming?" Paulina demanded.

"She surprised me."

"Romantic," Meera raised her brows.

"You could say that," Karina chuckled. "Michel is in Dresden for a conference, and my work schedule opened up unexpectedly.  I thought—why not stop by Prague before joining him for a little weekend getaway?"

Seeing a few quizzical looks, I clarified, "Michel is husband number two. Brave man," which drew a few chuckles.

"Spontaneous and pragmatic," Hugh raised his glass in approval. "I like it."

"How long are you staying?" Venky asked.

"I've got an early train tomorrow," Karina smiled. "Heading back to the hotel right after dinner."

"Karina is best experienced in small doses," I deadpanned, eliciting a fresh round of laughter.

"Keeps the mystery alive," Karina agreed, joining in.

She gave me a small, knowing smile—seemingly amused by how comfortable I was in the environment.

A spectacular seven-course dinner was unfurled in waves of savory excess.

In hushed tones, Karina and I exchanged notes with the practiced efficiency of long-divorced, amicable co-parents.

After the tables were cleared, we were led into a lavish hall where a string quartet played in a bar area.

Many couples were slow dancing, including Hugh and Paulina, who struck poses that rivaled those on romance novel covers.

Venky and Scott whisked Karina and Meera away, leaving me at the bar, distracted by images flashing across a white screen from a projector flickering in the corner.

The initial photos were those captured by the EMBA staff—mostly staged, formal ones.

As the mood loosened, the tone of the images changed—to candid, informal. Scenes from the previous evening started appearing, clearly the handiwork of the Czechs.

The hoots and hollers grew particularly raucous when a video of Paulina, Meera, and me appeared.

I was sandwiched between them on a dance floor, looking quite unburdened by dignity. Our movements were—to use a kind word—"spirited."

A soft intake of breath indicated Karina's nearby presence.

"Well, now," she murmured, swirling red wine in her glass. "That's a sight you don't see often."

"Mercifully," Scott chuckled by her side. "But rather him than me, I suppose."

"I'm impressed," Karina turned to Venky. "He might be ready," she added in a conspiratorial tone.

"I think so," Venky nodded solemnly.

I choked on my beer and emerged, sputtering, "Ex—excuse me?"

Karina turned to me, "To be unleashed into the dating world, silly."


# Day 5 of Class

Everyone welcomed the lighthearted informality of Day 5, which was wholly dedicated to team bonding exercises.

The curriculum was academically meager and socially packed.

Once again, the cohorts were randomly organized into teams and faced mental and physical challenges, each designed to underscore the superior problem-solving abilities of collaborating groups over individuals.

The exercises were made short work of, as someone or the other in every team was familiar with the solution. The curriculum had not evolved to stretch the abilities and acumen of seasoned business leaders, or their consumption of widely published business leadership tropes.

The ensuing void was filled with levity and leisure, which even the EMBA staff joined in.

Impromptu contests were organized, including rubber-band archery, paper plane crafting, and wastebasket paper toss.

A few palms were greased, and beer bottles circulated.

The entire day had provided a welcome distraction. I had not pondered Karina's words from the previous evening. As I lay prone in my room, suppressed thoughts surfaced.

*Karina showing up was supposed to steady me. Recenter me. Slow things down.*

*But instead, she's gone and opened a new frontier.*

*Dating.*

*Dating? After all these years?*

*That's a bridge too far.*

*Or is it?*

*I have always been a "reply when asked, preferably via email" kind of guy.*

*And now?*

*I can initiate and hold my own in conversations. Navigate social dynamics.*

*Heck, even enjoy the company of relative strangers without seeking the nearest exit.*

*And, annoyingly, Karina had foreseen all this.*

*And plotted the next step.*

*Could she be right?*
*Nah.*
*Befriending people is one thing.*
*But opening myself up to romance?*
*That's an advanced-level course—no textbooks, no teachers, no tutorials, and definitely no tuition reimbursement.*
*And one I'd already flunked out of.*
*Dating?*
*No, thanks.*


# Prague by Night

Venky knocked on the door.

"Hey, I hear someone is organizing a street crawl tonight," he said. "We should join in. See the city at night."

"Why not?" I nodded.


We went to the hotel bar, where we found Meera downing quick shots of Becherovka.

She looked troubled.

"What's the matter?" I was concerned.

"Nothing," she shook her head and smiled.


Scott, Paulina, and more members from the Brazilian, American, and Czech cohorts appeared, swelling our ranks.

The plan was for the Czech ambassadors to lead separate contingents on foot.

Hugh walked in. "You all ready?'

"Yes," replied a chorus of voices.


Hugh eased into the role of a Czech guide—polished, courteous, and attentive. His maternal roots ran deep in Prague, and his knowledge of the city was extensive.

"This," Hugh began, leading us toward a statue, "was erected in honor of the city's founders. My grandfather used to bring me here."

Paulina, walking closely beside him, tilted her head. "That's lovely, Hugh. You seem to have a strong connection with this city."

Hugh smiled. "London will always hold a special place in my heart, but Prague is home now," he nodded. "Every corner, every street holds a childhood memory for me."

"Thank you for being a part of the tour," Hugh said, looking around at us, and his eyes lingered on Paulina. "I feel like I'm sharing a piece of myself."

Paulina batted her eyes playfully. "Well then, I expect the full tour."

Hugh chuckled, nodding.

Their chemistry was unmistakable.


Dusk cast its palette of hues across the radiant sky, reflecting off the smooth cobblestones of the street.

Meera and I lagged the others, my pace slowing to match hers.

"I overheard you the first time you mentioned Karina," she said quietly.

I frowned, trying to recall the context.

"About life steamrolling your marriage. What was that about?"

"Ah," I took a deep breath. "You've probably seen the cliches in movies—careers taking off, schedules misaligning, and gradually being consumed by too many moving pieces. Eventually, we were just managing logistics."

Meera nodded slowly.

"We weren't unhappy," I continued, surprised at how easy the words came. "Just … unconnected."

"So … you just ended it?" she asked, brows raised.

"It wasn't that simple," I shook my head. "We tried. Therapy. Getaways. Recreating moods and conversations from past romantic times. Long story short … we realized that the spark was gone. And the only functioning part was friendship. So, we decided to preserve that—and let the marriage go."

"That sounds …," Meera looked pensive, "sort of healthy."

"That was all Karina," I nodded. "She's just wired that way—for the long game. She could detach herself and view our situation objectively."

Meera looked thoughtful. "And you're still close?"

"Yeah. We talk. We co-parent. We hang out. She's always understood me better than I understood myself—and she isn't shy about giving me life pointers," I smiled wryly. "Big picture stuff—like doing this program. Not my day-to-day."

"And … her husband … Michel?"

"Great guy," I said. "The only thing I hold against him is that he managed to make Karina fall in love again. And now she feels that if she could a second time, I can too."

A minute or two of silence passed before Meera spoke.

"How did you become such good friends?"

"Well … that's how we started. As friends. She was in one of my classes at Ohio State." I paused to glance at her. "She frequently asked to borrow my notes," I said with a tentative grin.

She smiled back.

"I suppose …," she said slowly, "friendship is a solid foundation for a marriage."

"Perhaps," I nodded doubtfully. "It didn't save our marriage, although it made the divorce painless."

Meera looked away, her expression shifting. She paused for a minute or two, then drew a deep breath. "I am …," she hesitated, "getting … divorced."

"I'm very sorry to hear that," I said sympathetically. "Kids?" I asked gently.

"Thankfully, no," she gave a slight shudder. "But it's still hard."

"I can imagine."

We walked a few steps in silence. "The past couple of days," Meera said slowly, "I managed to take my mind off it. But I just heard from my lawyer … it's getting messy."

I let her talk. It seemed cathartic.

"Sorry, Srini," she smiled at me, eyes glistening. "Normally, I'd talk to Paulina."

I nodded.

"But she seems to have found a connection with Hugh," she laughed. "I didn't want to spoil her mood. Not on the last evening here."

I smiled. "I understand."

She straightened. "I've resolved to have a good time tonight," she declared. "I'll tackle the mess back home once I get back."

"That's the spirit."

"Thanks for listening, Srini," Meera said, squeezing my hand.

"Of course," I smiled. "But you know something?"

"What?"

"You are now part of a very exclusive club," I said solemnly.

She raised an eyebrow. "Oh?"

"People who've borrowed my notes and gone through life changes shortly after."

"Oh no," Meera burst into laughter. "I knew there was a catch."

"A well-documented one."

She was still laughing. "How bad can it get?"

"Well," I rubbed my chin, "some good, some bad."

"I hope it's all good in my case. I hope it leads to the start of …," Meera started, amusement lighting her eyes.

"… a beautiful friendship?" I completed her thought.

She nodded.

"There's a very high probability of that," I replied, nodding.

We caught up to the others, and Meera's mood was visibly lighter.

Our first stop was at an upscale restaurant for a Czech dinner. The fare was primarily Germanic, and the interior showcased an old-world charm. Rich wall tapestries depicted historical scenes, adding a sense of heritage. Itinerant musicians dressed in folk attire further enhanced the traditional ambiance.

After a couple of beverages, Meera's personality emerged in all its attractiveness. Her laughter was spontaneous and genuine, and her wit unmatched.

We indulged in people-watching, making up silly stories about the patrons around us.

In time, I noticed everyone at our table had rotated seats to take turns conversing.

But I was content to stay with Meera, and apparently, she felt the same.


A glassy rattling sound halted all conversation at the table. Hugh was drumming a fork against his empty beer mug.

He got up and spoke, sounding more British than ever. "Friends, it has been an absolute privilege to know each of you and collaborate with your brilliant minds this week. However, I find myself in a situation that demands my undivided attention."

Hugh placed a hand on his chest and paused for dramatic effect. "And so, I must regretfully take my leave. I wish you all a wonderful evening and safe travels on your journey home tomorrow. But duty calls—and I must return to the art of being a city tour guide."

With an exaggerated bow, he extended his hand to Paulina with a flourish. She rose and accepted it with a barely suppressed grin.

The table erupted into cheers and laughter as they hurriedly made a wholly unsubtle exit.


"I gotta hand it to them," I said, leaning back in my seat. "That was effortless."

"Ridiculously so," Meera agreed. "They meet, dance, flirt a few times—and now they're off on a romantic adventure."

"Guess some people are wired… differently," I shrugged. "Time has fried my circuits."

"And marriage has short-circuited mine," she sighed dramatically.

"To the jaded and the cynical," I said, raising my glass.

"To the hopeless, holding out hope," she smirked, raising hers.

The party broke up, and we all ushered to the front door.

A group of us commenced a self-guided amble.

We heard a lively rhythm.

"This place seems to have a live band," Scott gestured. "I hear rock and roll."

"Let's check it out," Venky said, pushing open the salon door.

We were in a cozy, medieval-themed bar bathed in the warm glow of concealed lighting.

A band was belting out a cover of a Led Zeppelin song.

"Does not look like the original at all," Meera joked.

The lead singer was a short, blonde woman in a pantsuit. The guitarist was Asian-looking, with neatly combed hair. The drummer and bassist had loosened their ties.

Everyone looked like they had just left their white-collar workplace.

But each chord, guitar riff, wailing solo, bass line, and drumbeat reverberated through the intimate space with electrifying intensity, and the raspy, feverish vocals were spot on.

Scott and Venky were rocking out, lost in the swelling crowd in front of the stage.

The noise was deafening, and conversation was nigh impossible.

The evening was advancing fast, and my attention began to wander, good though the music was.

I stole a glance at an equally restless Meera.

I could no longer deny an inexplicable yearning to be alone with her—to offer and receive undivided attention.

*What in the world is wrong with me?*

*A few months ago, I'd have hung out with the boys all night.*

I looked into her eyes and read the same unspoken sentiment.

"Want to go see the city?" I asked tentatively. "Unlike Hugh, my summers were spent in Pondicherry, not Prague. But I can find my way around."

She laughed at my terrible joke. "I'd very much like that."

As the music faded behind us, we set out into the night.

My mood was aglow with the magic of live music.

My heart fluttered with the promise of companionship.

*Or perhaps it was the onset of indigestion from all the bratwursts.*

Night had begun to cloak the ancient city, rendering it even more beautiful.

*Obnoxiously so.*

We took a scenic route back toward our hotel, weaving over the cobblestones while crossing iconic downtown landmarks.

The Charles Bridge was silhouetted against the Prague dusk, its span lit by the soft glow of antique streetlamps. We briefly halted to view the Vltava River below, its dark waters rippling under the emerging moon.

Continuing our stroll, we entered the enchanting Old Town Square, where the illuminated spires of the Astronomical Clock reached toward the heavens like ancient sentinels.

"Our Econ professor said his favorite thing to do in Prague was to sit at one of these tables and look at the clock. He swears with each drink, the clock gets bigger."

"I am sure he was having something stronger than beer."

The square was alive with the buzz of activity.

Meera casually hooked her arm in mine, catching me off guard

*Relax.*

*Her equilibrium must be challenged.*

*The surface, however inviting, is tough to navigate on heels.*

*And on alcohol.*

I gallantly did not pull away.

We joined the crowds gathered around street artists displaying their skills and hawkers selling traditional Czech handicrafts and delicacies.

We meandered solemnly through the narrow alleyways of Josefov, the historic Jewish Quarter. The ancient synagogues stood as silent guardians of a bygone era; their somber facades illuminated by flickering candlelight from within.

We passed by quaint cafes and cozy wine bars, their inviting glow offering travelers refuge from the Fall night air.

As we walked, I was transported in space and time—from Prague's winding streets to Pittsburgh's neighborhoods. There was a time when Karina and I would walk hand in hand through the local streets, planning our future and dreaming big for our family.

Those memories seemed like a lifetime ago.

But every step with Meera felt new and reminiscent.

I felt my heart sputtering—like an old car starting in winter.

*Maybe it is not indigestion but something worse.*

*A cardiac event would be ... somewhat inconvenient.*

We reached Wenceslas Square, a bustling hub of activity even late at night, and paused to admire the grand statue in its center.

Meera kept up a cheery chatter, admiring the elegant facades of the surrounding buildings.

I was content to smile and listen silently, avoiding any superfluous words or gestures that might have caused her to withdraw her arm from mine.

I was grateful to have it there.

*In case I keeled over from a sudden medical emergency.*

Food carts dotted either side of the Square, peddling freshly baked pastries and an assortment of street food.

"I think I am hungry again," Meera turned to me and smiled.

I was surprised to find that, despite my recent self-diagnosed discomfort, I was as well.

"What do you see that you like?"

"Everything. But it's your choice," Meera offered, "and my treat for being the tour guide."

"Thanks. I was all out of cash," I smiled, looking around. "This," I gestured towards an old lady with short silver hair who seemed to be making a roaring business of fried chicken and mulled wine, "seems popular."

"I was hoping you'd pick that," she exclaimed.

We sat on the steps, munching sandwiches and occasionally sipping steaming beverages.

"This is yummy," she sighed, resting her head against my shoulder. "Thank you. I needed this evening."

My heart seemed to do a couple of flips, and I furtively began scanning for the nearest medical clinic—until my mind, which was matching patterns from the past, sounded the alarm.

*Hoi!*

*This is how it started with Karina, remember?*

*An arm in yours. A head on your shoulder.*

*And before you knew it—romantic thoughts, romantic acts.*

*Ending in disappointment.*

*Abort, fool!*


I leaned away from her scented hair and broached harmless topics: college, graduate school, traveling the world, and running marathons.

I became intrigued by her quest to run a race on every continent.

"I killed my knees running the Great Wall last month," she rued. "I hope they recover soon, and I can start training for Antarctica."

"They will. But that sounds impressive … and crazy…" I shook my head. "How do you even get there?"

"Take a ferry from Chile."

"Maybe one of these days," I said wistfully.

"Oh, I'll join you. That will be fun," Meera exclaimed.
I felt oddly pleased, which unsettled me all over again.
*Wait—*
*I was a happy hermit.*
*Living on a pragmatic, emotionally unavailable island.*
*Now being trespassed upon.*
*Worse—occupied without a permit.*
*Evict or evacuate?*
*Do I even have a choice?*


As we took unsteady steps back to the hotel, her arm once again found mine.

Our conversation flowed unabated—our voices mingling with the sounds of the night.

We talked about professional careers.

We recalled our favorite moments and places in Prague, starting with our first meeting.

We joked about the long way we had come in the past few days.

I felt our connection growing with each step.

My heart felt full—of wonderful memories, but also something else.

A vague yearning.

For more moments like this?

*Stop!*

*Get a hold of yourself, man.*

*Tonight was a good time—but like all good things, it must end.*

*Come tomorrow, in the sunshine of reality, Prague's spell will break.*

*Bid farewell to this nauseatingly enchanting city … and move on.*

*With your life.*


Meera and I arrived at our hotel and walked silently into the deserted lobby.

I disengaged from her arm, still nestled in mine.

I offered to walk her to her room.

She nodded.

I summoned the elevator.

We stood awkwardly in front of her closed door, locked in uncertainty.

"Well," I channeled my most articulate self.

She exhaled, a small smile tugging at her lips, "That was ... great."

"Yes, it was."

She looked at me for a moment.

"Srini ...," she hesitated. "My flight home is very early in the morning, and I will probably not see you tomorrow."

"Oh," I said, attempting to mask the uninvited twinge of disappointment that momentarily ambushed me.

"I ... I ... need time. To sort things out."

"I get it," I said, telling myself not to overthink the situation.

"See you in Sao Paulo in a few months?"

"And in Pittsburgh after that."

"So, you're stuck with me from now on."

"I've survived worse."

She chuckled. "You forget I've met Karina."

"That was her good version," I laughed.

There was a pause.

*What is she waiting for?*

*What am I waiting for?*

Then Meera leaned in and kissed me softly on my cheek. "Goodnight, Srini."

I cleared my throat, which seemed to have gone bone-dry. "Yep," I croaked. "Night."

She disappeared into her room, and I stood gaping at the door like a stone gargoyle.

Eventually, I shook off my temporary rigor mortis and groggily walked toward the elevator.

My head spun.

*Over the past six months, I'd been easing into social life—*
*At my own pace.*
*A new interaction here. A conversation there.*
*Manageable. Predictable.*

I paused to take a deep breath.
*Then Prague comes along—*
*And gives me a shove.*
*Sideways. Off a cliff.*

I shuffled forward, thoughts in turmoil.
*Five days. That's all it took—*
*To transform me.*
*From a cautious hiker of unfamiliar but navigable terrain*
*To a cheek-kissed, disoriented, free-falling casualty.*

I summoned the elevator.
*As anticipated, I've learned new things in the classroom—*
*And the social lessons outside were not unexpected*
*But the emotional strike—that's an unwelcome spark.*
*In something I'd hoped had long gone ashen.*

I looked back.
*Meera and I? We make no sense together.*
*Geographically. Age-wise. Life stage-wise.*

I stepped in and absent-mindedly pressed a button.
*Yet, here I am. Looking forward.*
*To two more summits. And more such evenings.*
*With her.*

I rode the elevator, heart pounding.
*I'm so screwed.*

## Triple Bond

In 1990, Vikalp enrolled in the Bachelor of Electrical Engineering program at IIT-Madras and spent his first semester shuttling between his hostel, classrooms, library, and the campus dispensary while battling a series of respiratory ailments (later attributed to mold in his hostel room). His perpetually stuffed nose and a lingering aura of VapoRub earned him the nickname "Vicks."

Vicks held the Andhra Pradesh State Under-19 #2 rank in Table Tennis and had a chip on his shoulder for surrendering the #1 spot for the first time. During his first year of college, Vicks found that he had no real competition in the inter-college circuits of Chennai. So, he did some research and discovered that Pratik (nicknamed "Pong" for obvious reasons) had joined the Mechanical Engineering Bachelor's program at IIT-Bombay the same year, as the reigning Maharashtra State Under-19 champion.

Vicks became consumed by the desire to defeat Pong and salvage his wounded pride.

During the Summers of the 1990s, each of the six IIT campuses took turns hosting athletes from the others. All vied for honors in various sporting events during the Inter-IIT Collegiate Championships, while their supporters sought bragging rights. At the 1991 meet hosted in IIT-Kanpur, Pong and Vicks battled for the men's singles table tennis title. Pong triumphed in a thrilling five-set marathon.

A rivalry was born.

So was a friendship.

Pong and Vicks crossed paths each year during their remaining three years of college in India. Pong beat Vicks in 1992, taking an unassailable lead of 2-0 in the series, but Vicks had the last word by taking the consolation win in 1993.

Vicks secured a graduate assistantship at Ohio State University (OSU) and received a job offer from Reliance Industries for an entry-level engineering position. He had decided to study in the US, but the lure of lucre (in the form of Reliance's travel allowance to attend an in-person orientation) was irresistible. He took a train to Mumbai and a bus to Powai and moved into the room he had reserved at an IIT-Bombay hostel, only to realize he had landed right in the middle of Mood Indigo, the campus's famed cultural festival.

Room 218 in H6 was austere—just a spring cot, no mattress, and no pillow. Thumping music from the festival rattled the windows, and snippets of announcements blaring from loudspeakers bled into the room. Vicks winced, consoling himself that the hostel meals couldn't possibly be worse than those at IIT-M.

Vicks locked his room and went to the mess, where he ran into Pong.

"What are you doing here?" Pong asked after they greeted each other warmly.

Vicks explained the situation.

"That is ridiculous. Eat something, then come to 412," Pong said.

Vicks reached 412 and knocked. Pong opened the door.

"Ah, there you are. You can stay at 414. Hang on a second."

Vicks peeked inside 412.

"Wait, you guys have a balcony to yourself?"

"Yeah, man, we live in luxury. Come and look."

Vicks and Pong went to the balcony. Pong casually swung one leg over to the neighboring room's balcony and hopped across. He repeated the move until he was another balcony away. He disappeared inside the room.

Vicks chose to exit 412 via the more conventional front door and went over to 414, which Pong opened from the inside.

"This room is all yours—Calvin spends all his time at the festival."

"Who's Calvin?"

"You'll meet him soon enough."

Vicks entered Calvin's lair, furnished in utter luxury: a comfortable bed, thick curtains, a chair, and a desk. A bottle of Old Monk was sitting on a shelf. The sounds from Mood Indigo were barely discernible.

Vicks slept soundly that night.

The next day, Vicks completed his work trip, collected his travel expense reimbursement, and returned to H6 by nightfall. He met a super-excited Pong, who had received a letter from OSU offering him an assistantship. He waved a similar envelope with an OSU logo.

"Calvin got one too! In Chemistry!"

"That is awesome! Hey, want to be roomies in Columbus?"

"Yeah, man—ok if Calvin joins us? You see how neat he keeps his room and stuff. I am a slob, so he will even me out," Pong laughed.

"Sure. But wait," Vicks said, looking at the front of the envelope. "His name is Rajat?"

"Yeah, Calvin is his nickname. The dude hates doing laundry and keeps buying new underwear—mostly Calvin Kleins. Let's go meet him."

Pong and Vicks arrived at the heart of the campus, where outdoor spaces had been transformed to host Mood Indigo. They were greeted by loud music, crowded stages, and endless food stalls.

"You can't come to IIT-Bombay and not attend Mood Indigo," Pong declared, leading Vicks toward a packed crowd surrounding an open-air podium where a DJ was spinning an electrifying mix of dance music.

Suddenly, someone climbed onto one of the towering speaker stacks.

The crowd hooted.

Vicks squinted at the silhouette clad in an unbuttoned white shirt and ripped jeans, wearing a fedora.

The music dropped, the bass hit, and the figure leaped off the speakers into a perfectly timed dance move.

The crowd erupted, forming a circle around the dancer, who moved as if Earth's gravity were a mere suggestion. Feet gliding and arms renting the air, every move was timed to perfection.

"Who is that?" Vicks asked, stunned.

"That," Pong said, grinning widely, "is Calvin."

The next evening, Vicks and Pong were chatting in front of Room 412 when Pong cupped his hands around his mouth and bellowed, "*Abbe*, Calvin, come meet Vicks!"

Calvin emerged from the far end of the corridor, dressed in a Mood Indigo T-shirt, shorts, and sandals. He ambled over with an effortless swagger and a disarming smile. His curly hair framed his face perfectly, and his deep-set eyes exuded a relaxed confidence.

"Hi," Calvin extended a hand, his voice smooth and welcoming. "Pong's told me about you. His table tennis nemesis from IIT-M, huh?"

Vicks shook his hand, momentarily starstruck. "Th—thanks for letting me use your room, Calvin," he stuttered.

"You're welcome. And thanks for letting me hang with you guys in Columbus," Calvin said, his smile widening. "I'm pretty low maintenance—trust me."

"… as long as he has his dance music, a floor to move on, and clean underwear," Pong chuckled.

Vicks smiled, instantly liking Calvin.

## Social Circles

Six months later, Vicks, Pong, and Calvin moved into a modest two-bedroom apartment on West Lane Avenue north of the OSU campus in Columbus, Ohio. Calvin claimed the first rotation in the living room, setting up a bedroll alongside neat piles of laundry and unopened packs of Calvin Klein underwear.

"A toast," Calvin declared on the first night, holding up a bottle of Bacardi. "To freedom and friendships."

Long John and Little John from the adjoining apartment were their first visitors. Both were mechanical engineering graduate students like Pong. Little John was short, stocky, round-faced, and always dressed as if he'd just stepped off a golf course—preppy polo shirts tucked into neatly pressed shorts, regardless of the weather. Long John was tall and lanky, with a thin face and flair for cowboy attire. He rarely appeared without his signature Stetson, scuffed leather boots, and a weathered vest whose musky odor seemed to hold a history of its own.

After a round of introductions and handshakes, Long John let himself in with easy familiarity. "You're the guys with the constant *Bhangra* music, huh? Tinga-tinga-tinga-ting—" he pointed his index fingers at the ceiling and shook his shoulders.

"Not me," Calvin said, laughing.

"It's Indi-Pop," Pong corrected him coldly.

"Whatever. You got curry?" Little John followed in, sniffing the air. "We can smell it from the hallway."

"We made *dal*," Vicks sounded annoyed.

"*Dal?*" Long John asked, scratching his head. "You mean lentil curry?"

"No, just *dal*," Vicks replied firmly.

"Same thing, right? You just put curry on everything," Long John said confidently, glancing at Little John for support.

Little John nodded sagely. "It's like we have ketchup in America. Curry is Indian ketchup."

Pong stared at them, aghast, while Calvin burst out laughing. "*Dal* is not curry, and curry is not ketchup, you culinary geniuses."

Long John shrugged off the correction. "You got *naan*? I love dipping it in curry."

The two Johns became unofficial apartment members, popping in at odd hours with beer, engineering textbooks, and endlessly entertaining, if wildly inaccurate and borderline offensive, takes on international cuisine and culture.

Vicks' role as a teaching assistant in the electrical engineering department brought him in contact with numerous undergraduate students. However, one stood out: Abhinash "Beans" Dutta—an *ABCD* with a passion for fast food and a knack for fast-talking.

"It all started in freshman year," Beans explained during his first visit to the trio's apartment. "I ate at Taco Bell seven times in a single day. My roommate started calling me Beans. It stuck."

"And you're okay with that?" Calvin raised an eyebrow.

"Are you kidding? I love Taco Bell," Beans replied, holding aloft a wrapped taco. "The nickname is a badge of honor."

"Beans," Long John declared, shaking his head. "You're a walking cliché."

"Far from it. I'm the *Baadshah* of burritos—no one even comes close," Beans declared.

"I think I know why," Little John said, taking a few steps back.

"Sorry, dude. Had a couple of extra-beefy ones that are jamming the works," Beans affirmed ruefully, rubbing his abdomen. "A five-foot radius ought to do it."

Beans became a constant presence in their apartment, doling out unsolicited advice while markedly lowering the air quality.

"Pong," he said one evening, leaning against the kitchen counter, "you've got to chill out, man. Studying engineering isn't going to prepare you for life. You've got to embrace the vibes."

"I'm trying to finish this Thermodynamics assignment, and you're talking about vibrations?"

Beans shrugged. "Vibes, man. How it's all connected. Thermodynamics. Tortillas. You'll get it one day."

"All I'm getting is your thermodynamic inefficiency processing refried beans," Pong shot back. "Long John, for the love of humanity, crack that window open."

Calvin's winsome personality and dance moves during student mixers didn't take long to gain him popularity on campus. The trio first met one of his fans, Yang Wei, after they returned from an off-campus bar one night.

"Calvin, yes?" Yang called out, standing by their apartment building's door with a backpack slung over his shoulder, round glasses reflecting the streetlights.

Calvin paused, unsure. "Do I know you?"

"No, no. But everyone know Calvin," Yang grinned, nodding enthusiastically. "You are famous in international student group. For dancing, yes?"

Calvin laughed. "I guess."

Yang introduced himself as an older student from China who had spent seven years working in manufacturing before coming to the U.S. to pursue a master's degree in industrial engineering. "You can call me Mike. Perhaps I will stop by?"

"Sure."

At the apartment, "Mike" revealed that his American dream was to secure a high-paying job and make a future for himself and his wife, who was currently in Shenzhen, awaiting her spouse's visa. He had two notable goals: perfecting his American accent and "borrowing" homework. He believed that the former was essential for landing a good job, while the latter was his key to academic success.

"You all engineers, no? I only need small help with homework. My English ... not very good."

Thus began Mike's near-daily visits to the apartment. "Perhaps I will stop by ..." became his trademark phrase over the phone and always preceded his arrival at the apartment uninvited.

Once inside, Mike would grab a chair, adjust his glasses, and scrutinize notes or finished assignments that were lying around.

"Vicks, you are genius. I borrow this, okay?"

Vicks tried to protest. "Mike, you can't just take our work. You are here to learn."

Mike shrugged. "I know engineering, but I study in Chinese. I look at equation, I understand. Anyway, employers only care about GPA, no?"

Mike's obsession with mastering the American accent involved religiously watching the local, national, and cable news channels, mimicking anchors, and adopting catchphrases. His favorite was a nightly news show where the host often said, "Let me be clear."

During one of his "stop-bys," Mike started peppering his conversations with the phrase.

"Let me be clear," Mike announced one evening, pointing a pencil at Pong. "You have very strong accent. I think you need to improve."

Pong laughed. "My accent? At least I use grammar."

"Let me be clear," Mike repeated solemnly, "accent important for interviews. You wait. I talk better than Beans."

Mike appeared at the apartment one day.

"Vicks, you explain question three now, okay? I'm stuck."

"Mike," Vicks groaned, half-asleep, "I have chores to do."

"No time, no time. Let me be clear—this is life or death."

"Ok, ok," Vicks relented. "But let me at least chop vegetables—it's my turn to cook today."

"Cook? No time. You do question three. I bring food."

Mike surprised everyone by bringing over homemade dumplings and ingredients for stir-fried noodles. The aroma of his cooking drew Long John and Little John from their apartment.

"Smells better than Joy's Village," Long John extended a six-pack of Coors Light.

"Indians and Chinese setting aside their squabbles to give peas a chance," Little John sniffed appreciatively.

"First human to offend two cuisines and John Lennon in one swoop," Calvin chortled.

"We're all about peace, love, and dumplings, bro," Beans grinned.

Calvin shook his head. "What you all are is living proof that an engineering education doesn't guarantee intelligent conversation."

"Quiet, men are eating," shushed Pong, between mouthfuls.

"Mike, this is amazing. Where did you learn to cook like this?" Vicks marveled.

"In China, cooking is survival," Mike shrugged. "Good food ... key to happiness. I teach you."

By the end of their first quarter, Mike had become an indispensable part of their motley crew. His relentless pursuit of the American accent and unabashed borrowing of homework were undeniably endearing, but his exceptional culinary skills cemented his place in the group. Mike was older, married, and not necessarily wiser, but he was a wizard in the kitchen—with a heart of gold and a pair of catchphrases for all occasions.

The trio's world gained a feminine touch when Mike's wife arrived from Shenzhen. She had spent months waiting for her visa, and her coming was a cause for celebration—or so Mike declared when he entered the apartment one evening with a triumphant grin.

"Everyone," Mike announced. "My wife is here. Her name is Ying Hua, but she says she will be called Jenny now. Let me be clear—Jenny will bring much discipline to our lives."

"Discipline?" Calvin raised an eyebrow. "Sounds like loss of freedom, Mike."

"Perhaps I stop by more," Mike added with a wry chuckle, "because I not relax at home anymore."

From the moment Jenny set foot in the apartment for a welcome dinner, it became evident that she was utterly fascinated by the *Desi* trio.

"You," she said, pointing at Calvin, "look like American pop star. Like … Michael Jackson. Why these guys not look like you?"

Calvin grinned, leaning into the compliment. "I'm one of a kind."

Jenny nodded thoughtfully and shifted her attention. "And you, Pong. Always smiling with dimples and perfect, white teeth."

Her eyes widened as they rested on Vicks. "And you. So … hairy. This is normal?"

Vicks nearly choked on his *chai* while Pong burst out laughing.

"Uh, I guess so," Vicks said awkwardly, scratching his neck.

Jenny leaned closer, scanning him. "Your arms! Your legs! So much hair."

Calvin smirked. "Careful, Vicks. I think you've got a fan."

"Hey, hey," Mike jumped in, but his tone was sporting.

Jenny quickly integrated herself into their social lives, but Vicks became the unintended target of her attention. Having taken up badminton to "stay active," Jenny decided Vicks was the perfect partner. "Let's play every weekend. You are strong, hairy, and will make good partner."

Vicks found himself on the Larkins' badminton court with Jenny on Saturday mornings. While she was surprisingly agile, her enthusiasm for his hirsuteness remained unsettling.

During a break, Jenny sat beside him on the bench, studying him curiously. "Your hands and wrists … so strong. And … so hairy," she said, running a finger along the top of the hair on his forearm.

Vicks froze, his racket clattering to the floor. "Uh, Jenny, that's—uh—not appropriate."

Jenny, oblivious to his discomfort, smiled. "Hair is good. Very manly. Mike cannot even grow beard."

Later that day, a flustered Vicks stormed into the apartment and found Pong lounging on the couch. "I can't do this, Pong," he declared. "Jenny just touched me … inappropriately."

Pong sat up, trying not to laugh. "She what?"

"She's obsessed with my body hair. I'm scared to go near her now," Vicks said, pacing. "Can you please talk to Mike? I wouldn't even know where to start."

Pong broached the topic during one of Mike's "stop by"s.

"Mike, I think Jenny is … uh, overly enthusiastic about Vicks," Pong began. "She keeps inviting him to badminton, and it's making him uncomfortable."

Mike frowned, stroking his chin. "Vicks is good man. Why uncomfortable? Let me be clear—Jenny likes strong, athletic men—and badminton."

"It's not just that," Pong said, suppressing a laugh. "She's fascinated by his … hairiness."

Mike's face lit up in understanding. "Ah, I see. Hair very rare in China. Like … how you say … exotic."

Pong shook his head. "Mike, you need to tell her to tone it down."

Mike sighed. "Ok, ok."

Jenny eventually tempered her enthusiasm. Her arrival added a new layer to the group dynamic. Her initial quirks led to awkward moments, but her genuine curiosity and infectious enthusiasm quickly won everyone over. Beyond her bubbly energy, Jenny's presence subtly elevated the group's standards—improving their social cohesion and commitment to basic hygiene and the apartment's overall livability. Of course, Jenny's attention occasionally veered into personal territory, particularly with Vicks. Calvin, ever the observer, summed it up perfectly one evening as he raised a toast with his signature smirk: "To Jenny—the only person who can make Vicks sweat without lifting a finger."

For Vicks, Pong, and Calvin, their first year in Columbus sped by—a blur of cultures, experiences, and friendships. Their two-bedroom apartment on West Lane Avenue was not just a place to live—it became a melting pot where laughter, learning, and occasional chaos reigned.

## Game On

Fluorescent lights buzzed overhead in the dingy Columbus Ping Pong Club, reflecting off a cluster of battered tables. Vicks was adjusting his paddle grip, Pong was stretching dramatically, Beans was licking cheese dust off his fingers from a bag of Doritos, and Calvin was leaning casually against the wall, observing everyone.

Big John and Little John, dressed as if they were about to referee a rodeo and a golf tournament simultaneously, were discussing "optimal paddle angles and velocities" with an authority that had no basis in actual gameplay. Mike sat cross-legged in the corner, squinting at his phone, muttering in Chinese, and furiously typing replies to every notification from Jenny, who was home, trying to play along with an episode of "Wheel of Fortune."

The door to the club creaked open.

And then, she sauntered in, clad in a sleek athletic outfit—shorts that ended at the border of modesty and rebellion, a tight-fitting sports shirt that seemed painted on, and shoes designed to outrun a moderately determined greyhound. Her hair was tied back in a high ponytail, and she moved with the casual confidence of someone who had just been informed that the sun, in fact, orbited her. A ping pong paddle was elegantly tucked under her arm like a Louis Vuitton clutch on a red-carpet runway.

Every head in the room turned.

Beans' snack stopped halfway to its destination. Pong froze mid-stretch, one leg lifted awkwardly behind him like a Yoga instructor who'd forgotten the pose halfway. Vicks, already sweaty from warm-ups, exuded a fresh sheen.

Calvin cocked an eyebrow.

"Hi," she said, her American accent bright and clear. "I'm Ishika. I'm just checking out the tournament site. Is there someone I can talk to about registration?"

The Johns exchanged a glance, and Big John smoothly stepped forward, tilting his hat.

"Howdy, miss," he drawled. "Welcome to the wild, wild West Columbus."

Little John was less decorous in his greeting: "You play? Seriously, like, play?"

Ishika smiled confidently. "Well, I didn't bring a paddle to fan myself."

Beans, regaining motor control, accidentally crushed the Dorito in his hand and muttered something to Calvin about paddling and spanking under his breath.

Calvin chuckled, shaking his head.

"Excuse me?" Ishika arched an exquisite eyebrow at Beans.

Pong and Vicks exchanged nervous glances.

Big John intervened. "Well, miss, we're honored. You've already raised the average class of this crew by about … what do you think, Little John? 300%?"

"Easily," Little John replied. "But … are you sure you're in the right place? This is a serious competition, not a Bollywood film shoot."

Vicks groaned. Pong winced. Calvin rubbed his temple.

"First time I heard that from a dude," Ishika laughed disarmingly, dispelling the momentary awkwardness. "I suppose I'll need to find someone else to answer my question," she gave a little wave and walked back out the door, her ponytail swinging like a metronome of destiny.

The group stood in a loose circle, silently processing what had just occurred.

"She—she had a Butterfly racquet," Vicks stammered.

"Did you see her shoes?" Pong said, eyes wide.

Calvin shook his head exasperatedly and stepped forward. "Okay, listen up. She's here to compete, not to collect stares from awkward *FOBs*. Don't embarrass yourselves. And, more importantly, me."

Pong straightened up. "Calvin, with all due respect, we've got game."

Calvin raised an eyebrow. "Game? You forgot how to breathe for at least thirty seconds. And Vicks nearly fainted when she made eye contact. Even Beans forgot about snacking."

Beans let out a low whistle. "He's right, boys; we are in the pros now."

The Columbus Ping Pong Open featured a draw of sixty-four. Vicks and Pong had been placed in two of the four divisions: Long John, Little John, Beans, and Mike in the rest. Eight tables were laid out in a two-by-four grid, and participants were hitting practice rallies.

"See you in the finals," Pongs gave Vicks a first bump.

"Game on."

Vicks sailed through four rounds, winning his division and securing a spot in the semi-finals. He was toweling off when the two Johns came up to congratulate him.

"Thanks, how'd you guys do?"

"Got killed in the first round by a little old Asian man," Little John said. "My golf swings were off today."

"Beans and I had a slugfest," drawled Long John. "A heavyweight bout. Ali vs Frasier. Or, as you guys would say—Veeru vs Gabbar."

"They endlessly lobbed the ball at each other," Little John chuckled, "until the referee stopped the match and disqualified them for unsportsmanlike conduct."

"Speaking of epic duels," Long John continued, unfazed, "there's one in progress."

They joined Beans and Pong, who were watching Ishika's quarter-final duel with Erik, a tall, blond Dane.

Ishika was down one set.

"Dude looks like he is fresh off a Viking longboat," observed Little John.

Ishika's game contrasted brilliance and chaos; her lightning-fast smashes barely outpacing unforced errors.

"Killer forehand," Vicks observed.

"Kamikaze backhand," twanged Long John.

"Rusty brilliance. The spark's there, but the engine's misfiring," Beans commented.

"Incoming," Little John yelled, ducking as Ishika's wayward shot sailed toward them.

Pong checked his watch and stood up. "Gotta go—I'm up for my match."

Despite her mistakes, Ishika clinched the second set with a spectacular cross-court winner that left Erik lunging in vain. The boys erupted in raucous applause, causing Ishika to glance towards them and smile.

The third set was closely fought, with both players elevating their match play. Erik played a steady, methodical game, keeping the ball in play and patiently waiting for Ishika to err. His tactics worked, and he took the match two sets to one.

Ishika grabbed her towel and headed to the corner where the Johns, Beans, and Vicks were waiting. She looked both exhilarated and frustrated.

"Well played," Long John said, handing her a water bottle.

"Thanks," she smiled wryly, shaking her head, "out of practice, out of form—too busy with college."

"You're leagues ahead of me. I got demolished by a guy who looked like he was on a break from delivering dumplings," Little John said.

"Rusty or not, your wristwork is pure artistry," Beans gushed, "it's like watching Michelangelo sculpt with a paddle."

"I play Erik next," Vicks smiled. "And you have shown me how to beat him."

Ishika laughed, standing up. "Thanks for the pep talk, guys—I feel better already. I'd better get going." She waved and walked toward the exit door nearby.

Vicks' semi-final match started with Erik trying to replicate the same steady, defensive play he had used against Ishika. But Vicks began to exploit Erik's slower footwork and narrow range of shots. By the time the first set ended, Erik was outmatched.

"This is a snooze-fest," yawned Beans during the brief interlude. "I am going to check on Pong."

"I'll go with you," Little John said.

The second set was over even faster, ending in a blowout.

"Well, that was anticlimactic," Long John muttered.

Vicks shrugged. Just as he grabbed his bag, Little John ran up, breathless.

"You guys don't want to miss this. Some *Aunty* is giving Pong a tough fight."

"Wait, what?" Vicks blinked in confusion.

"You heard me."


They hurried toward the far side of the facility, where Pong's table was drawing a small crowd. A diminutive *Aunty* in a cyan-bordered maroon *saree* was poised to receive serve.

"Score?" Vicks whispered to Beans, who was biting his lip, shoulders trembling with suppressed laughter.

"Third and final set. Pong is down two match points," choked Beans.

Pong's eyes were locked on the ball he was bouncing on his paddle. With a fluid motion, he served a fast top-spin ace down the line.

"Yeah," Vicks cheered, raising a fist.

Pong tossed the ball to his opponent for the service change and made brief eye contact with Vicks.

Vicks froze.

He recognized the expression on Pong's face all too well.

He had seen it in the faces of many opponents.

Resignation.

"He has no chance," Beans muttered, his hand cupped over his mouth, eyes glistening, and face crinkled with barely contained giggles.

*Aunty* paused to run a forefinger over her right ear, tucking away a stray wisp of hair. She tossed the ball high, her wrist snapping with supple fluidity as she flipped her paddle—a seamless shade of red on both sides. Her bangles clinked, and the ball zipped across the table, spinning viciously away from a wrong-footed Pong.

"Game, set, match to Mrs. Uma Athreya," intoned the referee.

Beans collapsed to the floor and burst into obscene laughter.

"Couldn't read it, man," Pong shook his head ruefully. "Couldn't take a single point off her serve. It became a mental thing. And Beans in the crowd did not help."

Beans started to apologize, but Pong waved him away. "All good. I bet it was entertaining to watch."

Mike came over, "Pong, got pointers? I play her next."

"What? You won your division?" exclaimed Vicks.

"Let me be clear. I have many talents," Mike wagged a finger.

"Just move her around the table," Pong said plainly. "Her serve is her main weapon, and she disguises it well. Oh, and her racket sides are the same color but different rubbers—she flips them at the last second."

"I play ball on merit," Mike declared confidently.

Mike breezed through to the final as well—his defensive pencil grip stabs producing a mix of sharp, unpredictable drops with backspins that the petite *Aunty* could not reach even at full stretch.

Vicks and Mike got pats on their backs when the whole gang regrouped during a break.

"Mike, where did you learn to play like that?" Pong exclaimed.

"In factory ... we play ... during breaks. No boss can beat me."

"You know we play almost every day at the Larkins Center. Why didn't you ever join us?" Vicks asked plaintively.

"No time for play, only school," Mike declared. "But let me be clear: I win this tournament."

"Not unless you change your grip," Pong grinned.

Vicks unleashed a merciless attack on Mike's backhand corner, winning the tournament in straight sets.

They all gathered in the bleachers to watch the third-place match. Poised in her *saree*, Uma *Aunty* unleashed cunning serves and sharp placements, leaving Erik lunging helplessly.

"Go, Mom," Ishika's voice rang out as she joined the group, her ponytail bouncing and her bright eyes locked onto the table.

"Wait, she's your mother?" Pong stammered.

Ishika nodded. "Had a class to attend, but glad I get to watch her now," she smiled, setting her backpack down.

The gang collectively gasped, then joined Ishika in a chorus of enthusiastic cheers.

The match raged on—*Aunty* played serenely while her opponent grew increasingly flustered. With a final, elegantly placed drop shot, she secured victory.

"Game, set, match to Mrs. Uma Athreya," the referee announced.

The crowd erupted.

As they all jumped up and down in celebration, Ishika spontaneously hugged Pong, leaving him stunned.

Uma *Aunty* smiled graciously, giving a slight bow to acknowledge her supporters.

The winners' podium was set up near the central table.

Vicks stood tall in first place, Mike beside him in second.

"I am glad I didn't have to play you, *Aunty*," Vicks smiled down at Uma *Aunty*, who beamed with her bronze medal.

Ishika rushed forward. "Congratulations to the champs," she exclaimed. She high-fived Vicks and Mike before enveloping *Aunty* in a hug.

"So, Ishika, your mom is a ping-pong legend?" Calvin said with an easy smile.

"She taught me how to play," Ishika replied affectionately. "But engineering coursework takes up most of my time now. I transferred from the University of Cincinnati last year after my parents moved here. I start my junior year at OSU next term."

"Oh," Beans exclaimed. "These are the best engineering minds at OSU. Vicks and Pong are teaching assistants; the two Johns run all the labs, and Mike has tons of industry experience. As for me … well, I'm an engineering student like you … name's Beans."

Ishika laughed. "Nice to meet you all. I could use tutoring help; I didn't do too well in my sophomore courses."

"Anytime," Pong replied. Vicks nodded vigorously, seemingly tongue-tied.

"Thank you, Pong," Ishika gave him a dazzling smile. "Mom said your game was fantastic, and she had no business beating you."

"Just couldn't figure out her serve," Pong grinned at *Aunty*, who laughed.

Ishika casually glanced at Calvin. "I've seen you around. You're kind of a legend in the local dance clubs."

Calvin smiled, "Guilty as charged."

"Congratulations, again," she turned to Vicks, her gaze lingering on him a trace longer than necessary. "Ready to head home, Mom?"

The crowd dispersed, leaving the gang to themselves.

"Guys, I think she likes me," Vicks blurted. "You see how she looked at me?"

"She looked at everyone," Pong countered. "But hugged only me."

"Gentlemen," Calvin intervened. "A word of advice: No."

"No?" Vicks asked.

"No?" Pong echoed.

Calvin shook his head. "She's way out of your leagues. Plural."

"Way to be supportive, Calvin," Long John frowned.

"She has confidence and looks," Mike added thoughtfully. "Let me be clear—such women … dangerous."

"Calvin," Vicks beseeched. "Come on, man. Can't you see? This is our moment!"

"Moment?" Calvin smirked. "Sure. One of delusion."

Long John slapped Vicks on the back. "Listen, kid, I like your chances. You're smart. And you got masculine energy."

Pong frowned. "What?"

"Women can't resist male pheromones," Long John explained with exaggerated patience. "With proper use of deodorant and manscaping, his hair and sweat give him a courtship advantage."

Pong blinked, turning to Little John. "Is he serious?"

Little John shrugged. "Hey, love is war, buddy. One fights with what one has."

Beans turned to Pong, nodding consolingly. "Don't worry, bro. You've got something too … an electric presence."

Vicks raised an eyebrow. "What does that even mean?"

"Circuit board energy," Beans said, arms crossed, radiating the confidence of a man who'd never let facts obstruct his flights of fancy. "You know—sparks, connections …," he paused for effect, then chortled, clearly pleased with himself, "… and occasionally, things short-circuit."

Pong blinked. "Like … a malfunctioning appliance?"

Long John grinned. "Nah, man. He means you'll bring … high voltage romance."

"I see it," Little John giggled. "Just … don't … blow your circuits."

"But," Beans cautioned, "you need a strategy. You just don't plug into the grid without proper grounding."

Seeing the confusion on everyone's faces, Beans puffed out his chest like a rooster addressing a befuddled barnyard. "What I mean to say is that you two need help. I understand *ABCD*s, like Ishika. I will be your guide, your sherpa, your love guru. And may the best man win."

"Sounds reasonable," Long John nodded.

"Yeah," Little John added, squinting thoughtfully. "After all, she probably can't understand half the stuff you mumble in your accents. It's like listening to engineering drawings read aloud by a blender."

Pong and Vicks looked at each other, nodded, and turned to Beans.

"Alright," Pong said.

"Sounds good," Vicks agreed.

Beans grinned and clapped his hands. "Game on."

Calvin rolled his eyes.

Mike adjusted his glasses. "Perhaps I will stop by sometimes ... to see wreckage."

## Dead Even

It was a drizzly afternoon in Columbus, the kind of day that makes one stay indoors, sip one's favorite beverage, and philosophize about life—or, in Beans' case, hold court.

Beans assembled everyone in the living room of their apartment and took center stage in front of the window, on which several A4 sheets of paper had been affixed with cello tape. With a theatrically grave expression and a marker held aloft like a wizard's wand, he cleared his throat.

"I am laying down the Rules of Engagement for what will henceforth be known as the Great Courtship Ping Pong Match of Columbus."

Calvin sighed and crossed his arms. Pong and Vicks sat upright, their faces wearing expressions of terrified curiosity. Little John whispered something about popcorn to Long John, who nodded in agreement.

Beans took a deep breath and launched in.

"I am going to explain this in terms you understand." He pointed the marker directly at Vicks and Pong, who flinched as if he'd aimed a curse at them.

"Think of your courtship of Ishika as a ping pong match, and I am the organizer and referee. For the next four months, I will carefully orchestrate situations that bring the three of you together—academic battlegrounds in the Engineering Library, feats of strength at Larkins Gym, and skill face-offs at the Larkins ping pong tables."

Calvin raised a hand. "Can I sit these out?"

"Yes and no," Beans said, turning to Calvin with exaggerated seriousness, "You don't have to witness events as they unfold. But you are the philosopher-king in this grand contest. The arbiter of appeals. The keeper of the competitive flame. Your services will be needed if they tie, and a deciding vote is needed."

Calvin sighed dramatically, shoulders slumping. "Guess I have no choice."

Beans turned back to Vicks and Pong. "Listen carefully. I will award points based on wit, charm, physical or mental brilliance displays, and overall poise under fire."

"When one of you pulls into the lead by two clear points, it's game over. At that moment, I will transition from referee to personal coach and do everything I can to help the victor."

Vicks, sweating as though already in the gym, raised a tentative hand. "Uh, Beans, what about … accidents? What if I trip and fall in front of Ishika?"

Beans grinned knowingly as if he had anticipated this line of questioning.

"Ah, excellent question, Vicks. Points can also be negative. Screw-ups, blunders, unforced errors—they will all incur deductions. For example—spilling coffee on Ishika's textbook—minus one point. Body odor—minus two points. These are standard fouls."

Pong piped up. "What about … things beyond our control?"

Beans said gravely. "The same goes for acts of others that nevertheless result in catastrophic embarrassment—stepping on doggy-doo on High Street, ripping your pants on a bench at the Oval, or your mother showing up unannounced on campus and insisting on meeting Ishika as her future *bahu*."

Calvin snorted into his Coke.

Pong nodded seriously. "So … what happens if our score goes below zero?"

Beans leaned forward, dropping his voice. "If your score dips below zero, gentlemen … you are out. Disqualified. Kaput. Banished from the Ping Pong Court of Love."

Beans straightened, standing tall. "So, what say you, brave gladiators? Are you in?"

Pong and Vicks nodded hesitantly.

"Excellent," Beans beamed. "Let the games begin."

The duel kicked off with Vicks explaining electromagnetic fields. "Imagine this wire as an expressway," he sketched diagrams on a notepad. "The electrons are your traffic. Now, if we add a magnetic field here—"

Ishika leaned forward, eyes wide, her head tilted slightly in admiration.

"That's so cool, Vicks," she exclaimed. "You make complicated concepts sound so … simple. I was not quite getting Pong's method."

Vicks blushed. Pong, sitting across the table, folded his arms in chastened silence.

Ishika left that day with her textbook hugged to her chest and a bright smile directed at Vicks.

Beans, who had been pretending to read a textbook, muttered, "Point to Vicks."

The following week, Ishika's class project, which involved building a small motor, was in trouble. No matter what she or Vicks did, it just wouldn't run.

"Please allow me," Pong said dramatically, tying a bandana around his head like he was entering battle. After five minutes of tinkering with wires and making vague references to "rotor dynamics," the unit whirred to life.

"Whoa," Ishika clapped her hands. "You're like … an engineering superhero, Pong."

Sitting with a chagrined Vicks and a near-empty bag of corn puffs, Beans whispered, "And Pong ties the game. It's 1-1."

Beans arrived at the Larkins' weight room with Ishika in tow.

"Engineering is lifting heavy mental stuff, but you need a healthy body for a healthy mind," he philosophized. "As exemplified by these two."

Pong was running on the treadmill. Vicks was at a weight bench, drenched in sweat after completing a set of deadlifts.

"Hi Pong, nice form," Ishika said brightly. "Vicks … you look … strong."

Vicks paused mid-wipe with his gym towel and looked at her sheepishly. "Oh, uh … you want help with anything?"

For the next twenty minutes, Vicks patiently coached Ishika on proper form for dumbbell exercises. Every so often, she'd glance at him with admiration.

After she waved goodbye and left, Beans, who had been doing hammer curls with water bottles, announced, "Vicks pulls ahead. 2-1."

Pong was at mid-rally, his paddle rhythmically attacking Mike's defensive blocks. Ishika, standing at the sidelines, was watching with bright eyes, occasionally letting out little gasps at particularly sharp returns.

Midway through the rally, Pong executed a forehand loop, sending the ball across the table and dipping it at the far corner. Mike lunged and missed, his paddle slicing the air.

"Hey, Pong," Ishika called out, her voice cutting through the sound of bouncing balls. "Your forehand loop is so smooth. You make it look easy."

Pong looked up and grinned, adjusting his grip on the paddle. He turned back toward Mike and, with the confidence of a man used to being in the spotlight, unleashed a fierce down-the-line smash so powerful that the ball ricocheted off the far edge of the table and careened into the bleachers.

The other players fell silent for half a beat before Ishika clapped her hands together in delight.

"Look at that," she said, her face glowing. "You should play professionally."

The compliment hung in the air like a golden trophy. Pong turned slowly, his paddle tucked under his arm, and shot Vicks a triumphant smirk.

Beans, seated like royalty on a stack of gym mats by Vicks, a bucket of buttery popcorn on his lap, muttered, "We're tied again, 2-2."

"Beans, is this going anywhere?" Vicks glared.

"This is what you both signed up for," Beans shrugged, tossing a handful of popcorn into his mouth. "I am now moving this contest to the social phase."


Exhorted by Beans, the trio's apartment received a makeover in preparation for hosting Ishika for an evening of "Tea and Tutoring." The walls got a fresh coat of paint, and the carpets underwent a round of steam-cleaning. Jenny scoured local garage sales and spruced up the decor.

Long John perched on the armrest like a cowboy surveying the plains while Little John sat on the couch, flipping through a golf magazine. Calvin, Beans, Mike, and Jenny hovered over a Monopoly board. Ishika, her ponytail swinging lightly, sat between Pong and Vicks at the table in the nook, thoughtfully studying a dog-eared textbook. A mostly barren plate of Mike's excellent dumplings and a ceramic Oolong tea kettle had been confined to the kitchen counter.

Long John interrupted a temporary lull in the hubbub, waving his beer bottle. "Hey, you three—what are your real names again? Your *Desi* names."

Calvin leaned forward with a grin. "I'm Rajat, which means 'silver.' You know, like something valuable."

"Aptly named," Long John tipped his hat.

"And easy to remember," Little John nodded. "Like 'Raj' plus an '@' sign, like an email address. Now, what about you two? Spill it."

Pong leaned back in his chair and shrugged. "It's not a mystery. My name's Prateek. It means 'symbol' or 'hopeful sign.'"

"And mine's Vikalp," Vicks added. "It means 'hope' or 'possibility.'"

"Wait, wait, hold on," Long John blinked. "Both of your names mean 'hope?'"

"Did your moms, like, coordinate this?" Little John asked. "But … why didn't they pick normal names? Like 'John'?"

"Hey, at least our names mean something," Vicks frowned. "Hope. Possibility. Ambition. Big ideas."

Pong followed up, "Meanwhile, your moms named you after disciple number four."

Little John opened his mouth to respond, closed it, and burst into loud guffaws. Long John started chuckling, nudging him in the ribs.


The laughter in the room had barely subsided before Beans let out a fresh peal. The Coke he was sipping shot straight up his nose, and he doubled over in a coughing fit, clutching his stomach.

"Bit slow on the draw, isn't he?" Long John remarked.

"Oh my God," Beans wheezed. "So, the three of you … are like … wait for it … Calvin and Hopes!"

For a second, there was silence. Then, Ishika giggled uncontrollably, followed by Calvin's deep laugh. Long John clapped like a seal, and Little John cackled so hard he nearly fell off the couch.

"Calvin and Hopes," Long John repeated, pointing at Vicks and Pong. "Oh, that's gold. That's absolute gold!"

Ishika, still laughing, wiped a tear from her eye. "Beans, that was really funny. I'm impressed."

Beans blushed at Ishika's rare compliment.

Vicks groaned. "You know what? Fine. At least it's better than being named after an apostle."

Little John, still red-faced from laughing, pointed a finger at Vicks. "Hey, apostles are cool. Have you ever seen a painting of them? Very distinguished."

Mike, quietly observing from the corner, deadpanned. "Distinguished? Let me be clear—you put mayo on dumplings and call it 'Asian Fusion.'"

The room erupted again; this time, even Pong and Vicks cracked smiles.

Beans leaned back on the carpet, looking triumphant. "I'm telling you, boys. You're Calvin and Hopes from now on. Trademark pending."

Ishika's eyes were fixed on Beans, whom she seemed to be regarding in a new light. "That was a clever pun, Beans. I like a quirky sense of humor," she said in a husky voice.

Beans beamed, soaking in her admiration like a sunflower on a bright summer day. "I'm not just a pretty face. I'm a cultural bridge." He raised his drink, "To Calvin and Hopes."

Several months later, on a tranquil night, Vicks and Pong sat brooding in separate corners of the couch. Ishika had gone home after a tutoring session, cheerfully thanking them for their "amazing help."

Beans, feet propped up on the coffee table and munching on a leftover taco, broke the silence. "You two realize she's equally impressed by both of you, right? Like it's a perfect equilibrium of hope and despair. The score's dead even. Maybe Calvin needs to cast a deciding vote."

From across the room, Calvin shut his book with a decisive snap, stretched, and wearily strolled toward the kitchen. "You know what fascinates me? She's not even playing the game. You two are. Back and forth across the emotional table, trying to score points. And all she wants is help with her circuits and equations."

"I think you're right," Pong sighed heavily, staring at the ceiling light fixture as if it held the answers to life.

"Yeah," Vicks groaned, burying his face in his hands and muttering something unintelligible.

"Hey, hey, don't stop now, fellas. It'll all be over soon. I promise," Beans grinned, leaning forward to pat them on the back. "Plus, this is the best show in town, and I've got front-row seats."

Calvin chuckled softly as he walked to his room, iced tea bottle in hand, leaving Pong and Vicks and their fates at the mercy of more emotional ping-pong rallies conjured and orchestrated by Beans.

## Acts of Men

The note on the apartment door was written in bold black marker on graph paper, complete with crude sketches of a burger and a bowl of noodles:

"INDO-CHINESE FUSION DINNER NIGHT! Hosted by Long John & Little John. Come hungry, leave culturally stuffed. FRIDAY, 7 PM. Dress code: anything with elastic waistbands."

"Oh no," Pong said flatly.

"Oh yes," Beans said with a gleeful grin.

"Didn't they spike Coors with *garam masala* last time?" Vicks asked warily.

Beans shrugged, chewing on a churro like an expensive cigar. "Relax, boys. It's all good. I helped them with the menu. Like my *paneer* tacos, every bite will have cultural harmony."

Mike muttered. "Let me be clear … this will end in regret."

Long John and Little John's apartment was decorated in what could only be described as "chaotic diplomacy." Red and gold streamers encircled an American flag pinned to one wall. A singular incense stick smoked ominously on the table next to a pizza box, and in the corner was a small, crooked printout of the Taj Mahal taped beside a picture of Jackie Chan.

"Welcome, peace ambassadors," Long John announced proudly, tucking a wooden spatula in his belt like a ceremonial sword while bowing deeply.

"Indians and Chinese have been squabbling for centuries," Little John bowed, his palms pressed together in a *Namaste.* "Tonight, we honor your ancient tribes with food."

With a flourish, the two Johns gestured towards the table, where dinner was laid out. The menu included Mac and Cheese laden with cumin powder and sporting an ominous glow; yellow-tinted mashed potatoes aggressively dusted with curry powder; pizza topped with fried paneer cubes, spinach, and drizzled with soy sauce; burger patties dusted with mustard powder and smothered in duck sauce; and Coke infused with pink rock salt.

Everyone hesitantly filled their plates, eyeing each item with suspicion.

Beans announced, "I suggested adding cumin to all the dishes. It helps with digestion. Relax … you'll all be fine."

Mike sniffed the air. "I smell something … chemically aggressive," he remarked ominously.

Long John hovered proudly over them, pointing out the "cultural nuances" and "flavor bridges" in every dish.

"See, Ishika, every dish has … uh… harmony. A cosmic balance."

Ishika giggled politely.

As the evening progressed, Pong began to monopolize Ishika's attention entirely. Most of the time, they were engrossed in private conversation, and now and then, she would throw her head back and laugh at something Pong said.

Vicks noticed and began to panic, his anxiety triggering a chain reaction in his stomach. A dull ache was growing—it felt like a cement mixer had started inside him.

Beans leaned over, noticing Vicks' face. "Hey, man, you good?"

"No," Vicks said through gritted teeth. "Something's wrong. I can feel … chaos in my gut."

"You've played ping pong matches through cramps. This is just abdominal turbulence. Stay in the game, man," Beans said encouragingly, tilting his head toward Ishika.

Vicks took a deep breath. The pain was temporary. Ishika and Pong? That could be forever. He took a deep breath, clenched his gut, and inserted himself into Ishika and Pong's conversation.

"So, Ishika," he said, attempting to sound casual, "did Pong tell you about the time he spent an hour trying to fix a PC whose power unit wasn't connected to the motherboard?"

Ishika shook her head and laughed.

Pong glared daggers at Vicks.

Vicks grinned back.

"*Prrt.*"

The noise, although ignorable, was unmistakable.

Vicks froze mid-grin. Calvin's shoulders started shaking. Beans' eyes widened. "No. No, Vicks. Control it," he whispered in Vicks' ear.

Vicks tried to recover. He laughed nervously, but the floodgates had opened. Every awkward chortle triggered a volley of auditory betrayal from his rebellious gut.

"*Prrt.*"

"*Pfft.*"

"*Parp.*"

Long John sniffed the air. "What is that? The rock salt?"

"That …," Little John tilted his head gravely. "And a whole lotta something else."

Mike removed his glasses and pinched the bridge of his nose. "This is dumpster fire."

Pongs had turned his head away, face buried in his hands, shuddering with silent laughter.

"Abort! Abort mission!" Beans leaned in again and hissed. "Leave. Now. Take it with you."

Vicks didn't need to be told twice. Pale as a ghost, he muttered something about "gastric destabilization" and dashed out of the apartment.

Vicks sat slumped in a corner chair in the trio's apartment. His face was pale, and his stomach had settled into a quiet, post-chaos grumble.

Beans entered, munching on a slice of pizza.

"Feeling better, champ?" he asked concernedly.

"No," Vicks groaned.

"Ah … hmm …," Beans scratched his chin thoughtfully. "I … um … might've forgotten to tell you something."

Vicks squinted at him wearily. "What?"

"I didn't think it was that big a deal," Beans shrugged. "You're sensitive to Ajinomoto, right?"

"Yeah, but Mike always uses the Chinese MSG, which I can handle," Vicks seemed confused.

"Well," Beans said slowly, "I knew. But I forgot. Look, man, there were burgers, mashed potatoes, a lot was happening."

"What are you trying to tell me?" Vicks scowled.

Beans raised his hands defensively. "It's not like I added it. Blame the Johns and their … cooking skills. I gave them a pack of Ajinomoto that I had. They must have used it liberally. Did you notice the sheen on all the food they served?"

"That … that … would explain it," Vicks gasped.

Beans shrugged. "Ah, buddy. That's … rough. Chinese MSG vs. Japanese Ajinomoto. Same formulas, isomer impurities, different effects. Science strikes. But hey, the cumin will flush the system—you'll be fine by morning."

"That … er … performance by Vicks," Beans said, leaning against the kitchen counter, "although attributable to no fault of his, has disqualified him from the tournament."

"An act of God," Pong said sympathetically.

Calvin patted Vicks' back. "More like an act of the apostles," he commiserated.

"I will now become Pong's coach. Cool?"

"I suppose," Vicks grumbled. "But I am not giving up … just going to lie low … for a bit."

"Prudent," Beans nodded. "So, Vicks will sit out Ishika's family potluck dinner get-together this weekend. Calvin?"

"I'm out as well," declared Calvin. "Got to hit the books."

"I thought as much," Beans raised an index finger. "I can't make it either—I promised Mike and Jenny I'd help them shop for a new television. So, Pong, this is your chance to dazzle Ishika's whole family. The Johns will be there for support. You in?"

"Absolutely."

"Good. Now," Beans paused, "when it comes to potlucks at strictly vegetarian families like the Athreyas, you need to think outside the wok. Don't go with boring old plain white rice or *dal.* You want flash. You want pizzazz. You want colors."

"Colors?" Pong asked, suspiciously eyeing the Ziploc filled with assorted food dyes that Beans was displaying like a door-to-door *rangoli* merchant.

"Yes, my friend," Beans said, tapping the bag. "A vibrant plate of Indo-Chinese vegetable fried rice is in order." He emphatically slapped a Post-it note on the fridge. "Mike's written out the recipe. Think of the dish as … fireworks on a plate. A technicolor feast for the eyes—like those sweet mouth fresheners you get after a heavy meal at *Desi* weddings."

Pong nodded slowly.

"Trust me, Pong," Beans said, walking toward the door, "this is the dish. Plates of vibrant, edible gemstones to dazzle the Athreyas. Playful, festive, and they'll be talking about it for all time."

The day of the Athreya event dawned bright and auspicious. Pong and Vicks stood in their apartment kitchen, sleeves rolled up and faces set with the grim determination of soldiers entering the trenches.

*Basmati* rice was boiled, fluffed, and separated into batches. Food coloring—red, green, yellow, and blue—was carefully added to each portion.

"I'll fry the batches separately, so the colors don't run into each other," Pong said confidently, tossing the first batch into the sizzling wok. "Are the veggies ready?"

"Mike's recipe calls for desiccated red carrot cubes from the fridge—this will complement the green peas and yellow corn I've just defrosted."

"Bring them all forth, my man." Pongs appeared to be enjoying himself.

Later that night, Pong, Long John, and Little John were slumped on the apartment couch, wearing the expressions of men who had survived a natural disaster.

Calvin sat on the kitchen counter, sipping iced tea. Beans was at the coffee table, wearing the expression of someone who had just lit a fuse and walked away whistling. Jenny and Mike sat beside him, fussing over their shopping bags.

"Alright, quiet everyone," Vicks announced. "Let's all hear it. From the top."

Pong sighed deeply and sat up. "Okay. It all started when we walked into the Athreya residence carrying … the dish. Look, I'll admit, things were already looking dicey. The rice wasn't exactly multi-colored anymore—the colors ran, and the grains congealed—it became more like … muddy cement. But, you know, Ishika looked gorgeous in a *saree* and was all smiles, her parents were polite, and I thought maybe—just maybe—the lighting in the dining area would hide the disaster."

"It was a good call," Little John nodded pedantically. "All the food looked off-color under the festive orange, red, and yellow lights."

"Anyway," Pong continued, "we placed the pot of rice on the buffet table. There were fragrant flowers, burning incense sticks, and a brass lamp. Very classy vibes." He paused. "I can't do the next part," he added faintly and sank into silence.

"Okay, okay, so here's where things went sideways," Long John sprang up. "Picture this—*uncles* and *aunties*, all decked out in silk *sarees* and *kurtas*, floating around the dining room like butterflies performing ballet to lounge music. We were blending in, sorta keeping a low profile as we lined up for the food."

"And then?" Jenny asked, biting her lip and on the edge of her seat.

"One *Uncle*—a massive guy with a mustache that spilled into the neighbor's yard—paused mid-chew. He froze. His eyes bulged like he'd swallowed a lit *Diwali* cracker."

Little John piped up. "He looked straight at Ishika's dad and said—in a ghostly whisper, 'Ramesh, is this … non-veg?'"

Everyone in the apartment gasped in unison.

"It was like someone had pulled the plug on the entire party," Long John shook his head dramatically. "The garlands seemed to droop. The flame on the lamp flickered. Somewhere, a few *sitar* strings droned discordantly."

"At this point," Little John continued. "Pong's face was the color of overcooked pasta. Ramesh Athreya turned to us. His eyes … oh man, his eyes glittered like the lasers in our precision machining lab. Dude must play tennis—he knocked the rice pot off the table with a sweeping forehand."

"Someone turned on the lights, and our dish lay exposed," Long John rued. "It looked like a concrete mixer had suffered an explosion inside a Skittles factory."

Pong clasped the sides of his head. "One *Aunty* yelled 'rat poison' and started sobbing. Another clutched her throat like she was resisting a chain-snatcher. And a bearded *Uncle* declared—very loudly—that he could 'smell meat three feet away!'"

"Answers were angrily demanded, and the culprits quickly identified. That's when the sandals came," Little John said.

"Wait, sandals?" Vicks asked, eyes wide.

"Oh yes. One *Aunty*—undoubtedly an excellent fielder in the deep—threw her *chappal* at me. It missed by an inch, but I could smell the leather." Pong's voice was low and haunted. "We were then escorted out. By two *ABCD* kids who looked like they bench-pressed *idli* grinders for fun. They walked us out—firmly."

"Did Ishika say anything?" Jenny asked softly.

Pong shook his head. "She wouldn't even look at me. She was helping her mom clean up the rice disaster while her dad glared daggers into my soul."

Long John sighed. "And we didn't even make it to dessert. I heard they had *Ras Malai*."

"The biggest loss of the evening," Little John rued.

"So," Calvin deliberately took a long sip, "let me get this straight. You guys made mud-colored rice, offended an entire vegetarian crowd, got sandal-bombed, and bounced out of the premises?"

Long John nodded solemnly. "That'd sum it up accurately, yes."

"But how did the meat get in there?" Vicks asked, his face contorted with confusion. "I helped Pong prepare the rice. I remember adding only vegetables."

Pong's face lit up slowly, like a lone sodium vapor streetlamp reluctantly flickering to life in a quiet *nukkad*.

"Wait," he walked to the kitchen in a trance, opened the fridge, and retrieved a packet. He shuffled back to the living room and extended it toward Mike. "What are these?"

Mike adjusted his glasses, squinted at the packet, and declared confidently, "Dried red carrots. I use in fried rice. They give crunch."

"As it said in your recipe," Beans added, seemingly entertained, chewing noisily on a tortilla chip.

Jenny snatched the packet from Mike, opened it, and sniffed exaggeratedly. Her face froze, her nostrils flared, and she turned toward Mike with the slow menace of a chef who caught one of her minions about to drizzle ketchup into a pot of Mapo Tofu.

"Mike. These. Are. Pork. Cubes."

There was a collective gasp.

Somewhere in the distance, a cricket chirped.

"Ah," Mike blinked, his expression clearing. "Perhaps there was … a mix-up?"

"A mix-up?!" Pong exclaimed, clutching his forehead.

"How you not smell it?" Jenny looked at Pong and Vicks like they were toddlers, blissfully unaware of their soiled diapers.

"I thought it was the MSG," wailed Vicks.

"Or the oyster sauce," Pong whimpered, glancing around desperately for support.

"Unfortunate," Beans interjected nonchalantly, "Well, on the bright side, you're famous among the local *Desis* now. For all the wrong reasons, but famous nonetheless."

There was a heavy silence.

Finally, Vicks spoke, his voice small and defeated. "No question that we are well and truly out. After the Johns' dinner … and now this … Ishika's never even going to look in our direction."

Pong's shoulders slumped. "Yeah. It's … it's over."

"Good game?" Vicks said, extending his hand.

"Not quite … but I know what you mean," Pong replied, shaking it firmly.


## The Final Rally


The Pan-IIT Reunion was in full swing at a convention center in downtown San Francisco. The halls were abuzz with engineers who had swapped their half-sleeved shirts and cheap cafeteria coffee for ill-fitting suits and espresso martinis. Banners hung from the rafters, groups clustered around buffet tables, and laughter echoed through the lobby.

Vicks and Pong stood near a ping pong table tucked away in a quieter corner, having spotted it almost immediately after arriving. They weren't wide-eyed graduate students anymore; both had graying hair, paunchy guts, and crow's feet at the corners of their eyes.

But their eyes sparkled with the same competitive fire.

Their families stood nearby, chatting and occasionally throwing curious glances toward the table. The kids were excited—they'd grown up hearing stories about their fathers' legendary rivalry.

"Ready?" Vicks challenged, spinning a paddle in his hand.

"Game on," Pong shot back, adjusting his glasses.

They began playing, their reflexes slower but their vigor undiminished. Back and forth, paddle to paddle, the ball zipped across the table. The kids cheered every point, the wives clapped politely, and for a while, it felt like they were back in the Columbus Ping Pong Club, two decades younger, with Beans munching on a snack and Calvin smirking in the background.

Between sets, they caught up.

"You remember the Johns?" Vicks asked, wiping sweat from his brow.

"Of course. They left OSU and started that solar panel company in Arizona. Made a killing when the market boomed," Pong replied.

"And Mike and Jenny? Detroit, right?"

"Yep. Mike works in the automobile industry, and Jenny is with a business consultancy. Last I heard, they were doing well. Two kids—a boy and a girl."

They fell silent momentarily, their paddles tapping absently on the table.

"Calvin?" Vicks asked softly.

Pong shook his head. "No idea. He disappeared after ditching OSU Chemistry and going to NYU for an MBA. Wall Street, I think?"

"Typical," Vicks said with a wry smile.

The match continued into the fifth set, both men panting slightly, shirts sticking to their backs.

Pong paused mid-serve and looked around. "Um … where is everyone?"

Their entire audience had vanished.

Refrains of festive music drifted in—the unmistakable beat of dance tracks, clapping hands, and distant cheers.

"Sounds like Mood Indigo. What's going on?" Pong asked.

"Let's find out," Vicks said, tossing his paddle aside.

The rivals stepped into the outdoor atrium. Strings of lights crisscrossed the sky, casting a soft glow over a crowd gathered around an impromptu dance floor. At the center, a dancer moved with unmatched grace and energy, effortlessly spinning, leaping, and twisting to the beat.

The crowd, which included their wives and kids, cheered every move, mesmerized.

"Brings back memories," Pong murmured.

"Kid's got moves," Vicks agreed.

They exchanged a look.

*Could it be? Calvin's son?*

The dancer completed his routine, whipped the fedora off his head with a final flourish, straightened up, turned to face the crowd, and smiled.

It was Calvin himself.

His hair had the same windswept charm, his face barely seemed to have aged, and his trademark smirk was firmly in place.

An hour later, the trio sat nursing drinks at a small table in a quieter corner of the garden. Calvin leaned back in his chair, all smiles.

"So … Manhattan, huh?" Vicks asked.

"Yep. Wall Street suits me," Calvin replied casually. "I have an apartment near Central Park. The views are great. You guys should visit. There's plenty of room."

"And you're still single?" Pong raised his brows.

"Of course," Calvin said with mock indignation. "This—" he gestured broadly to his face, "—is the result of staying unattached. Honestly, you two began to age when you started wooing Ishika."

Vicks sputtered into his drink.

"I still can't believe the Athreyas felt so humiliated they moved back to Cincinnati after the potluck debacle," Pong groaned.

"Tragic," Calvin shook his head with mock sympathy, then leaned forward, his smirk fading slightly. "You guys ever hear from Beans?"

Vicks frowned. "No. He kind of … vanished. We lost touch after he graduated."

Calvin's smirk returned. "Well, brace yourselves, gentlemen. I've got a story for you."

He leaned in conspiratorially.

"You remember the day Beans came up with 'Calvin and Hopes'?"

Both men nodded.

"Well, apparently, something clicked in his head when Ishika repeatedly complimented him. Beans realized he wasn't just the referee—he was in the game."

Pong and Vicks froze mid-sip.

"So, he decided to eliminate competition," Calvin continued smoothly. "First, he convinced the Johns to add Ajinomoto to every dish. Vicks, my man—that was a targeted strike."

Vicks' jaw fell.

"And the dried carrots debacle? Yeah. Beans swapped them for pork cubes. Pong, you never stood a chance."

Pong slammed his glass down on the table and swore vehemently.

Calvin chuckled. "And here's the kicker. After the chaos settled, Beans came clean to Ishika, confessing everything—the Ajinomoto sabotage, the pork swap, the whole tangled courtship arbitration. It was a superbly calculated gambit. Instead of being furious, Ishika … well, she fell for him. Turns out, she admired his boldness—or maybe just his weird charm. Either way, they're married and living somewhere in San Jose."

There was silence. The weight of revelation hung heavily in the air.

Vicks shook his head in disbelief. "So … Beans played us. All of us."

Pong sighed. "The greatest game of ping pong wasn't even on a table."

Calvin raised his glass. "To Beans—the only man who beat you both."

The three of them clinked glasses, their laughter echoing into the night.

As they sat there, drinks in hand and nostalgia in their hearts, Vicks couldn't help but smile.

Ultimately, his friendly rivalry with Pong had endured through time, distance, and the absurd chaos masterfully orchestrated by Beans, with unwitting assistance from their delightfully quirky friends.

From somewhere in the distance, faint music beckoned.
Calvin stretched, stood up, and grinned.
"Alright, gentlemen. Nice catching up."
And just like that, he was gone.
Forever young, forever free.

# Eyes of Truth

## Family Bonding

Vikram Malik stared at Pramod Dutta's hunched-over back with mild annoyance. With a gloved hand, Pramod carefully moved a golf ball from the rough edge of the fairway to a favorable spot.

"It was on a divot," Pramod declared with a crude laugh.

Vikram shrugged.

They were colleagues. The healthcare provider community in Johnstown, Pennsylvania, was replete with *Desis* of all specializations. As a pathologist at Conemaugh Memorial, Vikram often crossed paths with many of his colleagues, including Pramod, a cardiothoracic surgeon.

Pramod's shot curled away to the right, out of bounds.

Pramod glowered at the fairway as if it were at fault.

"These bloody idiots cannot maintain a course," he swore vehemently, his face instantly darkening with rage. With a primal grunt, he raised his 5-wood high above his head and smashed it violently onto the ground, splintering the steel shaft. Breathing heavily, he flung the broken pieces into the nearby lake.

Vikram stood stoically—it was not the first time he had witnessed Pramod's outbursts. During tense surgeries in the operating room, Pramod was known to throw instruments and scream at everyone, his mood unpredictable and sometimes dangerous. Maintaining a nonplussed veneer usually brought Pramod to his senses. The tantrum was overdue. Pramod's game had been off all morning, and his escalating misanthropic grumbling required an outlet.

Vikram avoided playing with Pramod, but his hand was forced today. He was trying to squeeze in a quick nine holes before a family road trip, and the club had paired them for an impromptu tee time. Vikram was no stranger to Pramod's frequent transgressions of golfing etiquette and was well beyond the point of letting them affect his own game. Despite the undesirable company, he finished two strokes under par.

The men, of similar athletic build but disparate height, drove their golf cart to the parking lot. Pramod was 5'7", with a sallow face, pointed chin, pencil mustache, and a head of closely cropped, spiky hair dyed jet-black. He had an air of furtiveness about him. Vikram was six inches taller. His face and chin were square, and his nose sharper. He had neatly groomed salt-and-pepper hair and beard and an amiable demeanor.

"Have you met the new *Desis* in town? Morali and Haresh Shah?" Pramod asked, sliding his bag of clubs inside a grey SUV.

"No," Vikram said, shutting the trunk of his bright red Porsche parked in the adjoining spot.

Pramod whistled, sketching an exaggerated hourglass figure in the air. His roving eyes and hands were notorious

among the *Aunties* in town. Since his wife Pratibha sold her
General Practitioner medical practice and moved to
California to be closer to their daughter a year ago, Pramod
had treated every attractive woman in town as a potential
target for his advances. In an all-male company, he frequently
and insistently shared his thoughts and exploits in explicit
detail.

"For once, I wish I were a GP," he winked lasciviously.
"Hers."

"Uh … what do they do?"

"Gas Station."

"The Sunoco on Goucher Street?"

"Yeah. The dude seems to be a real wuss. If I were
married to her, we would never leave home, if you know
what I mean."

Pramod seemed eager to prolong the conversation, but
Vikram wasn't interested. "Gotta go, buddy. Driving the
family to a wedding event in Canada," he said, glancing at his
watch.

"Oh? Where? The Shahs are from Canada as well."

"Toronto. Anshu's distant cousin Nikhil got hitched. She
is not close to the family, but we got an invitation. Figured
Nitya could use the distraction—she has been working hard
on her college apps."

"What about Om?"

"Still in Africa."

"How long is he going to waste his time and talent with
that volunteer crap?"

"He finds it rewarding."

"Kids these days. Whatever. Anyway, have a safe trip.
Wish I was going—weddings are full of horny women."

"Catch you later, PD."


Vikram arrived home—a stately two-story brick house on
Stardust Lane with meticulously maintained landscaping,
large windows, and an arched entryway. As he eased his car
over the paved brick driveway that curled towards the side

entrance of the garage, he noticed Anshu by the family minivan, stowing a couple of suitcases inside.

Vikram parked his car and glanced in the rearview mirror at his wife of more than twenty years. In her early 40s, Anshu had retained much of her petite, youthful figure. In the sunlight, auburn highlights rippled through her long, dark hair. A pair of stylish sunglasses adorned her high cheekbones and slightly rounded face.

When their match was arranged, Anshu was a 21-year-old college graduate, and Vikram was a medical student at Ohio State University. Despite being six years younger, Anshu's maturity and wisdom grounded Vikram's impulses and whims, steering them through the typical crises and challenges in a marriage.

"Oh, hi, honey," Anshu greeted Vikram as she entered the garage, pushing her sunglasses into her hair. Her expressive brown eyes smiled affectionately, hinting at a thoughtful and intelligent personality. She wore jeans and an ornate kurta, blending her dual heritage as a first-generation Indian American.

"Thank you for indulging me," Vikram said, hugging and kissing her.

"You're welcome. Let me grab some snacks for the road, and we can leave."

"Did you pack all my stuff?"

"Yeah."

"You're the best. Be right back after a quick shower."

Vikram discarded his dirty golf cleats in the garage and hurried up the spiral staircase in the living room just as Nitya emerged from her bedroom, wheeling a large suitcase.

"Think you packed enough?" he teased.

"It's my first *Desi* wedding, Dad. I don't want to be underprepared," Nitya smiled back.

The three-member Malik family drove leisurely, stopping for lunch and dinner enroute. By nightfall, they reached the wedding venue, a downtown Marriott.

They were woken by a knock on their door the following morning.

Arya and Nikhil greeted them warmly. Nikhil touched Vikram's feet, per Anshu's family tradition. Even after all these years, Vikram had never gotten used to the gesture. He was prepared to stop Arya from doing the same, then remembered that unmarried girls were exempt.

Although four years apart, the siblings closely resembled each other in appearance and mannerisms. Nikhil's distinguishing facial feature was his French beard, which was meticulously groomed to compensate for his prematurely balding temples. Arya's big, light brown eyes and broad smile accentuated her vivacious charm on full display.

"Arya, you were just a little girl in pigtails the last time we met! You look so much like *Chachi*," exclaimed Anshu, referring to the siblings' mother, who was Anshu's distant aunt by marriage.

"Where are Om and Nitya? They must be all grown up as well," exclaimed Arya.

"Om is volunteering for Doctors without Borders. He is somewhere in Nigeria. Nitya is a rising senior in High School. She must still be sleeping," Anshu replied.

"I'll go get her." Vikram started towards the connecting door to Nitya's room.

"No, *Jijaji*, please let her be," Arya beseeched. "The events do not start for another couple of hours." She turned to Anshu, "But *Didi*, we could use your help with some of our friends and their sarees."

Vikram was pleasantly taken aback by the hospitality and reverence they were being accorded. Anshu, who had only met her cousins a couple of times when they were much younger, effortlessly eased into the role of being their *Didi* and was promptly whisked away.

Vikram decided to go on a leisurely run along the lakefront.

Vikram returned to an empty room. He knocked on the connecting door.

"Mom and I are getting ready for the *Haldi* ceremony. Take your time, Dad. But please do not miss the *Baraat*," came a muffled voice.

Vikram smiled, sensing Nitya's excitement.

"Ok."


After a brief nap, Vikram showered, meticulously dressed in an ornate, regal *Sherwani,* and went downstairs. The groom's party was already gathered outside the hotel lobby. Vikram's eyes sought and found Anshu, who was wearing a black and gold *saree* adorned with an intricate floral pattern. Her jewelry, including dangling earrings and a delicate necklace, added a touch of understated elegance.

Vikram walked to Anshu's side.

"You look utterly gorgeous," he whispered. "How do I look? Don't want everyone to think you married me for money."

"When it was the other way around?" she laughed. "You look good as always, babe."

"Thanks. Where's Nitya?"

"See if you can spot her," Anshu said mysteriously.

Vikram looked around and immediately located Arya, who was waving to them. He did a double-take at Nitya standing beside her, clad in a vibrant blue *saree* with delicate gold embellishments and earrings that sparkled in the midmorning sun. Nitya's long, dark hair was styled in a loose updo, accentuating her youthful complexion. She looked radiant.

Vikram gulped, reflexively waving back.

"What happened to our little girl?" he asked Anshu, who was gazing at the girls lovingly.


The rest of the day was a blur of pomp and splendor.

Vikram was shaken awake early Sunday morning by Anshu. Utterly hung over, he forced himself to attend the family breakfast but could barely keep anything down.

Vikram yielded the driving to Anshu and lay curled up in the back seat. Nitya prattled on about the previous evening—recalling how Arya *Mausi* had done her makeup and had led the *Baraat* with Nikhil riding the ceremonial horse, the colorful Hindu wedding ceremony, the black-tie cocktail reception dinner, speeches by the newlyweds, friends, and relatives, and Arya's skills on the dance floor starting with the surprise flash mob she had choreographed.

"I should have laid off the Canadian Whiskey. I don't remember much of anything following the ceremony," Vikram groaned.

"You were having a great time, honey," Anshu smiled at him through the rear-view mirror.

"Uh … hope I did not embarrass anyone," Vikram rued.

"You were a huge hit—especially your flamboyant outfits and dancing," Anshu reassured him.

"I vaguely remember the *Baraat* and the *Shaadi* ceremony."

"Arya was teasing Nikhil *Mama* that your outfit matched the horse's better than his," Nitya giggled.

"That's funny," Vikram laughed despite his discomfort.

"There was that one awkward moment, though," Anshu said.

"Uh oh."

"You asked Arya how she was still single, what with her looks and personality."

"There it is," Vikram sighed.

"No, it was ok," Nitya reassured him. "She did not seem to mind."

"Whew."


## Newcomers and New Mysteries

The Maliks returned home to their small-town routines, punctuated by occasional phone calls and text messages from Arya and a brief visit by Om.

Three months passed.

It was an unusually warm Saturday afternoon at Windber Park, where the Johnstown Indian Association's annual summer potluck picnic was in full swing. *Desis* were scattered across the park benches and picnic tables around the Oak Shelter.

"All hands, as usual," Anshu said disgustedly, taking a seat beside Vikram.

"Who?" Vikram asked reflexively.

"Who else?" Anshu tilted her chin toward Pramod, among the men congregating around the smoking grill nearby. She reflexively hugged her bare shoulders and shuddered. "One can't even wear a tank top around him."

"Sorry about that. You should tell him to back off."

"We shouldn't let Nitya get anywhere close to him."

"What?"

"I don't trust that man around women—of any age," Anshu said protectively, folding her hands. "And Nitya is now an adult."

"Peace," Vikram raised one hand placatingly and watched Pramod lurch toward the women organizing the food under the picnic shelter.

A silver Honda Accord pulled into an empty spot in the designated parking area, causing Pramod to veer off course. The doors opened, and a couple stepped out. A woman in her early 30s, clad in abbreviated shorts, a translucent white shirt, and a straw hat, waved animatedly at Pramod. A short, overweight man in jeans and a golf shirt, presumably her husband, opened one of the rear doors and extracted a lidded aluminum chafing dish.

"Must be the Shahs," Vikram muttered to Anshu.

"Oh? It seems they have already met Pramod." Anshu's eyebrows were arched.

"Uh-huh. Ok, he is waving us over. Let's go be nice."

The Shahs contrasted in looks and personalities—a typical pattern among *Desi* couples in arranged marriages.

Morali was conventionally attractive and outgoing, even flirtatious. Her outfit was meticulously coordinated in a floral motif, with the most striking aspect being the matching white ribbon and white rose that circled her neck and straw hat.

Haresh was nondescript and spoke mainly in monosyllables. He took Anshu up on her offer to introduce them to the other families present.

Morali declined, preferring to chat animatedly with Pramod.


"Dad, do you want to play tennis?" Nitya appeared by Vikram's side. "We're one player short and have an extra racket."

"Sure."

Nitya and her friends were superbly coached, and playing with them elevated Vikram's game. The matchup soon attracted a small, vociferous audience, including Anshu and Haresh. After a closely fought set, Anshu discreetly waved to them, and they broke for lunch.


"That was great."

The voice made Vikram turn around in his seat.

Haresh stood with a plate of food in his hand. "The tennis match," he clarified. He had a heavy *Desi* accent, and his halting English was adequate.

"Thanks," Vikram said, "please join us."

"Appreciate. We didn't know what to expect when we moved here. Not this *Desi* community. Everyone—so nice, so nice," Haresh beamed. "And we love our new home in Westmont."

"Yeah, small-town mentality. We tend to look out for each other. Westmont is a lovely residential area."

"… with many, many Doctors and Engineers."

"Only jobs in town," Anshu chimed in. "But seeing a *Desi* joining the business community here is great."

"Thank you, thank you. I was feeling … er… embarrassed," Haresh laughed nervously.

"Don't be. I heard you guys moved from Canada. If you don't mind my asking, why Johnstown?" Vikram asked.

"Oh. Morali's family owns gas stations in the Philly area. Looking to expand, you know. I am only an employee. Um …," he broke off abruptly and stood up, his gaze becoming distant. Without a word, he hurried towards Morali and Pramod, seated on a park bench, conversing animatedly.

Vikram's eyes tracked him. A frown creased his face as he observed Pramod occasionally stroking Morali's bare thigh while they spoke, sitting closer to her than necessary.

"All hands alright," he mumbled darkly.

Nine months passed.

Acceptance letters came in from multiple colleges, and Nitya announced her decision to attend Pitt-Johnstown. "I need a strong computer science foundation for grad school. The class sizes here are small, and the faculty are excellent," she declared.

Vikram and Anshu agreed wholeheartedly, silently rejoicing over being able to have their baby close by for four more years. They headed out to celebrate over dinner at Asiago's Restaurant on top of the Johnstown Inclined Plane.

"Ugh, need gas," Vikram announced, looking at the gauge. He pulled into a Sunoco.

"Hey, isn't this the Shahs' gas station?" Anshu asked.

Vikram nodded, getting out of the car.

"Appears closed," he muttered, looking at the pump.

"Maybe they aren't open on Tuesdays?" Anshu offered.

"Let me check."

He walked up to the store and returned.

"Looks like they are shut for good."

"Weird."

At Asiago's, they ran into the Shindes, a *Desi* couple who lived in Westmont. They learned that the Sunoco had been closed for a few months, and the Shah residence seemed no longer occupied. The Shindes speculated that the Shahs had abandoned their business and returned to Canada.

"Local woman declared missing," screamed a headline in the Johnstown Tribune-Democrat. The article noted that Morali Shah's parents had filed a missing persons report, insinuating foul play. Haresh, wanted for questioning, was allegedly absconding.

The news spread swiftly through the *Desi* community. For many, the Shahs were unfamiliar faces, while for others, they became the center of conversation. Speculation arose that Morali had left the marriage, and Haresh was hiding out of shame. A more salacious theory was that Morali had moved in with Pramod, and the pair was keeping a low profile.

Several months passed, yet there was no sign of the Shahs.

Vikram got a call from the local Coroner's office. The police had found a potential burial site in the Shahs' backyard and were planning an exhumation. Vikram was asked to be the Pathologist onsite.

"Oh, the poor girl," Anshu commiserated. "Do you think Haresh did it?"

"I don't think so. He seemed quite harmless, didn't he?" Vikram said.

Anshu nodded.

"But you never know in Johnstown," Vikram added bitterly. He had assisted the local authorities in homicide cases in the past when people with money and power had subverted criminal investigations. Whenever Vikram had raised his concerns, he had been told in no uncertain terms not to interfere. Experience had taught him to be wary of personal and professional repercussions, typically disguised as bureaucratic actions.

It was raining heavily the morning Vikram left on his assignment.

He returned after two hours.

Anshu helped him strip off his muddied clothes in the garage.

"So?"

"False alarm. The site was too small. It turned out to be a dog. The Police confirmed with the Westmont Veterinary practice that the Shahs' pet had been ailing for some time, and Haresh had brought it in about a year ago to be put down," Vikram shrugged.

The exhumation created a brief stir within the community, but the story died quickly, and the Shahs again became a distant memory.

## Family Transitions

Vikram and Anshu were having breakfast in the nook of their home. It was one of Vikram's favorite spots—a tranquil oasis of natural light flooding in through a curved, greenhouse-style, black-metal-framed window that extended outwards into the lush backyard.

The comfortable silence was softly interrupted by the ringtone on Anshu's phone.

It was her mom who lived alone in the Washington, DC area.

After a brief conversation, Anshu hung up, looking conflicted.

"I think … I should take Mom to India to see a holistic specialist for her arthritis. Her medications are not working, and she sounds depressed. There are excellent centers in the South for pain management. Plus, seeing family might lift her spirits," Anshu began tentatively.

"Uh … for how long?"

"I'd say … a month if not two …," her voice trailed off.

"Just go," Vikram smiled understandingly.

"Are you sure?" Anju asked, looking dubious but also somewhat relieved. "You'll be alone when Nitya leaves for her senior high school trip."

"It's totally ok. We'll manage."

Anshu left within a month.

Vikram and Nitya occasionally hung out in the nook at mealtimes, supplementing the freshly frozen food Anshu had left in the freezer with takeout from Szechuan East. Both got busy with their routines, especially Nitya, who had decided to work part-time as a hostess at Balance, a downtown restaurant.

Vikram was practicing his chip shot in the backyard when Nitya approached him, her eyes sparkling.

"Uh, Dad?"

"Yeah?"

"Remember Arya *Mausi*?"

"Yeah."

"She wants to talk to you." Nitya handed her phone to Vikram.

"Hello?"

"*Namaste, Jijaji*," came the cheery reply.

"*Namaste*, Arya. How are you? How are the newlyweds? And your parents?"

"All good, all good, *Jijaji*. How are you and Nitya holding up without *Didi*?"

"Oh, we miss her," Vikram laughed. "But we are managing. What's up?"

"My cousin Arjun needs a favor from you, *Jijaji*. But please be under no obligation to say yes."

"Cousin?"

"Yeah, on my mother's side."

"Oh. Sure, what is it?"

"Arjun is in Pittsburgh, doing a project as part of his master's research. He needs to work with a Pathologist."

"Happy to help," Vikram said. "What is the project about?"

"I will let him explain when he meets you. He can come by this weekend if you are free; he says everyone at Carnegie Mellon University is off for the holiday."

"Sure, does he have our address?"

"Nitya just gave it to me, and I will pass it on."

"Sounds good."

"Oh, Nitya also invited me to come by this weekend and stay a week."

"You are most welcome."

"Ok, I will coordinate with Arjun, and we will see you soon," Arya exclaimed.

"Ok," Vikram said, returning the phone to a highly excited Nitya.


Nitya and Vikram prepared a July 4th barbecue lunch in the backyard, an annual Malik family event. An outdoor table covered by a red picnic-themed tablecloth and surrounded by four black chairs sat on a patio paved with uniform stone tiles. Various potted flowering and green plants stood by the side door leading into the house. A path of stepping stones led away from the patio and blended into the manicured lawn. A line of tall, well-trimmed trees and bushes provided privacy.

They were sipping lemonade when the doorbell rang.

Arjun was a slightly smaller, slimmer, and younger version of Nikhil. He had a sparse French beard and wore jean shorts, a button-down crimson shirt, a white-felt Panama hat, and dark sunglasses.

Vikram liked the stylish flamboyance of Arjun's appearance, which was meticulously coordinated with the holiday's red, white, and blue theme.

"*Namaste, Jee,*" Arjun greeted Vikram in a deep voice, bending to touch his feet.

Arjun's informal abbreviation of "*Jijaji*" amused Vikram. "*Namaste,* and welcome to Johnstown," he smiled.

"Thank you. And you must be Nitya. Nice to meet you."

"Good to meet you too, Arjun *Mama*," Nitya smiled.

"Arya got delayed," Arjun explained. "She should be here in a couple of hours."

They ushered Arjun to the backyard, and Vikram offered him a beer. "I don't think I met you at Nikhil's wedding, although I did not get to know all the family members on Nikhil's mother's side."

"Dad lost recollection of most of the day," Nitya giggled, explaining Vikram's frequent trips to the bar during the reception.

Arjun gave a short, vaguely bitter laugh. "I missed out on all the fun."

He did not elaborate.

They were interrupted by Anshu's FaceTime call. Vikram answered, and Anshu's face appeared.

"Hi, honey, how are things going?"

"Still jet-lagged." Anshu looked tired but excited. "But today, we are heading to a remote tea estate resort in Kerala. Sort of a spiritual retreat. We have to surrender our phones, so I may be unable to communicate for a week."

"Sounds like a great way to unplug."

"Sorry for missing our annual cookout. You guys are doing it, right?"

"Yes, and today we have a special guest," Vikram said, passing his phone to Arjun.

"Hi, *Didi*," Arjun greeted Anshu. "Good to meet you … virtually. "

"Likewise. Nitya had filled me in. Wow, you look so much like … Nikhil," exclaimed Anshu.

"I get that a lot," Arjun laughed.

"I am afraid I do not know a lot of *Chachi*'s side of the family. Where are you located?"

"I am right now in Pittsburgh, *Didi*. But I was doing a project in Seattle during Nikhil's wedding and could not attend. Home is in Ottawa."

"Sorry I'm not there to meet you in person," Anshu said apologetically.

"No worries, *Didi*. I hope your trip is going well."

"Yes, Nitya around?"

"Yes, *Didi*. I'll pass the phone to her."

"So, what is the nature of your research?" Vikram asked, poking at the kabobs on the grill.

"Data Fusion. Processing data from multiple sensors and making sense of it."

"Sounds cool," Nitya said.

"At CMU?"

"No, in Ottawa. We are collaborating with a CMU team to develop a GPR sensor that can be put on drones."

"GPR?"

"Oh, sorry. Ground Penetrating Radar."

"So, do you get to fly drones?" Nitya asked excitedly.

"Sometimes. I brought one along. Want to fly it?"

"Yes!"

Vikram watched the video feed on an iPad as Arjun and Nitya took turns flying the drone around the neighborhood. He was impressed with the drone's capabilities and Arjun's command.

Arjun showed Vikram how to work the controls and excused himself to use the bathroom.

He emerged, looking glum.

"What's the matter?" Vikram asked, handing the controls to Nitya.

"I just spoke to Arya. Not so good news, I am afraid."

"Is Arya *Mausi* ok?" Nitya asked concernedly.

"Yes, but her car broke down before the US border. She managed to get it towed. It will take a day to fix, so she's staying the night with a friend in Hamilton who's picking her up. She apologizes for not being able to make it this time."

"Oh …," Nitya said in a disappointed voice.

"So long as she is safe," Vikram commiserated.

"Yes, yes. She is."

Vikram started serving items from the grill, and the three had lunch.

"We got distracted by your flying machine," Vikram started, "But how can I help you? Arya said I should let you explain it."

"*Jee*, I want to demonstrate using a multi-sensor drone to detect buried objects—for my thesis."

Arjun paused, seeing Vikram frown.

"Our research lab in Ottawa uses only optical sensors ... I mean, cameras ...," he explained.

Vikram nodded.

"... but we have a tie-in with CMU for using GPR sensors, which is why I am in Pittsburgh."

"I think I understand. But, still, I'm not sure how I can help."

"I have developed an algorithm to fuse and correlate optical and radar data to classify objects using pattern recognition. I need a pathologist to help me fine-tune the identification of human remains. One of our project sponsors is the Canadian Archeological Society."

"Oh, I can help with that. But I do not know anything about sensor data."

"My software can display the rough outline of objects the sensors might have found. It will also approximately identify them using biological patterns I have already programmed in. You just need to validate my software and help me identify additional ones I may have missed. As a pathologist, I am sure you have seen plenty of buried human remains."

Vikram nodded. "Sounds easy enough. And cool."

As dusk set in, they moved indoors and sat in the plush living room.

Arjun seemed more relaxed and comfortable. He broached the topic of Nikhil's wedding.

"So … the word is that you were quite the life of the party, *Jee*," he teased.

"Arya was the star. We were all just trying to keep up," Vikram laughed.

"She is something else," Arjun agreed. "I may have a link to the flash mob video."

"Ooh … let's see it …," Nitya urged.

"Ok, I'll send it to you."


Nitya cast the footage shot by the official videographer on the TV. Arya was on the screen, kicking off the flash mob.

Vikram watched amusedly as Nitya and Arjun paid rapt attention.

Arjun started a running commentary, laughing whenever Nitya appeared on the screen. "Nice moves, Nitya. Especially flinging your *dupatta* in the air."

"I'm so embarrassed," Nitya laughed. "I was hyper and clearly out of my depth."

"Oh, look at *Jee*," he exclaimed. "He is owning the floor."

"I have no recollection of any of this," Vikram chuckled, causing Arjun to laugh uproariously.

The footage went on and on, as did Arjun's remarks.

Vikram sensed that Nitya was beginning to get annoyed at her younger self on the screen and Arjun's incessant teasing.

"Sorry to break up the party, but I have an early tee time tomorrow," he announced, trying to change the topic.

Arjun's mind seemed to snap back to the present. "Oh, I am so sorry. I lost track of time. I'll take your leave," he said, sounding abashed.

"Arjun, you have had more than a few beers. Just stay the night—there is a guest room in the basement," Vikram offered.

"Oh, thank you," Arjun said gratefully. "I was hoping you would offer," he loudly whispered, winking at Neha. His charm was back. Nitya smiled.

Vikram brushed his teeth and went to Nitya's bedroom to bid her goodnight.

Nitya was on the phone. She briefly placed her hand over the mic. "It's Arya *Mausi*. She is apologizing for not being able to make it."

"Oh, tell her that's all right. Is she ok?"

"Will do. And yes—she is still at her friend's, and her car won't be fixed until late tomorrow."

# Sensing

Vikram slowly descended the spiral staircase from the loft to the living room. Arjun was sprawled on the couch, palms locked behind his head. He rested against a cushion at one edge, hirsute legs dangling over the other. A mild frown indicated that he was deep in thought.

"Morning," Vikram said, snapping Arjun out of his reverie.

"Morning, *Jee*," Arjun rose with alacrity, his long limbs flailing before settling into a rigid, formal sitting posture. He seemed somewhat abashed at being found making himself a little too comfortable in his *Jijaji*'s home.

Vikram absent-mindedly waved a hand, indicating that he did not mind in the least, and Arjun relaxed visibly.

"You're up already? Was your room comfortable?"

"Yes, *Jee*. I am an early riser."

"Something bothering you?"

"*Jee*, I am having second thoughts about something. I was thinking of flying my drone over the local cemetery and taking scans of the gravesites, but that feels like violating someone's privacy. I do not feel good about it."

"Oh … yeah, that is certainly a bit shady … but … why do you want to do that?"

"I want to practice calibrating the drone's sensors and processing software for the terrain around here, which requires trial and error. Scanning the cemetery would enable me to figure out settings such as the drone's speed, altitude, flight patterns, signal strength, and other parameters."

"Hmmm … would an animal burial place do?"

"Oh," Arjun smacked his head. "Of course. Is there a Pet Cemetery close by?"

"Not that I know of. But I know a residence where a dog is buried in the backyard."

"Really?"

Vikram explained the exhumation in the Shah case.

Arjun's forehead wrinkled slightly at the mention of the Shahs. He seemed to start to say something, but stopped.

"That will do perfectly fine. What is the address?"

"It's in Westmont. I will take you there after lunch. I would like to see the drone's view of the nearby downtown area if you don't mind."

"It would be my pleasure, *Jee*."

Vikram parked his Porsche on the street in front of the Johnstown Inclined Plane visitor center. He and Arjun climbed the stairs to the flagpole with a giant Stars and Stripes fluttering in the mild breeze. Johnstown's historic, once flood-prone city sprawled in the valley beneath them. The whole area was brilliantly lit by the mid-morning sun.

Arjun sent the drone into the azure sky.

"Over there," Vikram pointed towards the edge of the Stackhouse Park woods, and the drone followed the line of his extended arm and forefinger. The iPad now displayed scenes of canopies of trees along wooded trails and rivulets that emptied into the main creek.

"Follow that trail," instructed Vikram.

"There," he exclaimed as the drone approached the edge of a tree line.

Arjun made the drone swerve into a backyard and descend lower, until they could visually discern a mound in the grass on the iPad display.

"That looks like the spot," Vikram confirmed.

Arjun pressed his finger several times on the iPad, and the video footage went blank. A blinking "Sensing" message indicated that the drone had switched its camera off and its sensors on.

"How does this thing work?" Vikram squinted at the screen.

"It sends radar pulses into the ground," Arjun explained, "and detects signals that bounce back when they hit buried objects."

Vikram nodded, intrigued. "And you can see bones with this? Like an X-Ray?"

"Not directly, but we can see anomalies—things that shouldn't exist. Then, we analyze the data to determine what those anomalies might be. It's like putting together a puzzle."

Arjun fiddled with the screen again, cycling through various sensors until satisfied that he had gathered sufficient data.

"Do you think you found it?" Vikram asked.

"I hope so. I won't know until I transfer all the sensor data from the drone and process it on my computer."

At Vikram's behest, Arjun flew the drone over the downtown area. He and Vikram squinted at the live video footage on the iPad screen. The whirring of the propellers slowly faded as the drone soared, enthralling them with scenes of the three winding rivers, industrial structures, and pockets of lush greenery.

"Wow," Vikram muttered as Arjun expertly controlled the drone's flight over a broad sweep of the valley until the iPad display flashed a "Low Battery" message.

"Ugh, the sensors use a lot of power. I am afraid I must bring the drone back, *Jee*," Arjun apologized.

"No problem. Would you be able to give me a copy of the downtown footage? It was fantastic!"

"Of course."

Upon Vikram's insistence, Arjun agreed to spend another night at the Malik residence.

Vikram and Nitya drove him around and showed him the local sights.

They returned home for dinner.

After helping clear the table, Arjun excused himself to go to the basement.

He emerged, extending a USB drive towards Vikram, "Here, *Jee*."

"Plug it into the TV," Vikram instructed, handing the remote to Arjun.

Nitya and Vikram marveled at the aerial views of downtown Johnstown.

"4K footage, 4K TV," Arjun explained.

"It's incredible," Nitya exclaimed.

"Can we see the video from the earlier flight?" Vikram asked. "From Westmont?"

Arjun pressed a few buttons, and the footage shifted to scenes from the top of the Inclined Plane.

"There we are," Vikram observed. "And now, on to the Shah residence."

"Why?" Nitya asked.

Arjun explained as Nitya followed the drone's journey to the Shah residence's backyard.

Suddenly, the screen went blank.

"That's when the GPR sensors were turned on," Arjun explained. "The camera powered down, but the video will come back."

As if on cue, the screen lit up once again. The backyard receded as the drone ascended.

"And that is that," Arjun said.

"Superb. Thank you for the scenic tour of Westmont and downtown," Vikram said.

"My pleasure, *Jee*."

"Wait," exclaimed Neha. "Who's that?" She was pointing at a male figure at the edge of the frame, who was crouching at one corner of the Shah's backyard.

"Whoa," Vikram took a sharp breath as Arjun hit the Rewind button and paused at a frame. "Looks *Desi*. I can't tell with the cap pulled over his eyes."

"I can grab zoomed frames on the computer," Arjun offered. "You don't think someone is taking a shortcut through the yard?"

"Could be, but it looks suspicious, doesn't it?"

"It does."

"Have you processed the radar data, Arjun *Mama*?" Nitya asked, her face shining with excitement. "Maybe you will find something?"

"I'll go get it started, but it is going to take all night, I'm afraid," Arjun responded. "My laptop just does not have enough processing power."

"Well," Vikram looked at his watch. "I'm going to turn in."

"Early tee time, *Jee*?"

"Yup," Vikram nodded. "I'm through to the next round of the club tournament."

"Oh, congrats, Dad. Who are you playing against?"

"Pramod."

"Ugh," said Nitya with a grimace.

Arjun looked curiously at her.

"He is a creepy *Uncle*," she explained.

"Ah."

Vikram looked agitated. "Has he ever misbehaved with you, Nitya?"

"Uh, no, Dad. Growing up, we heard our moms talk about Pramod *Uncle*, and we stayed away from him."

"Smart."

"Is *Uncle-ji* married?" Arjun asked.

"Yeah, but Mom says Pratibha *Aunty* suffers in silence or pretends not to believe what she hears or sees. Wonderful lady otherwise. And now she is out of sight and apparently out of mind."

"Yeah, I have seen that type," Arjun commiserated.

Vikram bade them good night.

"So, how is the bachelor life?" Pramod winked.

"More like a single-parent life," Vikram replied evenly.

"Nitya still around?"

"Yeah, she leaves for Europe this coming Friday."

"Are we still on for Bridge on Saturday?"

"Yeah, everyone is coming."

"We are going to get so wasted."

Vikram paused, then added, "You've been off the radar."

Pramod chuckled nervously. "Yeah, out of the country."

"Work? Or pleasure?"

"Bit of both. I had a two-week workshop in Singapore and decided to take a break right after. Things were … er … tense here for a while," Pramod said vaguely.

Vikram raised an eyebrow but didn't press. "Well, welcome back."

"Glad to be back," Pramod replied, smiling tightly.

Despite the handicap difference, Vikram was ahead by six strokes at the 12th hole. Pramod forfeited the match, and Vikram came home earlier than anticipated.

"Dad, is that you? Come see this, quick," came Nitya's cry from the basement.

Vikram descended the stairs leading to a poker table under an arched entryway. A green felt poker mat, stacks of colorful poker chips, and a deck of cards were neatly arranged, ready for the next game.

Nitya and Arjun were perched on two upholstered chairs, poring over a tiny laptop on a small side table for refreshments and snacks.

Vikram approached them, putting on his reading glasses. "What am I supposed to be looking at?"

"The mystery man," Nitya said, getting up enthusiastically and motioning Vikram to take the seat she had vacated.

"Anyone you know?" Arjun asked, zooming in on the face.

"Hard to tell for sure with that baseball cap on, but it looks like Haresh Shah …," Vikram said uncertainly.

"Maybe he wanted to get something from the house, Dad," Nitya said excitedly, "without anyone noticing."

"Got something else." Arjun brought up a highly pixelated black-and-white image. There were outlines around clusters of dots.

Vikram squinted at the screen. "Wow, skull and bones. This is like looking through dirt," he whispered in amazement.

"That's GPR for you," Arjun said proudly. He started spinning the graphics on the screen, and the outlines and dots moved in space.

Vikram sat back in his chair, amazed. "And you can capture buried objects in 3D?"

Arjun seemed to be enjoying his reaction. "Absolutely. It would be harder to identify them otherwise."

Vikram frowned. "Hmm … but wait … this is only a part of the dog's skeleton. And some of the bones look like they have been sliced."

"I used a quick-and-dirty algorithm and did not let it run on the full dataset, only to a specific soil depth," Arjun explained. "Otherwise, processing on my laptop would have taken several days."

"Ah."

"Also, the soil clay limits the radar's effectiveness. I would like to do a scan at a higher power setting."

"But why?" Vikram asked. "We know their dog was buried there."

"I wouldn't mind having a go with the radar at full power and capture the entire skeleton—it will help me fine-tune the calibration," Arjun said, scratching his chin.

"Ah, ok."

"There is a catch. I would have to preserve the drone's battery by limiting its flying time."

"We can hide in the intruder's spot and fly the drone from there," Nitya exclaimed.

"Why do I feel like I'm trespassing?" Vikram asked.

The three of them were crouched in the gap in the tall hedge behind the Shah residence, fully shielded from the neighboring house and the Stackhouse Park trail.

"This should be quick," Arjun assured him, fiddling with the drone's remote-control unit.

The drone whirred, rose a few feet above the ground, and reached the burial spot.

"Wait, what is all that stuff on the ground?" Nitya was peering into the drone's video feed on the iPad in her hand.

Vikram looked over her shoulder. "Looks like … flower petals. Must have fallen from the bushes nearby."

"What bushes?"

Vikram looked around. There was nothing in the backyard that was flowering.

"Strange."

Arjun piloted the drone's landing, and its propellers slowed to a stop.

After about 5 minutes, he brought the drone back.

"Let's get out of here, Arjun. We are on private property," Vikram urged.

"Oh, for sure."

They crept back to the nearest point on the trail.

Arjun checked the power level of the drone's battery.

"Cool. That did not use as much power as I had thought. Do you both mind if I go down the trail and do some low-power scans of Stackhouse Park? I researched this area—it contains buried artifacts from indigenous tribes."

"Coming, Dad? It'll be a nice hike," Nitya urged.

"Yeah, why not?"

## Bidding Adieus

Vikram was on call at Conemaugh Hospital the next morning. His day started very early, and no one was home when he returned around noon.

Vikram made himself a sandwich and took a nap.

Nitya gently shook him awake.

"Dad, Arjun's leaving."

Vikram shook his head to dispel his grogginess.

They went downstairs, where Arjun was waiting by the garage door in the living room.

"*Jee*, I cannot thank you enough for hosting me this weekend. It was great to spend time with you and Nitya and get some work done. Overnight, I ran a low-resolution analysis of the data to a soil depth of about 4 feet. The entire dog's skeleton was visible. I was able to calibrate the radar. All morning, I scanned more areas around Stackhouse Park. I think I have enough data for analysis."

"Glad to hear it. So, back to Pittsburgh?"

"And to Ottawa this weekend, *Jee*."

"Oh? For some reason, I thought you would be around for a few more weeks. Well, I hope you stay in touch, Arjun."

"I will come visit after *Didi* returns," Arjun stated earnestly. "And … if my thesis advisor thinks I should collect more data from this area …," his voice trailed off.

Vikram understood. "You are welcome to visit whenever and stay as long as you wish, Arjun. It is not a problem."

"Thank you so much, *Jee*. I did not want to impose."

"Not an issue at all. We enjoyed your company."

Nitya nodded in agreement.

"I will reach out as and when my software needs your expertise, *Jee*."

"I was about to ask if you needed my assistance at all, as your software already does a fantastic job," Vikram smiled.

"Long way to go, *Jee*. The grand prize would be to identify human remains with high accuracy."

"Happy to help whenever you need it."

Arjun picked up his backpack and suitcase.

Vikram and Nitya walked him to the driveway.

"Oh," Arjun paused after he got into the driver's seat. "Something else is buried in that spot in the Shahs' backyard.

I will drop the full dataset with one of the CMU professors we work with and ask him to do a deeper analysis. He is a busy guy, and there is a lot of data—it might take a couple of weeks."

"Oh?" Nitya's ears perked up. "What do you think it is?"

"Wouldn't it be a wonderfully weird coincidence if historical artifacts were buried in the same spot?" Arjun smiled.

"Arjun, please let me know what you find. The Johnstown Area Heritage Association would be very interested to know," Vikram said.

"Will do."


Vikram hardly saw Nitya around the house for the next couple of days. She was out shopping for her trip to Europe, which included London, Barcelona, and Rome.

Thursday night, Vikram knocked on Nitya's bedroom door.

"Hi, Dad." Nitya's hair was disheveled, and the large suitcase on her bed was overflowing with clothes.

"Just checking in. Do you need help packing?"

"No, Dad. Mom is back online, and she's helping me," she exclaimed.

"Hi," came a voice from behind her.

Anshu's face was visible on the iPad on the dresser.

"Oh, hi," Vikram exclaimed. "You are back among civilization. We missed hearing from you this week. How're things going?"

"We left the resort yesterday and reached Kochi late at night. On the way, Mom must have eaten something that did not agree with her. We had to check her into a hospital this morning. Everything is fine, but we are staying in the hotel here today. Hopefully, she will come out of it soon."

"Oh, sorry to hear that. Give her plenty of fluids."

"Yup. Did Arjun leave? I was hoping to say bye to him."

"I can add him, Mom," Nitya offered.

Arjun joined the call. He wore shades, and his face was very close to the camera on his phone. He seemed to be in a high-noise outdoor environment and kept holding his phone to his ear.

"Hi, Arjun. I'll be back home in a couple of weeks. You should visit again," Anshu exclaimed.

"I will, *Didi*. I promise. Arya and I have been planning it."

"Sounds like a plan. OK, gotta go. Talk to you all later."

There was a chorus of goodbyes, and Anshu left the call.


"So, Arjun, all set to head back to Canada?" Vikram asked.

"Yes, *Jee*. When are you and Nitya coming tomorrow? Maybe we could meet?"

"Will be tough, Arjun. I cannot leave work until 2 pm, and her flight is at 6 pm. There is going to be traffic to deal with as well."

"Ok, ok, no worries. Have a safe and fun trip in Europe, Nitya."

"Thank you, Arjun *Mama*."

"Oh, *Jee*. My CMU team is taking me to dinner at the Mintt *Desi* restaurant in Monroeville. It is on your way home from the airport. Would you be able to stop by? I can also introduce you to Dr. Ned Hawkins, who now has all the radar data we collected the other day."

"Oh, I can do that. I may be able to get there by 6 pm. Would that work?"

"That would be perfect."


Friday descended into chaos as Nitya constantly fussed about her luggage, which was considerably overweight. Tempers started fraying, and at one point, Vikram had to tell her to get a hold of herself and not overthink things. With Anshu's calming presence on a video call, they repacked her suitcases. Much as she rued the now greatly diminished choice of clothing, Nitya grudgingly acknowledged that none of the essentials had been sacrificed.

All said and done, they reached Pittsburgh airport in a more relaxed mood and were able to exchange goodbyes on a harmonious note. Vikram slipped her some extra cash, which fully restored the smile on Nitya's face.

"Take care of yourself, Dad."

"I will. And you be safe. Keep us updated daily if possible."

"I will. Heading to Arjun's farewell event now?"

"Oh, yeah. Thanks for reminding me."

They hugged, and Nitya headed towards the TSA pre-check line.

Vikram waited until she was done with security, and she could turn and wave before boarding the airport train to her terminal.

Despite encountering the usual traffic at the Fort Pitt and Squirrel Hill tunnels, Vikram made good time from the airport to Monroeville. He had never been to Mintt, which had only recently opened. The exterior was straightforward and welcoming, with a glass front that allowed passersby to see the inside of the restaurant. A sign indicated the restaurant's offerings: South Indian, North Indian, and Indo-Chinese cuisine.

Vikram went inside. He was greeted by a clean and spacious dining area with rows of neatly arranged wooden chairs and tables set with white napkins and cutlery. Soft, warm lighting hung from the ceiling, and the floor was carpeted. Beyond, an empty buffet station lay.

It was easy to spot the university crowd, which had taken up a large table in the dining section on the left. The place did not serve alcohol but allowed its patrons to bring their own. And there appeared to be no shortage of beverages—several coolers laden with ice and a variety of wine and beer were stationed at the nearest corner.

"*Jee*," Arjun waved, indicating an empty chair across from where he was seated.

Vikram took his spot and was introduced to Dr. Ned Hawkins, who was seated in an adjacent chair.

Dr. Hawkins was stocky with broad, muscular shoulders. Bald and middle-aged, he wore glasses and a plain black T-shirt. He was nursing a dark beer and a bright smile.

Vikram took an instant liking to him.

"Pleased to meet you, Dr. Hawkins."

"Likewise, Dr. Malik. Please call me Ned."

"And please call me Vikram."

Arjun got Vikram a beer, and the three made small talk.

The topic slowly drifted to Arjun's research.

"I haven't gotten around to analyzing the data you sent me," Ned turned to Arjun, "But I will get it done next week. Maybe as early as Monday."

"No hurry, Dr. Hawkins."

Vikram had dinner, bid Arjun a safe journey to Canada, and returned home.


Later that night, Vikram got a text from Nitya that she had made it to the youth hostel safe and sound. Her friends were already there.

Vikram also spoke to Anshu, whose mother had been declared fit to travel after being released from the hospital. However, they both decided to shorten their India trip and return home.

Vikram slept soundly that night, looking forward to Anshu's imminent return.


## Digging Deeper

Pramod arrived at the Malik residence the following evening for their monthly Bridge tryst. Shinde, a gynecologist, and Dubey, a proctologist, joined them.

After a few rounds, Pramod suggested they switch to Poker and play for real money. Shinde claimed he was pretty good, while Dubey and Vikram admitted they were novices.

Within an hour, Pramod was up by about two grand. Shinde was the heaviest loser, as Dubey and Vikram folded almost every round.

"You guys play like your specializations. I'm a heart guy, and I play with courage. Vikram and Dubey, I knew your game would be crappy," Pramod paused, and the others laughed out of politeness.

Pramod seemed pleased with his scatological wit.

"And you," he turned to Shinde. "You play scared—like a woman." He roared uproariously.

Shinde's face was flushed. "Well, at least I like women," he retorted.

"What are you talking about? Everyone knows I sleep around," Pramod laughed. "Including Pratibha." But he sounded nervous.

"Guess you crossed a line? That's why she left you?" Shinde stood up, breathing heavily, hands curling into fists.

"No idea where you're going with this," Pramod stood up, facing Shinde across the table.

"Come on, guys," Vikram tried to calm them down. Dubey leaned back in his seat, seemingly entertained.

But Shinde wouldn't back down. "I heard Pratibha caught you with a dude when you were in Thailand," he said, laughing derisively.

Pramod looked stunned. There was a brief silence as he gritted his teeth. "Who told you that?" he asked in an ominous, low voice.

Shinde seemed to regain his senses and appeared somewhat embarrassed.

"Forget it," he said and headed toward the stairs.

Pramod's face was suffused with rage as he violently lunged at Shinde's receding figure. However, Vikram grabbed Pramod in a tight embrace, holding him back with great difficulty despite their height difference.

Vikram had never seen Pramod so upset.

"PD, that's enough." Vikram held on until Pramod's body stopped shaking.

Pramod finally sat down, heavy of breath and short on words.

Dubey stirred. "I think I'd better get going as well, Vikram."

Vikram nodded. "I'll see you out."

They went upstairs to find Shinde sitting alone on the front porch, staring into the distance.

"Hey, you okay?" Vikram asked, sitting down beside him.

Shinde sighed. "I just ... I hate being made fun of. Especially by Pramod."

Vikram nodded. "He can be a real jerk. But why does it bother you so much?"

"I've always felt like I had to prove myself, you know?" Shinde hung his head. "Being a gynecologist, being stereotyped—it ... gets to me. And Pramod ... well, he knows ... how to push my buttons."

"You're a damn good doctor, Shinde. Almost all the *Desi* kids in town have been delivered by your ObGyn practice, including Pramod's. Don't let him get to you," Dubey added.

Shinde nodded.

Shortly, both he and Dubey left.

Vikram returned to the basement.

Pramod had not moved an inch.

"PD, come on, the party's over. Let me drop you home."

Pramod didn't say anything. Vikram walked over, gently pulled him to his feet, and walked him to the garage. Pramod, still silent, got into the passenger seat of Vikram's car.

They drove in silence.

"I did not know, ok?" Pramod finally spoke as they pulled into his driveway.

"What?"

"Pratibha was drunk and passed out in the bedroom. I ... um ... went downstairs to the hotel bar, where there were many attractive women ... including this ... Lisa. You know ... sometimes I cannot help myself. The mistake I made was to bring Lisa back to our suite."

He paused. His speech was slurred but fluid.

"I figured Pratibha was going to sleep all night. The bedroom door was shut. We used the couch. I was not careful. Lisa … turned out to be a man … a female impersonator."

Pramod paused. Vikram did not react.

"But that turned me on. It was something new, and she … he … knew what to do. Pratibha woke up and saw us. When we returned to Johnstown, she said she couldn't unsee the whole thing. Said she couldn't be with me anymore."

"It happens," Vikram commiserated. "Sorry, bud."

"But I know she'll come back to me. She knows … that I need her," Pramod said simply, his shoulders slumping.

Vikram walked him to the garage door.

Pramod punched in a code. "I got it, Vikram. Thanks … for everything."

"PD, let me make sure you are ok."

Pramod shrugged. "Suit yourself." He opened the door and staggered his way into the ranch home. Vikram helped him to his bed in the master bedroom. Turning to switch the bedside light off, he saw a framed picture of Pramod and Pratibha on the table.

"She was my everything, Vikram," Pramod muttered, following Vikram's gaze. "It all went so wrong, and I blame my wandering eye, my cursed need for excitement. Our arguments, the cold silences, and the final, painful goodbye haunt me. Thailand was supposed to be a fun escape for both of us, and it turned into my biggest regret. I have never felt so alone as I do now."

Anshu called on Sunday. She had rebooked her return flight from India for Tuesday, but would be staying at her mother's place in the DC area for about a week.

Work kept Vikram busy during the week.

Wednesday evening, he received a call from Arjun.

"Hello, *Jee*. Heard *Didi* is back from India?"

"Wow, news travels fast. Yes, Anshu and her mom made it safe and sound. How'd you know?"

"Arya had added me to a chat group with Nitya, and I get regular updates."

"Lucky you. Nitya does not bother to reach me at all," Vikram laughed. "Guess you guys are the cool *Mausi* and *Mama*."

Arjun laughed. "Well, since *Didi* and Nitya will be back home by next weekend, Arya and I plan to drive down together if that's okay."

"Cool. That will be a nice reunion," Vikram replied enthusiastically.


"Thank you, *Jee*. By the way, Dr. Hawkins has already sent me the processed data from the Shahs' backyard. He found something that we would like you to look at."

"Oh? Something interesting?"

"Not clear. He said he will be in downtown Johnstown tomorrow and can show it to you," Arjun said mysteriously.

"He is coming to Johnstown just for this?" Vikram asked incredulously.

"Oh, no. Dr. Hawkins volunteers as a referee for some High School Ice Hockey intramural thing and occasionally officiates games at the downtown arena."

"Ah, that makes sense."

"I will send you his cell number, and you both can coordinate."

"Sounds good."


Vikram contacted Dr. Hawkins and met him for dinner at the Balance restaurant downtown.

"Long day, Ned?"

"Exhausting," Ned shook his head. "But rewarding. There were some great matchups."

Ned reminisced about how he occasionally visited Johnstown when his now-grown-up boys played Ice Hockey. "I do miss those days, hectic as they were. Being a referee is a great middle ground."

"Good for you." Vikram raised his glass.

Ned raised his in acknowledgment. "Thank you. Also, for dinner."

"Any time. And do look me up when you are in town next."

"I surely will."

As they were wrapping up dinner, Ned broached the topic.

"Vikram, is there a less public spot where I can show you our analysis of the data Arjun collected?"

"How about coming to my place? We can have a nightcap as well. And you can stay the night in the guest room."

"That is very generous of you, Vikram, but I have already checked into the Holiday Inn on Scalp Avenue."

"Oh, that is very close to where I live."

They were seated in Vikram's home office.

Vikram looked dumbfounded at what he saw on the large monitor Ned had connected to his laptop.

The screen displayed Arjun's software's Graphical User Interface (GUI). Ned was spinning the 3D visualization around. It resembled the one Arjun had shown Nitya and Vikram from the previous data set. The dog's skeleton was whole, and the outlines of the skull and various other bones were crisply defined.

However, there was an additional object below it.

"That is indeed a human skull," Vikram confirmed, his voice barely above a whisper. "The top section of it, at least."

Ned nodded. "Oh, and one more thing," he clicked some buttons on the GUI. "The soil above and below the dog seems to have been disturbed recently, likely at about the same time."

"Meaning?"

"The skull is not an ancient artifact like we had hoped. It seems to have been buried around the same time as the dog. But that is as far as the radar could penetrate, so we cannot see the entire thing."

Vikram's thoughts swirled with colliding theories, but the simplest, most logical one prevailed.

He explained the details of the stalled investigation of Morali Shah's disappearance.

"Ned, I must tell the coroner to sanction another exhumation. Would you mind going with me as an expert?"

"When?"

"Tomorrow is Friday, and I will tee it up first thing in the morning."

"Sure thing. My gig doesn't start until noon."

## Unearthing the Truth

Vikram leaned back on one of the beach chairs in the backyard and closed his eyes against the exceptionally bright summer sun.

Nitya and Anshu chatted animatedly, swiftly catching up on multiple topics.

Vikram heaved a sigh. He had somehow made it through a tumultuous week of twists and turns.

The doorbell rang.

"I'll get it," Nitya sped inside.

She returned with Arjun, who was dressed in shorts, a half-sleeved shirt, and sunglasses.

"Namaste, *Jee*. Namaste, *Didi*," he greeted them, bending to touch their feet.

Vikram stopped him midway and hugged him instead.

"Where's Arya?"

"She is on her way, *Jee*. A couple of hours ago, she said the line at the border was unbelievable. But at least she made it across this time."

"Oh, you guys did not travel together?" Anshu asked.

"No, *Didi*. I came to Pittsburgh yesterday to wrap up some work."

Vikram closed his eyes again, mentally rehearsing for the story time to follow.

"OK, can someone explain what's happening?" Anshu implored. "Those editions of the Johnstown Tribune-Democrat Vikram saved for me raise more questions than they provide answers."

"Don't want to wait for Arya?" Vikram asked.

"She knows everything, *Jee*," Arjun replied.

"Ok, then. Maybe Nitya and Arjun can start us off? Until the point where they left the country? I still haven't figured something out."

"Sure, Dad."

Arjun nodded.

Anshu listened with evident fascination, occasionally interrupting to clarify her understanding. She marveled at the story's human and technological elements.

"And Dr. Hawkins assisted *Jee* in persuading the coroner to excavate the site again," Arjun concluded, nodding towards Vikram.

"Wow, what a tale this has been so far," Anshu exclaimed, her eyes shining excitedly.

"My turn now, I suppose." Vikram slowly and carefully launched into his part of the narrative.

"The coroner and the DA scheduled another exhumation, and I was asked to be present. The dig revealed a full human corpse buried vertically below the dog's."

"Wow, quite ingenious," Anshu remarked. "Why are the papers not reporting these details?"

"According to them, it might inspire copycat crimes," Vikram explained. "… but that's not all," he paused dramatically.

"Oh, come on, Dad," Nitya complained. "You are drawing this out for maximum effect."

"That I am," Vikram laughed. "I feel like the star of a detective show."

"Anyway," he continued. "The exhumed corpse showed signs of about a year of natural decomposition. From the skull, I could already tell it was a man, and the pelvic and overall bone structure confirmed it."

"Oh, I thought it would have been Morali Shah's body," Anshu exclaimed. "Someone else was buried there? Wow—what were the Shahs up to?"

"There was no clothing, jewelry, or hair on the corpse. Dental records did not match anyone in town. Nor did DNA records. There is no way to identify the corpse."

Vikram paused for dramatic effect. "But the autopsy revealed something significant. Something … sinister."

"What?" Anshu asked, her excited demeanor reminding Vikram of her 20-year-old self.

"Based on the damage to the area near the Adam's Apple, this was a case of homicide by strangulation."

"Ah, so that is why the papers are seeking Haresh for murder. But … I would have thought both Shahs would be under suspicion."

"Well, Morali is still missing, per their investigation. But this is where Arjun comes in," Vikram said somberly. "He says he knows something we don't."

"Oh?" Anshu looked puzzled. Then it dawned on her, "Oh, a Canada connection?"

"Yes, *Didi*. I did some digging back home in Canada. Turns out I knew Morali Shah growing up."

"What?" The Maliks exclaimed in unison.

"She had a different identity."

"What?"

"And gender," Arjun said slowly, letting his words sink in.

"Oh …," Nitya broke the stunned silence, realization dawning on her face.

"So …," Anshu started hesitantly.

"So, the corpse might indeed be that of Morali Shah."

"Oh, my," Anshu's eyes were tearful. "The poor, poor thing. What a tragedy."

Nitya walked over to console her, her own eyes welling up.

Vikram was too stunned to move. His mind instantly remembered Pramod's confession about his escapade in Thailand, which reinforced the plausibility of his attraction to Morali.

"A lot of small things make sense now," Anshu exclaimed. "Morali would always wear something around her neck. To hide her Adam's Apple, maybe?"

"Her voice was somewhat deeper, too," Nitya agreed.

Arjun nodded.

"But why would Haresh murder her?" Vikram mused. "What would be the motive?"

"That is not clear to me either, *Jee*," Arjun confessed. "Without her, he would not have her family's financial support and no livelihood."

An hour passed, and casual conversation resumed.

"You look so much like Nikhil," Anshu remarked for perhaps the third time that evening.

Arjun laughed. "You keep saying that, *Didi*. I never saw it until I decided to grow a beard. I now realize how strong the resemblance is."

"Explain to me again—how are you related to Nikhil and Arya? Which of *Chachi*'s siblings is your dad?"

"Um …," Arjun hesitated. "Excuse me," he said, looking at his phone. "Oh, Arya is outside. Says she brought a huge indoor plant and needs my help."

"I'll come," Nitya offered.

"Thanks," Arjun said gratefully.

As they turned and walked towards the house, Anshu stared at them, a frown on her face.

Nitya returned alone. "They're coming," she said, misty-eyed.

Arjun walked over to them slowly and deliberately removed his sunglasses.

It was then that realization dawned on Vikram.

He had never looked deep into Arjun's eyes.

Big, bright, brown.

Previously sparkling, with a hint of mischief.

And life.

Now, sad.

Somewhat hopeful.

"Arya," Anshu whispered, stepping forward and embracing Arjun in a maternal hug.

Arjun broke down crying, his narrow shoulders heaving convulsively.

"You … you … knew?" Vikram haltingly asked Nitya, who was smiling through her tears.

It was all the words he could muster.

Nitya nodded happily and draped her arms around Arjun and Anshu.

Vikram joined her.

Arjun left the next day. In parting, he simply said that all he wanted, as Arjun, was to feel accepted by the Malik family, with whom, as Arya, he had experienced an inexplicably deep kinship.

The Maliks offered their unconditional support, which overwhelmed him with gratitude.

"Thank you for accepting me," he said through unshed tears. "I have struggled since childhood—with my confusion, my fear of being different. Others, including Nikhil and our parents, aren't so understanding, but now … I have you all."

Arjun promised to revisit them, update them on his ongoing gender transition journey, and seek their assistance and guidance as necessary.

Based on Vikram's tip, the police sought Morali Shah's dental records from Canada and confirmed the identity of the exhumed corpse. The newspapers picked up the story, although the gender issue was not revealed.

Haresh turned himself in within a few days of the story breaking in the press. He confessed that he had gotten their ailing pet euthanized and buried both bodies within a day of each other. According to his statement, he did not murder Morali but had found her corpse hanging from a ceiling fan in the foyer when he got home from work one evening. Fearing that Morali's parents would hold him responsible and cut off all financial assistance, he hid her body.

Haresh claimed his marriage to Morali was based on mutual trust and understanding and that he greatly loved her. When confronted with Arjun's drone footage showing him lurking in the backyard, he explained that he had come to pay his respects to Morali's resting place—by placing petals from her favorite flowers. Haresh added that Morali had battled chronic depression all her life, had exhibited suicidal tendencies before, and likely committed suicide.

However, Vikram's autopsy report noted that, based on the fracture to the Hyoid Bone and the Thyroid Cartilage, Morali had been strangled before her body was hanged. The lack of a suicide note further incriminated Haresh, who was arrested and charged with first-degree murder.

The trial began 6 months later and ended swiftly. Harsh maintained his innocence on the stand but was sentenced to life in prison.

A few months passed.

The family was having breakfast when Nitya's phone alerted everyone to an incoming FaceTime call.

"Hi, Arjun *Mama*. Mom and Dad are here. Let me put you on speaker."

Vikram and Anshu gathered behind Nitya, who propped her phone against a vase.

Arjun's face came into view.

"*Namaste, Didi. Namaste, Jee.* How're you all doing?"

"All fine here, Arjun," Vikram replied. "How are you?"

"Good, good. I have another update for you," Arjun began. "I learned more about the Shahs, confirming parts of Haresh's story. Morali's parents did believe that if she could live a normal life as a woman, it might help her heal mentally."

Arjun paused before continuing, "But it goes deeper. They also wanted to shield their reputation—her being a trans-man was something they didn't want their social and family circles to know about. Meanwhile, Haresh's parents in India had been deeply indebted to Morali's family for years. His father had borrowed heavily to keep their struggling business afloat, and Morali's parents used that leverage to pressure Haresh into marrying Morali and moving far away."

"The plan, in a way, worked. Morali was relatively stable, even though she was rumored to sleep around. As for Haresh, he could do little about Morali's promiscuity, focusing instead on the emotional companionship they shared. For him, the marriage was a way to support her mental health while repaying his family's debts, quietly fulfilling his role as both protector and partner in their unconventional arrangement."

There was a series of exclamations from the Maliks.

"And this is where the story takes a turn. Before her disappearance, Morali had been telling her parents that she had fallen in love with someone and planned to leave Haresh. Haresh must have found out somehow and realized they would have cut all ties with him when that happened. That could explain why he tried to hide Morali's death from them. It could also be a motive for murder."

"Wow," Vikram whistled. "Who knew Haresh had so many layers beneath that bland personality?"

"Morali said she had fallen in love with someone? Must be Pramod, right?" Anshu said.

"He likely led her on," Vikram nodded in agreement.

Nitya broke the silence that followed.

"But how did you figure all this out, Arjun *Mama*?"

Arjun grinned. "Most of the *Desi* community here knows me only as Arya. They assume I cut my hair short and wear loose clothes these days. And women tend to talk freely among each other."

"But your voice—it is so deep," Nitya exclaimed. "Although I could swear the one time you called as Arjun *Mama*, I thought you were Arya *Mausi*."

Arjun laughed. "The first thing I did when I began my transition was to practice my Arjun voice for hours. I learned to speak from the chest, not just by lowering my voice and carefully modulating each word. When I dress up as Arjun, the male voice becomes second nature. But as Arya, I use my natural one."

"So much you need to tell us about your journey, Arjun," Anshu said admiringly.

"Story for another day, *Didi*."


A few days passed.

"I've been thinking. Do you think he might have done it?" Anshu casually asked while getting ready for bed one night.

"Who? Did what?" Vikram responded absent-mindedly, still thinking about the lineup for the upcoming golf tournament at the club.

"Murdered Morali Shah," she said, turning to look at him.

Vikram paused, frowning slightly. "We now have a motive. She was planning to leave Haresh for Pramod, and he would have been out on the street here, and his family in India would be in trouble as well."

"I wasn't talking about Haresh." Anshu's tone was even, but her eyes were fixed on Vikram.

"What? Who?" Vikram blinked. "Pramod?"

"Think about it," Anshu continued, calm but insistent. "He started having an affair with Morali—she was attractive, and he was drawn to her. And we know Pramod. He's not the kind of man who handles rejection or ultimatums well. What if Morali pushed him? What if she threatened to go public about their affair or tried to force him to leave Pratibha?"

Vikram sat down on the edge of the bed, the golf match forgotten. "You think Pramod lost control? That he killed her in one of his rage fits?"

"Why not?" Anshu shrugged. "We've known about his temper. You've seen him smash golf clubs and throw instruments in surgeries. He could have snapped if she said or did something that enraged him."

Vikram rubbed his chin. "It's a dark theory," he admitted. "But … plausible."

"Exactly," Anshu said, leaning forward. "And he's cunning enough to hang her body to make it look like a suicide."

Vikram's brow furrowed. "It's just speculation. There's no evidence."

"Agreed," Anshu conceded, "but look at the timing. Pramod disappeared for weeks right after Morali's missing person story broke. Isn't that suspicious?"

Vikram exhaled, shaking his head. "If Pramod did it, he's fortunate Haresh unwittingly incriminated himself. It's convenient—too convenient."

Anshu nodded slowly. "But it fits, doesn't it?"

"Hmm," Vikram muttered, leaning back against the headboard. "It's hard to imagine, but maybe it isn't. Who knows what he's capable of in the heat of the moment?"

"And yet," Anshu added softly, "we'll probably never know the truth. The case is closed. And Pramod will keep playing golf, throwing tantrums, and having affairs like nothing happened."

Vikram stared at the ceiling, his mind racing. "I hate how plausible this sounds," he murmured.

"Sometimes, the scariest truths hide behind the obvious," Anshu said, slipping into bed. "Good night, honey."

"Good night," Vikram replied absently, his thoughts far from rest.

# Know Strings Attached   

## Barkatpura to Belvedere

As soon as Tripti Iyengar's brother Rohit completed high school and secured admission to the Indian Institute of Technology (IIT), *Appa* accepted a promotion, which meant the family had to move from Hyderabad to Kolkata.

*Amma* lobbied hard for Rohit to consider joining IIT-KGP (a short train ride from Kolkata), but Rohit's heart was set on IIT-M (in Chennai). Tripti understood—Rohit had always cherished their summer trips to Chennai. He loved the city and their aunts, uncles, and cousins, who doted on Rohit.

Rohit and *Appa* were oblivious to *Amma*'s and Tripti's emotions as they cheerily bade goodbye and took the train to attend orientation day at IIT-M. *Amma* was in tears—both happy and sad, but Tripti's demeanor was stoic, masking her frustration. While her parents saw *Anna*'s IIT admission as a significant milestone in their parenthood journey, Tripti felt uprooted. Hyderabad had always been home—safe, snug, and supportive.

*Appa* was back within a week, declaring that he and *Amma* could now check off one of their responsibilities—Rohit was housed safely in his hostel and enroute to an IIT degree, so his prospects were secure for life.

Arriving in Kolkata, Tripti felt out of place, overwhelmed by the city's chaotic charm. The narrow, winding streets, the cacophony of honking horns, the overcrowded buses, and the vibrant markets starkly contrasted with Hyderabad's laid-back vibe.

Per *Amma* and *Appa*, hearsay and hormones ran rampant on the Belvedere Central Government Officers Quarters campus, where the Iyengars were granted residence. They enrolled Tripti in a private all-girls school rather than the co-ed public institution most Belvedere kids attended.

Ashok Hall, Tripti's new school, was challenging academically and socially. Telugu, her "second language" in the Hyderabad school curriculum, was not an option, so Tripti was forced to choose Sanskrit. Her classmates were clique-ish, her *Hyderabadi* Hindi and accented English posed communication barriers, and her stern and unhelpful language teachers had impossibly high standards. There was no respite from the academic rigor in the form of arts or athletics.

On the Belvedere campus, Tripti's interactions with her peer generation were carefully orchestrated and constantly monitored by *Amma*—lest a stray word or wayward action damage the family's chaste reputation. Expressly forbidden from hanging out at the clubhouse (which, according to *Amma*, was a cesspool of teenage depravity), Tripti became acquainted with a few of the younger Belvedereans during dinners hosted by *Amma* for the families of *Appa*'s new colleagues. But everyone was older than her and belonged in existing close-knit circles. Tripti soon understood that subsequent invitations to potluck get-togethers that *Amma* grudgingly permitted her to attend were solely motivated by the growing reputation of *Amma*'s cooking. Once the food was devoured, Tripti was gently eased out of conversations and sometimes the premises.

The atmosphere at home was not ideal either. *Appa* was heavily distracted by his new position, and with Rohit no longer at home, Tripti became the sole focus of *Amma*'s attention. Tripti's natural streak of rebelliousness, coupled with *Amma*'s unnerving critical gaze, frequently got her into trouble. *Amma* bemoaned, "Your grades—how will you get into a decent college, Tripti? Like your *Anna*? And why were you talking to the girl who always wears short skirts—didn't I tell you she is a bad influence? Who was the boy with the camera? Be careful—don't let him take pictures of you. Who knows whom he might show them to and what he would tell them!"

Tripti's retorts rapidly led to recriminations, not resolutions. Once conflict fatigue set in, both recognized they had to pick their battles, and an uneasy truce prevailed. *Amma* pivoted to passive-aggressive expressions of her victimhood at having to parent a headstrong offspring. Tripti learned to temper her reactions by ignoring what was said and walking away or self-isolating in her room until emotions ebbed.

Tripti's life took a turn for the better during a school trip to the Birla Industrial & Technological Museum, where a video phone was on exhibit. She picked up the wired handsets and stared at a smiling face on her black-and-white console screen.

"Hello, I am Sneha … from Section B," came a disembodied voice.

"Hi, I am Tripti. Section C."

"Hey, this thing works. Tell me a joke."

"Ok … what is black and yellow and goes zub-zub?"

"Er … what?"

"A bee flying backward."

"That's terrible," Sneha giggled.

"You didn't say it had to be good."

Sneha was Tripti's first friend in Kolkata.

Sneha's unconditional support, unwavering friendship, and unbridled personality considerably eased Tripti's trials and tribulations at school.

Sneha spread the word that Tripti was a trained *Carnatic* vocalist. This sparked interest among several of the Ashok Hall girls and widened her circle of friends, who appreciated her musical talent, no-nonsense attitude, conventional South Indian beauty, and sharp wit.

Per Tripti's suggestion, Sneha started accompanying her to after-school tutoring. Tripti's improved grades and Sneha's conservative *Marwari* background put *Amma*'s mind at ease and slowly earned her trust.

In Sneha's company, Tripti was allowed to spend time outside of school playing ping pong or carrom at the clubhouse or taking long walks on the lush adjoining grounds of the National Library.

Rohit's visits home during his Summer and Winter breaks afforded Tripti even more freedom—his presence distracted *Amma*, who focused on cooking his favorite meals.

By the end of the first six months, Tripti was popular at school and embraced by Belvedereans as one of their own. Barring *Amma*'s occasional grumbling about her being friends with too many boys, life was getting better every day.

After three years, the entire Ashok Hall cohort of girls transferred to J. D. Birla Junior College. With a leaner slate of courses, Tripti's academic performance started to hit its stride. Tripti's social circles at school and Belvedere widened, and her popularity soared.

# Belvedere Banter

"So?" Sneha's expressive, almond-shaped eyes sparkled. "Where is he?"

"You are not serious," Tripti exclaimed, shaking her head in mock exasperation and opening the front door wider.

Sneha rushed in, dark, wavy hair bouncing around her shoulders. She paused, turned her head, and arched a thick, well-defined brow. Her smooth, warm brown cheeks were flushed in anticipation.

"Oh," Tripti said vaguely, closing the door. "I think he is upstairs … on the terrace."

Sneha made a disappointed face, walked over to the dining table, and tossed her well-worn backpack filled with textbooks, notebooks, and pens.

"Sneha, he does not walk around dressed like in the photos," Tripti laughed. Sneha's positive energy, matched only by her optimistic outlook on life, never ceased to amuse her.

Their dialogue paused at the sound of the front door opening.

Sneha's eyes widened, and she stared at Tripti in anticipation.

A tuneless yodel from a popular Kishore Kumar song preceded the physical entry of the topic of their conversation.

Tripti's brother Rohit was clad in a slovenly, once-white T-shirt and shorts that looked like they had not seen soap or water in weeks. Oblivious to the girls' presence, he belted out a few more bars while shutting the door behind him. He turned and stood frozen in place upon seeing the girls, the last echoes of his voice fading into the walls and ceiling.

"*Anna*, this is my friend Sneha."

"Uh …," Rohit seemed to be searching for words. "Nice to meet you." He blushed and ducked into the living room.

"IITians," Tripti smiled at Sneha. "Their brains stop working when they see a pretty girl."

Sneha smiled back.

"I warned you—*Appa* got him a three-piece suit before he left for America, and *Amma* made him wear it so we could take some family pictures. Clothes make the man, as they say."

"He is still good-looking," Sneha said defensively, gathering her backpack. "He thought I was pretty?"

"Only a blind fool would think you are not," Tripti replied. "But … don't *Marwari* girls get married as soon as they finish high school?" she teased.

Sneha stuck her tongue out. "I still have a year."

Tripti and Sneha engaged in small talk, prolonging their parting as they often did.

Sneha kept throwing furtive glances at the entrance to the living room.

"Oh, ok, I'll go get him," Tripti laughed.

"Wait for me."

They found Rohit on the living room balcony, hands draped over the railing, gazing at the street below,

Sneha hung back within earshot.

"Enjoying the Belvedere sights?" Tripti asked Rohit.

"Only *Aunties* about," Rohit replied. "Hey, you never told me your friend was this pretty."

"Tons of wannabe Romeos are constantly circling our school on mopeds because of her. Just so you know—she is still here and heard everything you said."

Rohit's head snapped around. Seeing Sneha, he blushed but regained his composure quickly.

"Thought your school was full of nerds like you," Rohit retorted. "Sneha, you should come by more often, especially when I am in town."

"Well, it took a picture of you in your new suit to catch Sneha's eye."

"And?"

"Disappointment," Tripti shook her head.

"Total," added Sneha.

Both girls giggled.

"Oh, well," Rohit shrugged, smiling at Sneha.

"Wouldn't have worked out anyway," Tripti said somberly. "Feel bad for her. She will be married off to some *paan*-chewing *Marwari* business dude next year."

"Hey, my parents will find someone nice," Sneha protested.

"What?" Rohit sounded incredulous.

"Yeah, it's common in our community," Sneha smiled ruefully.

"And here I was, thinking I would return to woo you with a graduate degree from Ohio State."

"Well, get your B.Tech first," retorted Tripti.

"Just have to go to Chennai and physically receive the paper."

"Lucky."

"You are the fortunate one. I would gladly repeat my college years."

"You will be doing that anyway, right? That's why you are going to grad school. What is it like—two years for an M.S. and another four for a PhD? *Amma* wanted you to do an MBA, get a job, marry a nice *Iyengar* girl, and stay in India."

Sneha giggled at the back-and-forth.

"What do *you* want to do?" Rohit deflected, looking directly at Sneha. "In life?"

Sneha blushed. "I don't know," she shook her head. "Manage a home?"

"Come on, Sneha," Tripti urged impatiently. "You are smart and talented; you can be whatever you want to be."

"Maybe all I want to be is a good wife and mother?"

"There is nobility and virtue in that," Rohit interrupted, seeing Tripti working up a speech. "Look at *Amma*."

Sneha shot Rohit a grateful glance—all year, she had been at the receiving end of Tripti's woman empowerment discourses.

"That … that's not the same … times were different …," Tripti sputtered. "*Amma* didn't know any better and had no encouragement from her family."

"I suppose that is true," Rohit conceded.


"So, you are going to America?" Sneha shyly asked Rohit. Her life had been relatively sheltered when it came to boys. She had no brothers, and attending a co-ed institution was out of the question for her conservative parents.

As Rohit spoke about his plans, Tripti occasionally interjected with her comments, and Sneha grew increasingly quiet. In her community, boys and girls had pre-defined futures: the boys would manage the family business, and the girls would take care of the home. Sneha had never considered becoming anything other than a homemaker, like her own *Ma*. But listening to Rohit and Tripti discuss prospective careers, she felt a pang of self-doubt—a quiet ache at the rigidity of her predetermined path.

The sun sank below the horizon, bathing Belvedere in a hazy dusk. Sneha consulted her watch and gave a start. With an exclamation of dismay, she bid a hasty goodbye and tore down the stairs.

A thought struck Sneha as soon as she reached the street two floors below—this might be the last time she would see Rohit.

*Ever?*

She glanced up.

Tripti and Rohit were waving goodbye.

Sneha waved back.


Tripti smiled at Rohit, who was craning his neck over the balcony to stare at Sneha's family car speeding towards the Command Hospital gate of the Belvedere campus.

"Kolkata girls," Tripti teased, "are charming. But Sneha is special."

"She seems fun," Rohit smiled. "Can't believe I only met her now."

"What can I say? She was never interested until she saw the photo of you in a suit."

Rohit laughed. "I think she liked what she saw."

Tripti rolled her eyes but joined in.

"Chennai is my first love, but this city is also magical in a different way. I don't know if it is the people or the way the sun hits it during mornings and evenings in Summers and Winters, but I will miss coming here," Rohit sighed.

"You could have done what *Amma* wanted and gone to IIM," Tripti retorted. "And enjoyed Belvedere for two more years." She hesitated, "well, one more year, anyway."

"I don't know what I want to do," Rohit said, shaking his head. "I feel like I did not learn much at IIT. I am curious to see what America has to offer. I can always do an MBA and join the corporate rat race." He frowned. "Wait, what did you say about Belvedere and one more year?"

"*Appa* is talking about moving back to Chennai next year."

"Why?"

"He says he is due for another promotion."

"Already? Wow, good for him. Wait, you do not seem happy about it. You missed Hyderabad when Appa moved us here. Now you will miss Kolkata?"

"Well, yeah, but that is not what I am worried about."

"What then?"

"The college reservation system in Chennai does not work well for Brahmins," she said glumly.

"Ah," Rohit paused. "And *Appa* mentioned you refused to take the IIT entrance exam?"

She nodded. "Yeah … lack of preparation."

"So, what then?"

"BITS Pilani for Computer Science."

"Great program."

"Yeah, but the hostel food is supposed to be terrible, and the campus is kind of rural."

"All hostel food is awful, and all college campuses are fantastic. I loved Pilani the one time I was there. You'll be at home; parts of it look like Belvedere."

"Hope so."

"And after that?"

"Follow your inspiring footsteps, *Anna*."

"Cool, we may overlap in grad school."

"I meant I want to go to America for a career, not another degree."

"Peace. Good luck convincing *Amma* and *Appa* to let you leave India—alone."

Tripti rolled her eyes in annoyance.

## Betrothed to Bereft

A year passed.

Sneha looked shyly at Kunal. Their families had negotiated their nuptials and arranged for them to meet on the National Library campus, which adjoined Belvedere. Sneha picked the venue—a nostalgic throwback to the times she and Tripti used to walk through it, chatting for hours.

Skinny, tall, and fair-skinned, Kunal carried himself with a faint stoop. He was a man of sparing pleasantries. When he spoke, it was with an air of bitterness and cynicism. He was disparaging of the *Marwari* community.

"No ambition to make their future," he remonstrated with a short, barking laugh. "Just content to do whatever their parents and grandparents did."

Sneha briefly considered the irony of the sentiment, as Kunal was managing the family electronic parts store on Park Street, but she found the perspective refreshing.

Tripti could not attend the marriage, citing a busy academic schedule at college. Sneha was disappointed but understood.

Sneha moved into Kunal's joint-family home in the same affluent Ballygunge neighborhood as her parents' and assumed the duties of a new *bahu*. She was treated reasonably well by one and all. She saw Kunal only during late evenings, which were inevitably spent in the company of family members. Nights were reserved for listening to Kunal's complaints about work and physical intimacy.

Sneha was happy—her life was as "normal" as she had hoped and expected. At first, no one begrudged her frequent visits to see *Ma*, who was only a short car ride away. But after three years had passed, and Sneha was yet to bear a child, the grumblings in Kunal's household turned more pointed. Sneha's frequent visits to her parents' home, once met with indulgent smiles, now elicited narrowed eyes. Her mother-in-law began to speak wistfully of grandchildren, while Kunal's aunts were more direct.

Kunal's words, couched in feigned concern, cut deeper. "You know, Sneha," he began one evening, his tone exaggeratedly patient, "it's just ... every woman in our family has had children without problems. Maybe you're stressing over this too much, or ... not trying hard enough."

Fighting words tumbled to the edge of Sneha's tongue, only to crumble under the weight of decorum. She withdrew unto herself, seeking solace in her parents' home whenever she could. *Ma* comforted Sneha, even though her own face was creased with worry.

Sneha's family offered daily oblations at the Kalighat temple until Mother *Kali* relented. A routine doctor's appointment revealed that Sneha was pregnant. Kunal's family met the news with joy.

Kunal's reaction was muted. "Finally," he muttered, his eyes refusing to meet Sneha's.

Within a month of the pregnancy, Sneha overheard Kunal's aunts gossiping: "It's a tradition in our family for a *bahu* to stay with her parents until the baby is born." "Yeah, why is she still here?" "Her parents should send for her already."

Sneha didn't need any further encouragement, feeling relieved to leave Kunal's somewhat oppressive home.

*Ma* and *Baba* welcomed Sneha with open arms—their joy at becoming grandparents clearly evident.

Sneha's pregnancy and Sahil's birth were devoid of complications.

When Kunal visited, his demeanor was inscrutable. After holding a week-old Sahil for a few moments, he handed the baby back to Sneha and declared, "I'm leaving for the US within a month. I've been admitted to a master's program in Dayton, Ohio. It's a great opportunity, and I'll finally be able to get out of this rut."

Sneha stared at him, stunned. "America? What about us?"

Kunal shrugged. "Once I've completed my degree and found a job, I'll send for you both. You'll both need visas, which'll take time—you don't even have passports right now."

Her protests were met with irritation. "Don't make this about you, Sneha. This is for all of us."

Kunal left a month later, his departure marked by courteous farewells to both her family and his. Sneha stayed behind, cradling Sahil and wondering what lay ahead.

Sneha gradually found a rhythm in her days. She took on parenting with quiet determination, splitting time between her two homes. Her in-laws supported her, but *Ma* was her rock, comforting her whenever doubts about her future assailed her.

Kunal's communications from abroad began to take a positive tone. Graduate school seemed to suit him, and his frustration at managing the family business in Kolkata was replaced by growing contentment. "It is going better than I'd imagined," he messaged. "The Wright State campus is small but nice, and I'm doing well in my coursework."

Kunal wrapped up his studies in two years and secured a job, taking advantage of the "practical training" opportunities permitted under his student visa. "I'll send the required documents for your travel," he told Sneha one evening. "Start planning."

Sneha threw herself into the preparations, envisioning her new life in Dayton—a place she knew only through Kunal's sparse, matter-of-fact descriptions. While apprehension lingered, hope persisted—this could be the fresh start their family needed.

## Bachelor to Bride

Tripti's interactions with *Amma*—whether over the phone during her semesters at BITS Pilani or in person during breaks at their Chennai home—always carried an undertone of *Amma*'s expectations. When Tripti shared stories about extracurriculars, *Amma* would listen but steer the conversation back to academics or future career plans. "Have you been keeping up with your grades? You must always aim for the top, Tripti. That is the road to finding a good husband and a professional career. I was never given the opportunity—you should use yours." Tripti often ended these conversations feeling both motivated and resentful, as if her achievements would never be enough to meet *Amma*'s exacting standards.

After graduating with high honors in Computer Science and receiving a job offer from a leading multinational IT corporation, Tripti felt both proud and excited about her prospects. She aspired to a flourishing career in the US tech industry.

However, the traditional facet of *Amma*'s expectations reared its head exactly as Rohit had predicted.

In the midsummer following the BITS commencement ceremony, Tripti found herself with *Amma* and *Appa* in the living room of their Central Government Quarters apartment in Chennai.

"Tripti, *ma*," *Amma* began gently. "You know we value your achievements and dreams. But we also have to think about your life in a broader sense."

Tripti sighed resignedly. "I understand, *Amma*. But you have always encouraged me to pursue a professional career. I have an offer from TCS, which has promised me a visa to work in the US."

*Appa*, who had been quietly listening, spoke up. "Please understand, Tripti. It's difficult for us to send you alone to a foreign country.'

"We have found a good match for you," *Amma* continued firmly. "Srikant is from a respectable *Iyengar* family and is pursuing his PhD at the Ohio State University."

Tripti's heart sank. Despite geographical distances, the *Iyengar* community was small and close-knit. She had heard about Srikant through the grapevine. His family was well-regarded, and he was academically accomplished, but the prospect of an arranged marriage felt like a needless constraint.

"But, *Appa*, I don't even know him. How can I marry someone I've never met? And am I not too young to be married? I do not know the first thing about running a household … and I can barely cook."

"If only you had helped me more in the kitchen …," *Amma* started mumbling but stopped when *Appa* held up a hand.

*Appa* smiled—but there was a tinge of regret and sadness behind it. His voice belied his conflicting emotions.

"You will get to meet him, *ma*. He's coming to India for a few weeks. Just talk to him with an open mind. It could be the best of both worlds—you can still go to the US, and you'll have a supporting partner there."

Moved by his beseeching expression and words, Tripti relented. "Okay."

The meeting was arranged over lunch at the Adyar Matsya, a neutral, informal venue where both families could converse freely while visiting the ample buffet.

Tripti felt a mix of anxiety and curiosity as she walked in, her parents flanking her.

Srikant was already there, seated with his parents. He looked up and smiled as they approached.

"Hello, Tripti. It's nice to meet you," Srikant stood up. Thin, bespectacled, and affable, there was nothing objectionable about him.

"Nice to meet you too, Srikant," Tripti replied, bowing her head.

*As a "good" Iyengar girl would.*

They sat down, and the conversation flowed surprisingly easily. Srikant spoke about his research, interests, and experiences living in Columbus. Tripti felt remarkably comfortable in his presence.

After the formalities, they were given some time to talk alone in a quiet corner.

"Tripti, I know this is awkward," Srikant began. "But I have always felt my parents knew what was best for me regarding a life partner. I am academically inclined and, frankly, quite incapable of finding someone on my own."

Srikant's self-deprecating words had the desired effect. Tripti acknowledged that she had not thought much about her marital prospects and future.

"Srikant, which is sort of true for me as well. I have always thought I would go through the arranged marriage process when the time was right. I just did not expect it to happen so early."

"Understood. All I can say is that I will consider myself very fortunate if you agree to marry me."

Srikant's words were guileless, and his earnestness touched something deep within Tripti.

"I think I feel the same," she replied.

The tension between them seemed to evaporate. Tripti reflected on the romantic trials and tribulations of several of her girlfriends at BITS.

*Is it really this simple? Can I just bypass all the effort and drama of finding someone on my own?*

Srikant seemed to read her mind.

"I think certain people know when they have met their life partner. I feel that way now."

"So do I." Tripti's involuntary response surprised even her.

They smiled at each other, equal parts relieved and apprehensive.

"So, how do you feel about moving to Columbus, Ohio? I hear your brother lived there?" Srikant asked, his eyes curious. "He must have graduated before I started my PhD."

Tripti thought about Rohit. His stories about life in the US had been spare but fascinating—a blend of struggle, adventure, and romance gone wrong.

"We haven't heard much from Rohit in recent years. After insisting that he did not want to do an MBA and join the corporate 'rat race' as he called it, he did exactly that. He abandoned his graduate program in Mechanical Engineering and switched to an MBA. He now works for an international business consulting firm and seems to live out of a suitcase, constantly hopping between countries."

"Well, not everyone likes to stay tied down in one place. Maybe it suits him," Srikant smiled.

Tripti smiled back and took a deep breath. "Honestly, I'm excited about the opportunity to move to America. But the idea of an arranged marriage is … daunting. I have career goals and don't want to lose sight of them."

Srikant nodded understandingly. "I get it. I've been living away from my family for a while, and it's given me perspective. I want a partner who wants to pursue her ambitions. We can support each other."

His words were reassuring, and Tripti felt a glimmer of hope. *Perhaps this arrangement could work out after all.*

# Vows to Visa

The wedding was a low-key event filled with the colors and vibrancy of *Iyengar* traditions. Tripti, dressed in a conventional 9-yard *saree*, felt a whirlwind of emotions as she sat beside Srikant before the ceremonial fire, imagining her professional and married life in America.

After the lengthy wedding rituals finally concluded, Tripti and Srikant found a moment to themselves as a married couple.

"You look stunning," Srikant broke the silence.

"Thank you," Tripti smiled. "I guess our new journey begins."

"Yes, and I promise I will always support you."


Srikant's Buckeye Village apartment in Columbus was cozy and minimally furnished. His graduate student stipend was extremely modest, so their lifestyle was pragmatically frugal, with every expense meticulously calculated and budgeted.

Tripti enjoyed the novelty of domestic life with Srikant. He was surprisingly skilled in the kitchen. His interpretations of traditional dishes like *sambar* and *rasam* were unconventional—recipes born from a bachelor's improvisation—but delicious.

Srikant was a considerate husband, helping Tripti transition smoothly by introducing her to their neighbors and his circle of friends. During the week, he devoted long hours to OSU's Fontana Labs but always found time to accompany her on walks around campus. Being surrounded by the lively and vibrant student community, along with the lush greenery, reminded Tripti of her college years and gave her a sense of belonging.

Weekends offered more adventurous outings. Srikant drove them to various Columbus landmarks and state parks in either a friend's car or a rented vehicle. These excursions accelerated Tripti's acclimation to her new life and strengthened her bond with Srikant, filling her with optimism for their future together.

One Saturday afternoon, Srikant urged her to wear *Desi* attire. "You'll love Anita *Mami*. Her home smells amazing, and her *prasadam* is to die for. She might ask you to lead a few songs. You will also meet people from the local South Indian community attending the *bhajan*."

"Rohit used to talk about this *Mami*," Tripti exclaimed. "She is quite an icon in Columbus, according to him. But … sing? I haven't done that in public in years."

"Trust me, *ma*. You'll charm her and everyone else."

Anita *Mami*'s home in the Dublin suburb blended Ohio's suburban charm with *Desi* touches. The foyer opened into a spacious living room with high ceilings and large windows. Ornate tapestries, brass idols, and framed paintings adorned the walls. A faint aroma of sandalwood incense lingered in the air.

Anita *Mami* was in her mid-fifties, with an energetic voice and a vibrant personality. Her skin was smooth and glowing, a shade of dusky caramel untouched by Ohio winters. She had sharp, expressive features, almond-shaped eyes that sparkled behind a pair of horn-rimmed glasses, and thick salt-and-pepper hair styled in a bun.

Anita *Mami* warmly greeted Tripti and Srikant. She was as welcoming as her home, with an easy, loud laugh that made Tripti feel at ease. As they talked about old connections in Chennai, Tripti thought of Rohit. He must have reveled in the company of Columbus' *Aunties* and *Uncles*. He had always charmed relatives at family gatherings, effortlessly making people laugh with his sharp wit.

"You are Rohit's sister, right?" Anita *Mami* interrupted her thoughts. "Where is he now?"

"Oh, somewhere in Asia … I think Singapore … I can't keep track anymore."

"Such an unassuming, modest young man … and so bright."

"Yes, *Amma* brags about him constantly. Makes it hard for me to measure up," Tripti forced a smile.

Anita *Mami* threw her head back with a hearty laugh, "Well, that's how it goes. I do not have an older brother but two over-achieving sisters."

Tripti and Srikant became regular guests at Anita *Mami*'s. Tripti welcomed her trove of advice, anecdotes, and gentle scolding, all delivered with endearing warmth. Tripti's singing became the highlight of Anita *Mami*'s monthly get-togethers, bringing her into contact with local *Carnatic* musicians and aficionados. Srikant and Tripti were frequent attendees at musical meetups, and their social circle expanded.

Yet, as six months passed, Tripti's uneasiness rose.

While their weekends were filled with activities and laughter, the weekdays were silent and monotonous. She religiously cleaned and organized their modest apartment, but the routine began to feel pointless. Her loneliness during the day and many evenings when Srikant worked late in his research lab amplified her frustration.

Phone calls home offered no relief, as conversations with *Amma* were no longer about adjusting to life in America.

"When are you going to start working, Tripti? Have you thought about your career? *Appa* paid a lot of money for your BITS degree—are you going to waste it?"

*Amma*'s questioning fueled Tripti's frustration with her professional stagnation.

One evening, over dinner, she couldn't hold it in anymore.

"Srikant, I can't keep doing this—house chores, watching TV all day, and waiting for you to come home. Our weekends are fun, but the weekdays are unbearable."

Srikant looked up from his plate, surprise and puzzlement on his face. "But … you're not just waiting. You're making this place a home for us."

Tripti's frustration boiled over. "A home? I wanted a career, Srikant. I didn't come here to play housewife."

Srikant put down his fork. "I understand, *ma*, but—"

"Stop calling me *ma!*" Tripti snapped, her voice rising. "I'm not your mother … nor a child. And what do you even know about a real job or a career? You're a student, and we are living off a stipend."

Srikant's face fell, but he held his composure. "I didn't mean to upset you. I guess you're right … I just … do not know how to help you."

"I'm sorry, I'm sorry," Tripti immediately relented. "That was not fair on my part."

"It's okay," Srikant replied quietly. "I know this isn't easy for you."

"My lack of a career is *Amma*'s favorite topic now. On top of that, she keeps saying, 'Be like Rohit. He manages everything so well.' He's practically a ghost now—always on the road, never home, and unreachable. I am not saying I want an all-consuming career like his, but I could use some job-hunting advice right now."

"I understand."

The cycle of arguments and apologies repeated for several weeks, until Srikant's friend, Kishore, moved to Columbus from New Jersey. His wife, Sudha, an *ABCD*, was a whirlwind of knowledge and confidence, the kind of person who seemed to have all the answers. Sudha was unlike anyone Tripti had ever met. One day, they were sitting on Sudha's couch, sipping tea, when Sudha leaned in conspiratorially.

"You need something for *you*, Tripti. Have you ever thought about running your own business?"

"Me? A business?" Tripti asked, startled.

"Why not? I've been in Avon for years. It's flexible, and you'd be great at it. You're organized, and people like you. Plus, the community is wonderful."

Tripti hesitated. "I don't know … selling makeup? I've never even thought about doing something like that."

Sudha waved a hand dismissively. "It's not just makeup. It's professional experience. And personal empowerment. You'll learn to manage clients, build networks, and train others. You'll love it."

Encouraged by Sudha's words, Tripti attended Avon events during weekday afternoons. On the drive to a meeting, she confided in Sudha. "I felt like I've been losing my identity since moving here. Thank you, Sudha—this is exactly what I need."

Sudha nodded, her gaze thoughtful. "I felt the same way when Kishore and I first got married. But you know what? Finding something to call my own—something I built— changed everything. You'll find your footing in America, Tripti. Trust me."

Tripti rapidly learned the intricacies of the Avon business software suite, including the customer sales and services modules. Within weeks, she was able to help others use the available tools to develop their franchises. It was not the corporate career Tripti had envisioned, but it gave her a sense of purpose and community. Her hours were voluntary and flexible, and for the first time since moving to America, she felt she had a way to contribute to the workforce.

But Sudha wasn't done pushing her. One Saturday morning, she arrived with a stack of flyers. "We're volunteering at the Columbus Literacy Council," she announced.

"Doing what?" Tripti raised an eyebrow.

"Teaching adults to read. It'll blow your mind to know how many people can speak English yet can't even recognize the alphabet."

After the first session, Tripti was hooked. "Sudha, this … feels so … satisfying."

"I know, right?" Sudha grinned.

"Love it … would do it over and over," Tripti's face lit up. "And by the way, I've been thinking about ways to streamline Avon's customer service software."

Tripti immersed herself in volunteering and business automation projects. As her self-confidence in her technical abilities and interpersonal skills grew, so did her desire for a career.

One evening, as they sat on the couch watching a Tamil movie on their rickety VCR, Tripti turned to Srikant.

"I've been considering applying for real jobs," she announced.

"That's great," Srikant said, his tone cautious. "But it's tough, *ma*. The market isn't great, and you'll need visa sponsorship, which few employers are willing to do."

"I know what I need, Srikant," Tripti said irritably. "Please help me instead of reminding me of what I cannot do."

He sighed. "I'm just saying it'll take time. We'll figure it out together."

Tripti scoffed, "Easy for you to say. You're in your lab all day, working on your grand ideas. Meanwhile, I'm stuck here, spending my talents on voluntary work. I could be earning a decent living for us both."

Seeing Srikant's expression, Tripti softened. "I am sorry. I … shouldn't have said that," she said quietly.

Srikant glanced at her, surprised. "It's okay. I know this isn't the life you imagined."

"It's just … I'm just … frustrated," Tripti admitted. "There are so many opportunities here in the US."

Srikant smiled and took her hand. "We'll make it work. Your dreams are just as important as mine."

After numerous unsuccessful attempts, Tripti finally got her break. During an interview, a *Desi* small-business owner recognized her potential and agreed to sponsor her visa. Tripti was thrilled, but her initial excitement was met with skepticism from Srikant.

"We might go to jail for visa fraud," he warned. "Some of these *Desi* employers play fast and loose with immigration laws."

But Sudha was supportive. "Nonsense, it's only illegal to work for pay on a student or spouse visa, not a work visa. And I did some digging—your employer is legit. "

When the visa finally arrived, she shared the news with Srikant. His face lit up, and he embraced her. "I'm very proud of you," he said.

## Dayton Dramas

Sneha stepped off the plane, three-year-old Sahil tottering excitedly beside her. Kunal met them at the baggage area of the Dayton airport. He briefly hugged Sneha and ruffled Sahil's curly hair as they headed to the parking lot.

"You'll like the apartment," Kunal said during their drive to their apartment. "It's three bedrooms, so there's plenty of space. I've set up the basics, so don't expect anything fancy."

Sneha glanced out the window, her nerves giving way to cautious excitement.

Their dwelling was modest—a cookie-cutter unit in a sprawling complex. It had beige carpeting, white walls, and pine cabinetry.

Sneha took it all in, including the mismatched furniture Kunal had acquired secondhand.

"This is all yours now," Kunal teased. "We cannot afford servants."

Sneha grinned, unfazed. "Don't worry," she replied, her voice brimming with quiet determination. "I'm ready for a self-reliant life in America."

Although the apartment lacked the opulence of their family homes in Kolkata, Sneha felt an undeniable sense of pride. This wasn't about luxury or inheritance but building something entirely of their own. Exhausted from the travel but resolute, she was ready for the challenges ahead.

Sneha's first hurdle in adjusting to life in Dayton involved the dryer. Accustomed to the sun and a sturdy clothesline back home, she was unfamiliar with the machine. After Kunal had given a brief tutorial, she tried it herself, only to find the clothes damp and the machine emitting a strange, overheated smell. Panicking, she called Kunal at work.

"You interrupted my meeting. What do you mean it's not working?" he snapped.

"I don't know!" she replied, frazzled. "I followed your instructions, but something's wrong."

Kunal returned home that evening and inspected the dryer with exaggerated patience. He quickly discovered the problem, pulling out the lint trap stuffed with fabric softener sheets.

"Sneha," he asked, holding up one of the offending items. "What … is this?"

"The lint," she said earnestly.

Kunal's expression alternated between disbelief and laughter. "You think this is lint?"

"Well, don't the sheets become lint after the clothes dry?"

For a moment, Kunal was silent. Then he exploded into derisive laughter.

The next day, Kunal relayed the story to Reema and Sanjay, a young *Desi* couple who lived a few doors down. "She thought she was supposed to put the fabric softener sheet in the lint trap. Can you believe it?"

Sanjay stifled a laugh, but Reema came to her defense, "Oh, Sneha, I remember when I first came here—I didn't know what half the appliances were for."

Sanjay added, "Yeah, Reema tried to light our electric stove with a match."

"See?" Sneha said defensively. "Everyone makes mistakes."

"Yes," Kunal said, smirking. "But not everyone tries to burn down the apartment complex by setting the dryer on fire."

Sneha forced a smile.

One afternoon, Sneha sat at Reema's kitchen table, nursing a glass of cold coffee. Reema, a stay-at-home mom, had invited Sneha over. Her toddler, Tanvi, played with Sahil on the living room floor, sharing Lego blocks and toy cars. Ever the animated storyteller, Reema leaned against the counter as she reminisced about her early days in the U.S.

"You know, Sneha," Reema began with a chuckle, "when Sanjay and I first moved here, I set off the smoke detector at least once a week."

Sneha blinked in surprise. "What? But … how?"

Reema grinned sheepishly. "Oh, every time I cooked *chapatis* or made a ghee *tadka* and forgot to turn on the exhaust fan, the beeping would start. Sanjay's job was to wave a dish towel like a *paagal* to disperse the smoke."

Sneha burst into laughter. "That sounds like something I'd do. Thanks for the tip."

"One learns from mistakes, Sneha, and it's part of the adventure."

Sneha smiled, feeling a little lighter. "I guess you're right. But I am so wary after the fabric softener incident. Kunal still won't let me live that down."

Reema laughed, shaking her head. "Okay, that's a good one, I'll admit. But I have you beat in the laundry disasters department. I once put a red *dupatta* in with Sanjay's white shirts. He looked like he was going to break out in a Bollywood dance number every day."

Sneha laughed so hard she nearly spilled her beverage. "Sanjay must've been furious."

"Oh, he was," Reema said, grinning, "but we also got a good laugh out of it." She placed a comforting hand on Sneha's arm. "You're doing great, Sneha. Seriously. I've been here four years, and I'm still figuring things out. Give yourself some grace. And hey—if you ever want to set off your smoke detector, I'll come and wave a towel."

"Deal." Sneha laughed, her heart warming at Reema's kindness.

"To burnt *chapatis* and lint traps—the true markers of survival in America," Reema raised her drink.

Sneha clinked her glass against Reema's, grateful for a friend in her new world.

A year passed.

The soft hum of the overhead fluorescent light filled Sneha's ears as she stacked bags of turmeric powder onto a shelf. The familiar scent of *masalas* made her feel at home, even halfway around the world.

Thanks to Reema, the small *Desi* grocery store had become her sanctuary.

"You're so good with people," Reema had urged. "Pushpa *Aunty-ji*'s life is getting busier, and she is seeking help. I sometimes lend a hand on weekends while Sanjay watches Tanvi. If you want to try it, you and I can take turns volunteering at the store and babysitting our kids at home during the week."

Sneha had hesitated. "I don't know … what will Kunal say?"

Reema made a dismissive gesture. "Kunal can handle his feelings. You should do this for yourself, Sneha. Trust me; you'll feel better having something that's yours, just like I do."

Three weeks into her new gig, Sneha felt a flicker of pride whenever she walked into the store. The customers, primarily fellow immigrants navigating a new country, were kind and chatty. She often helped them find the right kind of *dal* or recommended *masala*s for recipes they hadn't tried before.

Sahil adjusted well to her new routine.

Kunal was disdainful. "You're volunteering at a grocery store? Really, Sneha? Working like a servant?" he sneered one evening as they sat at the dining table.

Sneha kept her tone steady. "It's about doing something for myself, Kunal. It helps me feel independent."

He scoffed, leaning back in his chair. "By stocking shelves and selling rice? That's not independence, Sneha. You're wasting your time. Maybe you should consider doing a few community college courses and getting a real job."

The store held a small *Navratri* celebration a week later, inviting customers and staff to a gathering. Pushpa *Aunty-ji* encouraged Sneha to prepare a traditional Bengali sweet.

Her *rasgullas* became the talk of the evening, with customers raving about their balance of sweetness and texture.

Sneha found herself surrounded by appreciative smiles and compliments.

"You should start a catering business," many urged.

Sneha laughed, a blush coloring her cheeks. "Oh, I don't know about that."

But as she stood there, basking in the warmth of the community, a sense of accomplishment washed over her. This moment was hers—not Kunal's, her in-laws', nor *Ma*'s.

Sneha's small victories didn't go unnoticed by Kunal, though not in the way she'd hoped. One evening, overhearing a neighbor's praise of Sneha's work at the store, Kunal confronted her.

"You're spending too much time at that place," he said sharply. "People will … start talking."

Sneha frowned. "Talking about what? That I'm doing something worthwhile for the community?"

"No," he snapped. "That you're neglecting your responsibilities at home. This little job you are doing is pointless."

Sneha clenched her jaw. "It's not pointless to me, Kunal," she said through gritted teeth. "It gives me confidence and a sense of purpose. I'm not just your wife or Sahil's mother; I'm a person, and I need something of my own."

Kunal's face darkened. "You've been listening to Reema too much. She's filling your head with feminist nonsense," he said dismissively.

Sneha steadied herself with a deep breath. "It's not about her, Kunal. It's about me—I have every right to have a life outside our home, just like you do."

For a moment, Kunal said nothing, his jaw tightening. Then he grabbed his keys and stormed out, slamming the door behind him.

Sneha stood in silence, her heart pounding. She regretted allowing the argument to escalate, but there was also a grim satisfaction in standing up for herself.

## Balancing and Bickering

Tripti and Srikant's lives settled into a steady work-life rhythm.

Two years passed, and Tripti's career progressed rapidly as the IT consulting business grew. She was now managing a portfolio of high-profile customers.

However, notwithstanding her success, *Amma* found a new topic to harangue her. "You're always so busy, Tripti," she would reproach Tripti during their weekly phone calls. "You no longer have time to talk to your *Amma*." *Amma*'s complaints were now focused on how Tripti prioritized work over family: "I hope you remember, no matter how high you climb, your family is what matters most. I hope you are not ignoring Srikant like you ignore me and *Appa*." Tripti bristled at the comments, feeling a sense of injustice that *Amma*, who had constantly pushed her toward professional success, now appeared to resent hers.

One afternoon, Tripti was milling about the kitchen, distractedly conversing with *Amma* over the speakerphone. "*Amma*, I told you already. I can't come this Summer. Work is hectic, and Srikant is busy writing two papers. We can't just drop everything."

*Amma*'s voice crackled through the line, a mix of accusation and indignation. "It's been more than two years, Tripti. Everyone is asking about you and looking forward to seeing you at the wedding next month. How can you not be here?"

Tripti sighed, her free hand clenched into a fist. "Why does it matter what 'everyone' thinks? They're not paying for the plane ticket or giving me leave from work. Do they even know how hard it was to get a job, let alone keep one? I can't just leave whenever there's a family event."

*Amma*'s tone sharpened. "So, your work is more important than family now?"

That comment struck a nerve. "*Amma*, I'm trying to build a career here. Do you think it's easy—like it is for you and others to sit at home and judge how I prioritize things?"

*Amma* gasped audibly. "What has happened to you, Tripti? We always have differences, but you were never this rude to me. You have changed, Tripti."

"Maybe so," Tripti snapped. "Maybe it's because I've had to fight for everything here. You wouldn't understand what it's like." Without waiting for a reply, she hung up, switched her stove off, and threw herself onto the couch with a frustrated scream.

Srikant, quietly working at the dining table, looked up. He set his mug of coffee down and walked over. "Another rough call with *Amma*?"

"She drives me insane. Every single call is about how I'm neglecting my roots or failing the family. It's like nothing I do is ever enough." Tripti clasped her temples and sank into the couch.

Srikant sat beside her. "She misses you, that's all," he said consolingly.

Tripti shot him a glare. "Don't defend her, Srikant. She doesn't care what I'm going through here—only what I'm not doing to meet her unreasonable expectations."

Srikant reached for her hand, speaking softly. "That's not fair, Tripti. She's from a different world. It's hard for her to understand yours."

Tripti pulled her hand away, her voice rising. "So, it's on me to be the bigger person? To explain, to justify, to apologize? What about my feelings? Why does she not care about those?"

Srikant stayed quiet for a moment, then said gently, "Maybe because she's getting a lot of questions from your relatives?"

Tripti threw up her hands, her frustration bubbling over. "Great, take her side. That's what I need right now."

"I'm not taking sides," Srikant said, his tone even. "I'm trying to help. You're both under different pressures—yelling at each other won't resolve anything."

Tripti's anger deflated slightly as his words sank in. She slumped back against the couch, covering her face with her hands. "I just … I feel like I'm failing in life while being successful at work. *Amma*'s constant guilt-tripping is wearing me out emotionally."

Srikant placed a reassuring hand on her shoulder. "You're not failing, Tripti. You're trying to balance many things, and feeling overwhelmed is understandable. But maybe you should try to talk to her—not to argue, but to explain how you're feeling."

Tripti let out a long sigh, her voice softening. "You think that'll work?"

"You know," he began gently, "*Amma* does have a funny way of showing it, but she is proud of you."

Tripti raised an eyebrow, skeptical. "Really? Because it feels like she's constantly criticizing me."

Srikant smiled faintly. "Do you remember when you first started doing well at work? *Amma* would call you and say, 'You've done well for yourself.'"

"Very grudgingly," Tripti gave a small laugh despite herself. "Like it physically hurt her to admit it."

"Maybe," Srikant continued. "But she wouldn't even say it if she weren't proud. And didn't she tell some of your relatives about your promotion?"

"'Tripti had to work hard, of course—it wasn't easy,'" Tripti rolled her eyes, mimicking *Amma*'s voice. "The classic *Amma* move. Boast, but make it sound like a struggle."

"It's her way of acknowledging your efforts and success," Srikant said, leaning forward. "She just doesn't know how to be … straightforward about it."

Tripti sighed, her anger subsiding in exhaustion. "I guess you're right." She rested her head against his shoulder and closed her eyes, grateful for his steady presence.

## Threads of Fate

In a rare gesture of appeasement, Kunal proposed an outing to the Columbus Zoo.

"Let's go this weekend," he urged. "Sahil will love it, and … while we're there, we can stop by a real *Desi* store in Columbus—better than Pushpa *Aunty-ji*'s hut."

The jab about her workplace stung Sneha, but before she could retort, Sahil squealed with joy, "Zoo, zoo! Can we see tigers? And elephants?"

An outing in Columbus was just what the family needed.

Sahil, barely able to contain his impatience throughout the 90-minute car ride, darted from exhibit to exhibit, constantly chatting. His excitement was contagious.

Kunal seemed relaxed, snapping photos and indulging them with treats from the kiosks.

The little family fell into an easy rhythm for a few hours, domestic tensions fading into the background. Sneha couldn't stop smiling, relishing the sense of togetherness.

They headed to the *Desi* store from the zoo. Sneha wandered the aisles, enjoying the sight of neatly stacked items, when she heard a woman's voice.

"What a lovely *kurta*!"

Sneha turned to see a smiling, petite woman in her early fifties. She was clad in a perfectly draped silk *saree* that shimmered softly under the store's fluorescent lights. Her graying hair, pinned neatly in a bun, and a dot of maroon *sindoor* accentuated her sharp, expressive features.

The woman nodded toward Kunal and glanced at Sahil with a warm smile.

"And is this your son? He's adorable."

"Thank you," Sneha replied, smiling politely. "What do you say, Sahil?"

"*Namaste, Aunty-ji,*" Sahil put his chubby hands together.

"*Namaste,* Sahil. You all can call me Anita *Mami.*"

Anita *Mami* turned to Sneha and Kunal with a radiant smile. "We haven't met before, have we? Are you new in town?"

Sneha returned the smile, "Sahil and I moved to Dayton from Kolkata a year ago. I'm Sneha, and this is my husband, Kunal. "

"Oh, Dayton," Anita *Mami* exclaimed warmly. "That's not too far. I organize *pooja* gatherings for the *Desi* community here in Columbus. Please come today; it's a wonderful opportunity to meet people. Plus, you will get to hear Tripti, who leads our *bhajans.*"

Sneha froze. "Tripti?" she asked cautiously, her heart pounding.

"Yes. She's such a talented singer. So melodious and poised," Anita continued enthusiastically.

Sneha's voice wavered. "Tripti Iyengar? Does she have … long, wavy hair? Skin darker than mine? And … she'd be about my age?"

Anita looked surprised but nodded. "Yes, that's her. How do you know her?"

Sneha felt a lump forming in her throat. "She's my childhood friend. We went to high school together in Kolkata but lost touch after graduation."

"What a small world," Anita exclaimed. "You absolutely must come to our place then. You will not only get to see her again, but you'll also be able to surprise her."

Before Kunal could protest, Sneha responded, "We'd love to come. Thank you for inviting us." Her voice was calm, yet there was an unexpected yearning to reconnect with someone who had been integral to her happier, carefree days.

## Reunions and Realizations

Tripti adjusted the *dupatta* of her emerald-green *salwar kameez* and glanced at Srikant fiddling with Anita *Mami*'s harmonium.

"You cannot resist that thing," she teased.

Srikant looked up with a soft smile. "It's a musical instrument, *ma*. Not a 'thing.' It deserves respect."

Tripti was about to retort when she noticed Anita *Mami* bustling into the room, impeccably clad in a bright red *saree* and accompanied by a young *Desi* couple with a toddler. The woman stood awkwardly, darting glances around as if she were searching for someone.

Realization struck, and Tripti ran forward, "Sneha? Is it really you?"

Joy lit up Sneha's face, "Tripti! After all these years! I can't believe it!"

Within seconds, they were hugging, laughing, and crying.

"You look … the same!" Tripti said, pulling back to look at Sneha. "And now you're a mother?"

"Yes, this is Sahil," Sneha tilted her head towards the five-year-old boy by her side, a faint smile gracing her lips. "And this is Kunal," she added, gesturing toward her husband.

Kunal nodded curtly. "Hello," he said in a clipped voice. He glanced at Srikant, then back at Tripti. "And you are?"

Tripti introduced herself and Srikant. "Srikant's doing his PhD at OSU, working on some groundbreaking research."

Kunal raised an eyebrow. "Ah, a perpetual student, I see," he said, his tone dripping with condescension. "I finished my master's at Wright State last year and now work full-time in Dayton for an aerospace startup company. I was promoted to a VP position." Turning to Tripti, he asked pointedly, "Someone has to be the breadwinner, especially with an extra mouth or two to feed, right?"

Kunal's words hung in the air, awkwardly heavy. Tripti felt a flicker of annoyance but masked it with a tight smile. "So, Sneha, how's life treating you?"

Sneha hesitated, her eyes nervously darting toward Kunal before she replied. "Oh, I am so busy. Sahil keeps me on my toes, and Kunal's job has him traveling quite a bit."

Kunal cut in dismissively, "Sneha's main responsibility is managing the home. It's a full-time job, too, I suppose."

Tripti noticed how Sneha's shoulders stiffened at the comment, and it struck a chord. She had heard that same tone in her voice when speaking to Srikant—belittling, patronizing, as though his contributions were secondary. The thought made her uncomfortable.

The collective filled the room with melodious voices, but Tripti and Sneha sat away from the rest. Despite her youthful looks, Tripti couldn't help but notice how the spark of carefree exuberance in Sneha's eyes had dimmed. She remembered their close kinship in Kolkata, which had now faded with time and distance. She silently resolved to rekindle the bond.

"So, how have you been?" Tripti asked softly.

Sneha smiled, but it didn't reach her eyes. "Fine. Life in America is … an adjustment. Kunal's a good provider, but sometimes …," she trailed off, choosing her words carefully. "It feels like I'm invisible, you know?"

Tripti nodded in understanding. "I think I do. Srikant's amazing, but sometimes I feel … frustrated. He's focused on his research, and I'm stuck managing everything else."

Sneha gave her a wry smile. "Kunal … has this way of making me feel like what I do isn't important. Like my life should revolve around his."

The candid admission caught Tripti off guard. She glanced across the room, where Srikant was in animated discussions with Anita *Mami* and Kunal. Srikant's face was open and earnest, while Kunal's expression was one of bored detachment.

After the *bhajans* ended, people milled about enjoying snacks.

"Sneha, can you get Sahil ready? It's getting late," Kunal's voice rang out.

Sneha nodded silently, excusing herself.

Tripti couldn't hold back. "Kunal, don't you think Sneha deserves a break? She's been minding Sahil all evening."

Kunal looked at her, surprised and somewhat puzzled. "It's just how things are supposed to be, isn't it? She's great with our son and the house. I handle everything else."

Before Tripti could retort, Srikant placed a calming hand on her arm. "Tripti, let it go," he murmured.

His attempt to play peacemaker only irritated her further. "Why should I? It's unfair."

Srikant sighed, lowering his voice. "Because it's not our place, *ma*. Let's not ruin the evening."

The pet name grated on her nerves, as it always did when she was already upset. She shrugged his hand off and turned away.

During their drive home, the car was filled with tense silence. Finally, Srikant spoke. "Kunal might not be perfect, but he probably thinks he is doing what is normal."

Tripti stared out the window. "He doesn't respect Sneha. It's obvious."

"And do you respect me?" Srikant asked quietly.

Tripti turned to him, startled. "What kind of question is that?"

Srikant's hands tightened on the steering wheel. "You get frustrated with me and dismiss my opinions … I was wondering if you see me the same way you feel Kunal sees Sneha."

The accusation stung because it wasn't entirely untrue. Tripti opened her mouth to argue, but stopped. She had seen herself in Kunal's dismissiveness tonight, and it was a sobering realization.

"I'm sorry," Tripti said softly after a long pause. "I'll try to do better."

Srikant's expression softened. "Thank you."

In the stillness of the car, Tripti reflected on the evening. The encounter with Sneha and Kunal had held up a mirror, and she did not like what it showed.

Sneha sat on the worn beige couch in her living room, mid-morning sunlight streaming through sheer curtains. Sahil and Tanvi played on the floor.

Sneha's mind drifted to the previous week when fate had pulled Tripti back into her life.

A knock on the door interrupted her thoughts.

Reema had returned from Pushpa *Aunty-ji*'s store to pick up Tanvi.

"Coffee?" Sneha offered.

"Yes, please," Reema smiled, sinking thankfully onto the couch. "Now, tell me more about Tripti."

Sneha began to reminisce, her gaze softening. "We met during a field trip in ninth grade when Tripti was new to our school. We clicked instantly. Everyone said we made an odd pair—Tripti was organized and outspoken, and I was the chaotic, happy-go-lucky one."

"Really?"

"Yeah, I never gave much thought to my future, while Tripti had every detail of her life mapped out. Yet, we became inseparable. We'd drop our bookbags at her home and go on long walks for hours, discussing everything under the sun." Sneha's voice grew more wistful. "Now I realize how much I've missed having Tripti in my life." Sneha paused to steady her thoughts. "Seeing her after all these years feels like a part of me has come alive again."

They were silent for several minutes, Reema gazing at Sneha thoughtfully. Then she abruptly asked, "I have a surprise and a suggestion for you. Which one first?"

Sneha blinked, intrigued. "Um … suggestion?"

"Go see Tripti for a couple of days. Kunal is out of town on business all week, isn't he? I can take care of Sahil."

Sneha's eyes widened as she stared at Reema. "But … but how?" she spluttered, grappling with the impossibility of it.

"Take the city bus, then hop on a Greyhound. Ask Tripti to pick you up in Columbus. Reverse the directions to get back home. It'll take three hours each way. Simple."

"But … the bus tickets? Kunal makes me account for every dollar I spend."

"This is where the surprise comes in," Reema said, smiling as she extended a roll of twenty-dollar bills toward Sneha.

"Reema," Sneha exclaimed, her voice a mixture of astonishment and protest. "I can't take your money."

"This isn't from me. It's yours—a gift of thanks from Pushpa *Aunty-ji*. Her store has been doing so well, thanks largely to you."

Sneha stayed motionless, her hand hovering over the roll of bills, seemingly paralyzed by disbelief. Reema laughed and firmly placed the money in Sneha's hand.

"This is doable, and Kunal does not need to know," Reema said with a grin. "Go see Tripti. As my mother used to say—surround yourself with people who lift you."

Sneha stepped off the Greyhound bus at the Columbus station and immediately spotted Tripti waving from across the waiting area.

The drive to Tripti's apartment in Buckeye Village was filled with laughter and updates as they slipped back into their easy camaraderie.

Sneha took in the warmth of Tripti's apartment—with its neatly arranged furniture and shelves lined with books and trinkets.

"You have *Amma*'s sense of decor," she observed.

"I hope you also see *Ma*'s touches," Tripti smiled.

From the beginning of their friendship, Tripti and Sneha had adopted each other's preferred terms for their mothers. To both, Tripti's mother was *Amma*, a title that carried weight and tradition, and Sneha's mother was *Ma*, a word steeped in warmth and familiarity.

"I'll make *chai*," Tripti said, slipping into the kitchen. "It's been too long since we sat down and talked."

A familiar aroma of cardamom and ginger wafted toward Sneha, triggering her nostalgia. She smiled and called out, "Tripti, I am reminded of the *chai* we used to have after our morning walks around Belvedere—at that little *adda* by the Masjid."

Tripti emerged grinning from the kitchen, carrying two steaming cups. "I obsessed over it for months after I moved out of Kolkata, trying to replicate it."

"And?" Sneha's eyes widened.

"You be the judge," Tripti handed her a cup.

Sneha took the first sip. "It's perfect," she sighed.

Tripti's gaze softened. "Every time I have this, I think of you. Those mornings, those conversations were some of my life's best moments."

Sneha looked up, her heart full as the years of separation dissolved. "Mine too," she whispered, taking another sip.

The next day, at the Columbus Greyhound terminal, Sneha's eyes sparkled with mischief. "Kunal doesn't know I'm here."

Tripti raised an eyebrow amusedly. "Like Kolkata? How we used to sneak out? You to escape *Ma*'s house chores, and me to avoid *Amma*'s guilt-tripping?"

Sneha chuckled. "Guess I'm trying to recapture that rebellious thrill."

Tripti made a gesture of zipping her lips. "Your secret is safe with me."

Thanks to Pushpa *Aunty-ji's* additional money, Sneha met Tripti again within a few months. During the trip, Tripti took Sneha to a beauty parlor for an eyebrow threading session. Sneha insisted on paying for both. The simple pleasure of doing something for herself—and being able to treat her friend—lingered after Sneha returned to Dayton, buoying her spirits.

A few weeks later, an unexpected invitation arrived by phone. Tripti insisted that Sahil, Sneha, and Kunal visit their new apartment for dinner and a casual evening.

Kunal's reaction was surprisingly neutral.

"Tripti and Srikant, huh?" Kunal remarked, scrolling through his phone. "Sure. It's been a while since we've had a family outing, especially with all my travel."

Sneha hid her surprise, relieved that Kunal hadn't dismissed the idea.

The prospect of the trip excited her, and she looked forward to what the evening might hold.


# Tossed Dice and Crossed Lines

Their new apartment in Governours Square became a warm and inviting home for Tripti and Srikant. While it wasn't luxurious, the space exuded charm with its neatly arranged furniture, soft lighting, and the faint aroma of *agarbattis*.

Tripti was excited to host Sneha, Kunal, and Sahil.

Sahil was sprawled on the floor, happily engrossed in a pile of toy cars Sneha had thoughtfully packed while the adults sat cross-legged around a brightly colored Ludo board.

As they set up the pieces, Tripti thought of Rohit's competitive streak. He'd never let her win, even when they were kids. She smiled at the memory, but the thought left a bittersweet ache.

"Tripti, you're amazing at Ludo. Did you play this as a kid?" Srikant asked.

"I used to. Although Rohit never let me win. You guys are too easy."

"That sounds like an older brother," Sneha laughed. "How is Rohit?"

"Who knows? He's too busy to even reply to messages."

Sneha tossed the dice, her hand fumbling as she turned to check on Sahil, who had begun making zooming noises. "Wait … where was I?" she asked, blinking at the board.

"Red," Srikant said kindly, pointing to her piece. "You were here, just a couple of moves from home."

"Thanks, Srikant," Sneha said with a small smile, moving her piece forward.

Kunal leaned back against the couch, watching her with a bemused expression. "Seriously, Sneha, it's a simple game. Do you have to get distracted every single time?"

Sneha's cheeks flushed as she looked down at the board. "I was just making sure he's okay."

"He's fine. He's not going to break anything," Kunal interrupted with a short laugh. He glanced at Srikant. "You're too soft, man. Encouraging her like that. She needs to learn to focus."

"It's just a game, Kunal. We're trying to have fun." Srikant's brows were furrowed slightly.

"Fun? You truly live in a fantasy world, don't you?" Kunal smirked. "All theory and make-believe?"

Tripti, silent until now, felt a familiar irritation bubbling inside her. She glanced at Srikant, expecting him to brush off Kunal's remark. Instead, he gave a patient smile.

"Everything is not about a paycheck, Kunal," Srikant said. "You've attended graduate school—there's value in that."

Kunal snorted. "Where is the value in staying stuck in school while your wife's moving forward? Tripti's got the real job now. You're just messing around while she foots the bills."

Tripti flinched, caught between defending Srikant and acknowledging the kernel of truth in Kunal's jab.

"Well, I'm indeed the one earning now," Tripti said, keeping her voice neutral. "And sometimes, Srikant, you seem … idealistic about where this research will lead."

Srikant turned to her; his eyes clouded with hurt. "Idealistic? You've always supported what I do, Tripti."

"I do support you," she said quickly, but her tone wavered. "I'm just saying … Kunal has a point. It's practical to think about what's next, you know?"

Kunal laughed, clearly enjoying the tension. "See? Even she agrees. You're lucky to have a wife picking up the slack."

Sneha bristled, her quiet voice cutting through the room. "Kunal, that's enough. Stop making it sound like Srikant's doing nothing. And stop dragging Tripti into this."

"Why?" Kunal shot back. "Because you don't want to admit that I'm right? It's called reality, Sneha. Not that you'd know much about that."

Sneha's eyes filled with tears, but she blinked them away, her hand frozen over the board.

"That's unfair," Srikant said, his voice sharper now. "Sneha's doing her best, and being a parent and homemaker is no small task. You should recognize that."

Kunal shook his head in mock disbelief. "You have quite the savior complex, Srikant. Maybe if you focused less on defending everyone and more on finding a real job, you'd get somewhere."

The words hung in the air, heavy and cutting. Tripti glanced at Srikant, staring at the board, his jaw tight. She wanted to speak up, to say something that would put Kunal in his place, but a strange hesitation rooted her in silence.

Sneha quietly picked up the dice and rolled, her piece landing shy of home. "There." Her voice was barely above a whisper.

"Nice move," Srikant said gently, his encouragement like a balm.

Kunal rolled his eyes. "Yeah, whatever. Let's just get this over with."

The rest of the game passed in awkward silence: the earlier camaraderie replaced by tension so thick it seemed to muffle Sahil's playful noises.

Later that evening, Sneha and Kunal gathered their jackets. Sneha gave Tripti a brief hug. Kunal muttered a curt goodbye, clearly unfazed by the atmosphere he had created.

After the door closed, Tripti sank onto the couch with a sigh. Srikant was tidying up the board, his movements slow and deliberate.

"I shouldn't have agreed with him," Tripti said softly, breaking the silence.

Srikant looked up, his expression inscrutable. "No, you shouldn't have."

"I'm sorry," she said, her voice tinged with guilt. "I just … I didn't want to pick an argument with Kunal."

Srikant nodded but said nothing, turning back to the game pieces. Tripti watched him, the weight of the evening pressing heavily on her chest. She reached out, touching his arm in a gesture of appeasement. Srikant paused, then looked at her with a faint smile that didn't quite reach his eyes.

Sneha leaned her head against the car window, her mind replaying the evening at Tripti and Srikant's apartment.

Sneha thought of Srikant's quiet defense of her, a gesture she had deeply appreciated, though it redirected Kunal's criticism toward Srikant's academic pursuits.

Although Srikant had maintained his calm, what lingered most in Sneha's mind was the look of hurt when Tripti hesitated to defend him fully. It mirrored Sneha's moments of feeling dismissed and invisible in her marriage.

Sneha tried to shake off her thoughts by breaking the silence, "Tripti and Srikant are doing well, aren't they?"

Kunal snorted. "Well? She's working herself to death while he's still pretending to be a student. Some life."

Sneha frowned. "That's not fair. Srikant is finishing a PhD. That's no small thing."

Kunal let out a short, barking laugh. "A glorified excuse to stay in school forever. Meanwhile, Tripti keeps the ship afloat. Pathetic."

Sneha bristled. "Not everyone measures success the same way, Kunal. Srikant's research matters to him, and Tripti supports him. That's what a marriage is supposed to be."

Kunal's grip tightened on the steering wheel, his tone sharp. "Supports him? She barely tolerates him. And what do you know about marriage, Sneha? Playing house with Reema doesn't make you an expert. Maybe focus on fixing yourself before defending others."

His words stunned her into silence.

*Fix myself? Our marriage is far from perfect, but what exactly is Kunal blaming me for?*

Sneha opened her mouth to argue but stopped when she saw Sahil's wide-awake eyes fixed on her in the rearview mirror.

The engine's hum filled the silence, and Sneha's thoughts returned to Tripti. Her friend had always embodied fearlessness, refusing to let anything or anyone get in her way. Sneha had admired that fire for years, but now she sensed a sharpness in Tripti's demeanor that she hadn't seen before.

*Perhaps it is the pressure of balancing a demanding career with a home in a foreign land without domestic help.*

With a sigh, Sneha turned toward Kunal, his face set in a familiar expression of smug indifference. Despite his insensitive words that evening, she resolved to cut him slack.

*Adjusting to life in America isn't easy for any of us.*

*Like Tripti, Kunal is likely grappling with work struggles I wouldn't even begin to understand.*


## Wheels of Change


Reema first brought it up during one of their afternoon coffees.

Sneha was seated at Reema's kitchen table, watching Sahil attempt a jigsaw puzzle. He was grouping pieces using colors and patterns with methodical precision far beyond his years.

"You know, Sahil seems really bright," Reema remarked. "Have you thought about enrolling him in Tanvi's Montessori program? They're amazing for kids like him—so curious, so sharp."

Sneha hesitated, glancing at her son. "Montessori? Isn't that expensive?"

Reema shrugged. "It can be, but it's worth looking into. They focus on letting kids explore and learn at their own pace. Sahil seems like he'd thrive there. And he will have Tanvi for company."

"I'm … not sure what Kunal would say."

Later that evening, she discussed the topic over dinner, expecting resistance.

To her surprise, Kunal nodded thoughtfully. "It's not a bad idea."

Sneha blinked. "Really?"

Kunal leaned back in his chair, a contemplative look crossing his face. "When I was a kid, my parents didn't care about education. They conditioned me from the start to join the family business. It didn't matter what I wanted or what I was good at. It was the store or nothing. Breaking out of that to do my master's was … not easy."

Sneha stared at him, stunned by the rare moment of vulnerability. "I didn't know that," she said softly.

Kunal shrugged. "It's not something I talk about. But maybe … I don't want Sahil to feel the way I did—trapped. He should have the chance to figure out what he wants, even if it's not what we expect."

For a moment, Sneha saw a glimpse of a different side of Kunal—the man he might have been without the bitterness and the scorn. It warmed her, however briefly, and she nodded. "Then let's look into it. I think it'll be good for him."

Kunal's unexpected support extended beyond Sahil's education in the following weeks. Seeing how inconvenient it was for Sneha to rely on others for transportation, he offered to help her get her driver's license.

"It's about time you learned," he said one evening, handing her the driver's manual. "We'll get you a reliable car once you pass."

Kunal took her to a parking lot for practice that weekend.

Sneha took to driving with surprising ease. By their second practice session, she was comfortably navigating turns and parallel parking.

When Kunal grudgingly acknowledged her quick learning, she smiled knowingly. "Jaggu-*da* used to let me drive our Ambassador back in Kolkata when I was in high school," she said, referring to the family driver. "Mostly on the quieter streets when *Ma* wasn't home."

Kunal raised an eyebrow. "Really? You never told me."

Sneha chuckled, adjusting the mirror. "The hardest part here is getting used to driving on the right side of the road and the driver's seat on the left. Honestly, I miss stick-shift. That's where the real skill is."

"Well, I must admit, you're better at this than I expected. Let's get that license and start looking for a second car."

Sneha felt a flicker of pride in earning Kunal's rare, albeit grudging, approval.

They bought a secondhand Toyota Corolla. "Practical and efficient—it'll get you where you need to go," Kunal said gruffly, handing her the keys. "Just remember, it's strictly for getting around Dayton," he warned.

Sneha's heart sank at his remark. She had secretly hoped the car would give her the freedom to visit Tripti more often, but she bit her tongue and forced a small smile.

"I have installed Life360 on your phone—so I can always locate you."

Sneha felt another pang of disappointment. A tracking app felt like a leash on her freedom. Still, she resolved to focus on the positives of driving around on her own terms.

One afternoon, Sneha recounted the Life360 situation to Reema, her tone laced with frustration. "Kunal tracks every move I make," she said, shaking her head. "If I stop at a grocery store for five minutes longer than usual, he calls to ask why. And once, when Sahil and I went to the park without telling him, he accused me of being irresponsible."

Reema's eyes widened in disbelief. "Wait, he monitors you that closely? That's insane."

Sneha sighed. "I'm not supposed to drive anywhere without his permission, and if I did, we would have a big argument."

Reema's voice was indignant. "Sneha, that must be downright exhausting."

Sneha nodded, bitterness creeping into her voice. "It's like I'm not to be trusted. He says it's 'for safety,' but it's about keeping tabs on me. I don't feel like a person anymore—just a child or pet he has to monitor."

Reema sat back, visibly aghast. Her expression slowly shifted to one of determination. "You know there's a way around it, right?" she asked.

Sneha frowned. "What do you mean?"

Reema grinned conspiratorially. "You can spoof the app to make it seem like you are home, even when you're not. It's not hard. Let me show you."

Reema pulled out her phone and walked Sneha through the steps. It was surprisingly simple, and Sneha felt rebellious when she tried it out.

"This … this is amazing," she said, laughing nervously.

"You're welcome," Reema winked.


After practicing the trick a few times in Dayton, Sneha felt emboldened to use it to drive to Tripti's. With Sahil in preschool and Kunal at work, she felt a surge of exhilaration as she merged onto the highway, the car's hum steady beneath her. The wide, open I-70 stretched ahead. She rolled down the window, letting the cool breeze whip through her hair.

Sneha hadn't felt this free in years. She popped in a Kishore Kumar CD, and the yodeling instantly transported her back to when she first met Tripti's brother Rohit—and the crush she had once harbored on him. Curious about his life now, she resolved to ask Tripti about his whereabouts.

She sang along loudly, a grin spreading across her face.

The cityscape of Columbus glimmered into view, and Sneha felt a rush of emotions—excitement, defiance, and a sense of independence. She wasn't just Kunal's wife or Sahil's mother. She was Sneha, reclaiming pieces of herself, one mile at a time. She wasn't looking over her shoulder, worrying about what Kunal, his family, or her own would say. For once, the journey was hers and hers alone, and it felt like a small victory—a point of equilibrium between the dutiful roles of wife and mother and the impulsive freedom of her youth.

## Cracks Beneath

Tripti brought out two mugs as Sneha prattled on about Sahil. "I swear, that *bachcha* has more energy than an entire *bhajan* group," she said, tucking her feet under her. "Thankfully, he will be joining kindergarten in a few months."

Tripti grinned, handing Sneha her *chai*. "It's nice to have company, especially yours, on a weekday evening. Srikant's always buried in his research well into the night, and I can only watch TV for so long."

Sneha's face lit up mischievously. "Be prepared for more of my company. I hacked our Life360 app by putting my phone in airplane mode. I can now sneak out whenever—Kunal will think I'm home."

Tripti raised an eyebrow, half impressed, half concerned. "Sneha, that's bold—even for you."

Sneha shrugged, sipping her tea. "What choice do I have if I want to see my best friend?" Her voice dipped slightly, betraying an edge of bitterness. "Kunal tracks me obsessively."

"I can't believe this is your fifth visit to Columbus," Tripti said, changing the topic.

"Coming here is good for me," Sneha laughed. "After you took me out to get my eyebrows done last time, I felt like a new person."

Tripti smiled warmly. "I'm glad it helped. And now you have a car—how does it feel?"

Sneha's eyes sparkled as she replied, "Liberating. And with the money I get now and then from the grocery store I volunteer at, I feel self-reliant—something I never thought I'd feel again."

Tripti nodded, her expression proud. "Good for you, Sneha. You deserve this freedom—and more. Remember our school days in Kolkata? How we'd zip past those mini-buses in your blue Scooty and get verbally abused by the drivers?"

Sneha laughed, her eyes twinkling. "How could I forget? *Ma* hated that I rode a two-wheeler. She'd say, 'You'll break your leg, and then who will marry you?'"

"*Amma*'s still like that. She'll say something equally dramatic even now," Tripti smiled wryly.

Sneha grinned slyly. "I called *Amma* last week from Dayton."

"You what?" Tripti blinked in surprise.

"She was thrilled—told me I should visit you more often." Sneha's infectious giggle made Tripti join in.

"Then she brought up Rohit." Sneha's tone turned wistful. "And I started reminiscing to her about how I came to gawk at him in Belvedere that day."

Tripti groaned. "Oh no, not this again."

"What? I did have a crush on him," Sneha admitted, giggling. "He was so serious and studious, and those pictures of him in a suit and those glasses made him look like a Bollywood professor."

Tripti rolled her eyes. "Trust me, he's still just as nerdy, except now he's traveling all over the world getting paid to tell people what to do."

"Well, you better warn him. If we bump into each other, I'll still be the girl who made googly eyes at him."

Tripti couldn't help but laugh, shaking her head. "I think he'd like that. He is single, you know."

"So … how are things between you and *Amma*?" Sneha asked gently. "She used to push you so hard growing up."

"*Amma* is still *Amma*—back then, she constantly reminded me to aim high, to make something of myself. And now, when I have, she complains I'm neglecting her and the family."

Sneha frowned; her voice soft. "That must be exhausting. *Ma*'s never been like that. She just wants me to be happy, no matter what."

Tripti's anger bubbled to the surface. "What makes it even more frustrating for me is that *Amma* never places any expectations on Rohit. He has almost vanished from our lives, yet she still sings his praises if anyone asks. But there's always this … bar I'm always falling short of meeting."

Sneha placed a comforting hand on Tripti's arm. "That's not fair, Tripti. You've achieved so much. *Amma* might not say it as you want to hear it, but I'm sure she's proud."

Tripti sighed, her gaze distant. "That's what Srikant says. But sometimes, it feels like she's proud of what I've done, not who I am. And that's a hard thing to live with."

"Srikanth is right, and you have his unconditional support," Sneha observed wistfully, causing Tripti to turn in her direction sharply.

"Sneha, please talk to me about what's going on with you and Kunal," Tripti entreated.

"Topic for another day," Sneha drained her cup and stood up. "Gotta get home before Kunal finds out I am miles from home."

# Breakdowns

Sneha stared at the hood of her Corolla through her windshield, steam curling ominously into the evening air. She eased onto the highway shoulder, her heart pounding as cars sped past in a blur. The once-reliable vehicle, which had dutifully carried Sneha—and sometimes Sahil—on her previous trips to Columbus and back, now sat stubbornly lifeless.

Phone trembling in hand, she debated her next move.

For a fleeting moment, she considered calling Reema but decided to confront this situation head-on.

*This isn't about a broken car; it is about broken trust.*

Taking a deep breath, she dialed Kunal.

"What is it?" came the impatient voice.

"Kunal …," she began hesitantly. "My car broke down on the way back from Columbus. I don't know what to do. Can you—"

Kunal's incredulous voice crackled through the line. "Columbus? Sneha, why does the app show you're still in Dayton? Where exactly are you?"

Sneha winced, gripping the phone tightly. "Kunal, I'm sorry. I didn't want to worry you, so I tricked the app into showing me at home."

"You what?" Kunal's tone rose, his disbelief palpable. "You hacked the app? Are you serious?"

"Yes," Sneha admitted, her voice trembling. "I wanted to see Tripti. I thought—"

"You thought what, Sneha? That lying to me and sneaking off to another city was a good idea?" His voice turned icy. "Unbelievable. I'll call AAA. Stay there until the tow truck arrives. We'll talk about this at home."

Sneha opened her mouth to apologize, but the line went dead. She slumped in her seat, frustrated.

Kunal met the tow truck at a garage in Dayton, staring coldly as Sneha alighted. After a terse exchange with the mechanic, he gestured for her to follow him to the car.

On the drive home, Kunal's hands gripped the steering wheel, his knuckles pale with strain and jaw rigid in barely restrained fury. Sneha sat beside him, her hands clenched tightly in her lap. She realized explaining herself would be futile.

Kunal slammed the apartment door behind them, the sound reverberating through the small space, rattling the glassware on the kitchen counter.

Sneha took a deep breath, steadying herself. "Kunal, I didn't mean to deceive you. I just did not want to worry you. I needed this for myself. To see Tripti, to feel like—"

"To feel like what?" Kunal interrupted, his voice sharp. "A rebellious teenager sneaking out of the house? Do you realize what you've done? You lied. To me."

"I know," Sneha replied miserably. "And I'm sorry. But I just wanted to be with my friend, Kunal. To share a few laughs, to recharge—"

"Recharge?" Kunal let out a bitter laugh, his voice rising. "Using deception? Do you even hear yourself, Sneha? This isn't about taking a break. This is about being dishonest, not to mention irresponsible."

Sneha's voice trembled, but she stubbornly stood her ground. "Irresponsible? Kunal, I've been doing everything for our family—raising Sahil, managing the house, and keeping everything running while you're on business trips. So what if I indulged in a silly escapade once in a while?"

"Once in a while?" Kunal asked measuredly. "Once in a while?" he slowly repeated as the import of the sentence sank in. "So ... how many times have you lied to me, Sneha?" His breathing was heavy, and he was clenching and unclenching his fists.

Sneha exhaled shakily, her tone soft but steady. "Does it matter, Kunal? I've broken your trust. I know that, and I truly am sorry. But for what it's worth, you know I am a good driver—and that Sahil's safety is my top priority."

Kunal's eyes narrowed as he studied her face intently.

"You're being evasive and defensive, Sneha," he declared. "Is there something you're not telling me? Do you go to meet Tripti's husband, Srikant? Tell me the truth—are you having an affair with him?"

Sneha recoiled as though he had physically struck her. "How can you even say that, Kunal?" she exclaimed, her voice shaking with disbelief.

Kunal pressed on, his tone turning colder. "Tripti is a working professional. How does she even have time to meet you on weekdays? But Srikant … well, he's a jobless dreamer, isn't he? And you're always defending him, admiring how he supports Tripti. Maybe you wish I were more like him. Or maybe you wish you were with him instead of me."

"That's absurd," Sneha's voice cracked, trembling. "This has nothing to do with Srikant or Tripti or anyone else. It's about me trying to hold onto a piece of my past."

She steadied herself, her tone firm. "And yes, Tripti works hard. But she also values our friendship. She makes time— during lunch breaks or by adjusting her schedule. It's not about being busy, Kunal; it's about priorities."

Her eyes met his in rising defiance.

"For the record, my trips were never about anyone else. They were about me. About finding someone who listens, someone who doesn't belittle me."

"Don't you dare turn this around on me," Kunal spluttered indignantly. "You're the wife who lied to her husband. You're the mother who left her child behind. What kind of woman does that?" He threw his hands up in exasperation, vehemently shaking his head. "Don't even bother answering. I'm done with this conversation."

Snatching his car keys off the counter, he stormed toward the door. Pausing briefly, he turned back, his voice low and icy. "And let me be clear: I forbid you from ever contacting Tripti or Srikant again. Or else."

"Kunal, wait—" Sneha called out, but the door slammed shut, cutting her off mid-sentence.

A heavy silence pressed down on Sneha like an unseen weight. She sank onto the couch, burying her face in her hands. Her long-suppressed tears broke free and streamed down unchecked.

An hour passed before Kunal returned. Without a word, he went upstairs. Emerging with a suitcase, he paused to curtly inform her that he had booked himself into a hotel indefinitely, as he needed "time to think."

In the week that followed, Kunal ceased all further communications. Sneha moved through her motions mechanically, her heart heavy and her mind relentlessly gnawing at her.

*You are a selfish wife and mother who has caused turmoil in your family.*

Sneha felt trapped in an endless cycle of regret and self-recrimination. Her only moments of solace came from Sahil, innocent and pure. Every night, as she tucked him into bed, he wrapped his arms around her neck. "Mama, you're the best," he mumbled sleepily.

Tears pricked Sneha's eyes as she kissed his forehead.

*I need to figure out a way out of the mess I've created—for both our sakes.*

Kunal returned home a week later without forewarning. Sneha heard the jangle of keys at the door just as she was helping Sahil put away his toys. Her heart thudded as she looked up, and Kunal walked in, his face an unreadable mask.

"You're back," Sneha said quietly, trying to gauge his mood.'

"Clearly," Kunal muttered, dropping his suitcase with a thud. He glanced briefly at Sahil, who had run up to him, his small face lighting up. "Papa, look! I built a big tower!"

Kunal barely looked down. "Good for you," he said flatly. "Now, clean up this mess. I don't want to trip over your junk."

Sahil blinked, the brightness in his face dimming as he turned to his blocks. "Sorry, *Papa*," he whispered.

Sneha stepped forward. "Kunal, you don't need to talk to him like that. He's just excited to see you after so many days."

Kunal shot a stern look. "Spare me, Sneha. I'm not in the mood for lectures." He turned and walked upstairs.

The rest of the evening passed in tense silence. Sneha tried to distract Sahil by reading his favorite storybooks and coaxing him to finish dinner. Kunal ate alone in the living room, his eyes distant, barely acknowledging them.

The following day, Kunal's mood was no better. He emerged from the bedroom just as Sneha was preparing Sahil for school. "Where's my blue shirt?" he demanded.

"In the dryer," Sneha replied, keeping her tone neutral. "I'll iron it for you."

"Typical," Kunal sneered. "Why should anything be ready when I need it? You have one job, Sneha—just one."

Sneha bit back her response, unwilling to escalate the situation in front of Sahil.

Kunal glared at their son, who was fumbling with his backpack.

"Hurry up, Sahil. It's like you can't do anything right, just like your mother."

"Kunal, stop it," Sneha said sharply, kneeling next to Sahil and helping him zip his bag. "Don't take your anger out on him."

Kunal scoffed. "Oh, sure, defend him."

Then, with a smirk that made Sneha's blood run cold, he snarled, "Are we even sure he's mine?"

Sneha froze, her hands trembling as she gripped Sahil's bag. "How can you say that?" she whispered, her voice breaking.

Kunal shrugged. "With all the sneaking around you've been doing, who knows?"

Sahil looked up, confused and anxious. "Mama?" he asked softly.

"It's okay, *beta*," Sneha said, gathering herself and forcing a smile. "Let's go." She grabbed Sahil's hand and led him out, her shoulders rigid, refusing to let Kunal see her expression.

The week dragged on with Kunal's hostility permeating every corner of the apartment. He criticized everything Sneha cooked—"Is this supposed to be edible?"—and nitpicked about the house being "a mess" despite her meticulous cleaning. He ignored Sahil most of the time, except to bark occasional directions at him.

One evening, as Sneha tried to coax Sahil to eat dinner, Kunal leaned against the doorway, arms folded and a scowl on his face. "You're coddling him," he said icily. "No wonder he's such a baby. Just as useless as his—"

"Kunal, enough!" Sneha's sharp voice cut through the room, her eyes blazing with defiance.

The force of her words seemed to catch Kunal off guard. He froze, staring with narrowed eyes.

"Fine," he said, voice heavy with sarcasm. "I don't have time for this parenting nonsense anyway." He turned and walked away.

The following morning, Kunal stood by the front door, suitcase in hand. "I'm leaving for Cincinnati on business," he announced. "I'll be gone for a week. Maybe I'll get some peace and quiet while I'm away."

Sneha nodded wordlessly, more relieved than upset.

Sneha left Sahil with Reema for the afternoon and sat alone in the dim living room, finally allowing her pent-up turmoil to wash over her completely.

*For far too long, I have avoided confronting the truths about our marriage.*

Sneha recalled the early days—her quiet optimism, her eagerness to adapt, and Kunal's distant detachment, even then. *Has he ever valued me? Seen me as an equal partner in our marriage?*

As she sifted through more recent memories, Sneha realized it had been a slow unraveling, so subtle she hadn't noticed how far she had changed herself to accommodate Kunal. *His dismissiveness has always made me feel small and inadequate. And I have conditioned myself to accept it.*

The weight of Sneha's revelations pressed against her chest, threatening to suffocate her.

*I cannot introspect my way out of this. I am too close to the problem, and my emotions cloud my thoughts. I need to talk to someone. Anyone.*

Reema came to mind, but her shame surged; this topic was too intimate. Her thoughts drifted to Columbus, to the laughter and warmth she had found in Tripti's company, each tryst like an oasis in the emotional desert she had been navigating.

Without further thought, she reached for her phone.

"Tripti," she said, her voice trembling, "can you come to Dayton? Please? I need to talk to someone."

There was a pause before Tripti responded, her voice steady and reassuring. "I'll leave now."

"Thank you," Sneha exhaled a shaky sigh of relief.

The doorbell rang, cutting through the oppressive silence of the apartment. Sneha hurried to answer it with trembling hands. When she opened the door and saw Tripti standing there, concern etched on her face, tears sprang to Sneha's eyes.

"Thanks for coming," Sneha said quietly, stepping aside to let Tripti in.

Tripti touched her shoulder. "Of course," she said softly.

Sneha led Tripti into the living room, her movements heavy and robotic. She gestured toward a glass kettle on the coffee table.

"I made *chai*," Sneha said softly, her voice trembling but steady. "Not as good as yours, but would you like some?"

Tripti nodded, her eyes warm with concern. "Yes, please."

Sneha filled two mismatched mugs, steam rising between them like an ephemeral bridge. She cradled hers, staring into the swirling *chai* as if it held the words she couldn't yet say.

Tripti took a sip, her voice breaking through the stillness—firm yet gentle. "What's going on, Sneha?"

Sneha hesitated. "Kunal isn't here," she began, her voice trembling. "He left on a business trip this morning. But that's … why I needed to talk to you."

Tripti nodded, waiting patiently.

Sneha took a deep breath, her fingers tightening around the cup. "We … he and I … have not been good … for a long time," she admitted, her voice barely above a whisper. "He's … he's kind of cruel, Tripti. Not physically, but with words. And sometimes that feels worse. Like I can't fight back."

Tripti's expression darkened, her brows drawing together in concern. "Sneha, what are you talking about?"

The memories came rushing back, and Sneha forced herself to speak. "It started back in India after we got married. You know how young I was, Tripti—barely nineteen. Kunal would say I was naïve and didn't know anything about the world. At first, I thought it was teasing, but it wasn't—it was control."

She paused. "When we moved here, it got worse. I didn't know how to cook like his mother or his aunts. I didn't understand how things worked. He mocked every mistake I made. 'Why can't you be like other *Desi* wives?' he'd say. 'They figure it out.'"

Tripti's face was a mask of quiet fury.

"And then," Sneha continued, her voice faltering, "something changed after we met you and Srikant. Seeing how Srikant treats you made me think that maybe I deserve better. I started speaking up. Just small things. But Kunal noticed."

Tripti leaned forward, her tone sharp with concern. "What do you mean he 'noticed'? What did he do?"

Sneha exhaled shakily, her heart pounding. "At first, it was just little jabs. He'd say I was 'changing,' that I wasn't as agreeable as before. But then it got worse."

She swallowed hard, her hands trembling as she set her *chai* on the table. "One evening, I was driving back from Columbus after seeing you. But on the way home, my car broke down. Right there on the side of the highway. I had no choice but to call him."

Tripti's eyes widened.

"Kunal was furious. He met me at the garage in Dayton and didn't say a word on the drive home. I kept hoping he would calm down, but when we got back, it all poured out. He accused me of lying, of deceiving him. And then he …," Sneha's voice broke, her eyes filling with tears. "And then … he … accused me of having an affair with … Srikant."

Tripti's jaw dropped. "That's absurd!"

"It was like he couldn't see reason anymore," Sneha whispered, swiping at her cheeks. "And it didn't stop there. He checked into a hotel for a week. After returning, he said something I can't get out of my head. He asked if Sahil was even his son."

Tripti gasped sharply. "What? That's beyond cruel! How dare he say something like that?"

Sneha wrapped her arms around herself, rocking back and forth, trying to hold back the sobs threatening to spill. "I don't know what's happening to him, Tripti. It's like he's spiraling … into paranoia. Kunal's always had his moods, but this … this is something else. He's angry all the time … at everything I do. And now he's punishing Sahil, too. I don't even recognize him anymore."

Tripti's voice was calm, but her anger was unmistakable. "Sneha, this isn't your fault. Kunal is lashing out, and it's not okay. You can't keep absorbing his sadistic anger—it's breaking you."

Sneha looked at her friend, her voice small and weary. "I don't know what to do, Tripti. I feel trapped. I just … I needed to tell someone. You're the only one who understands."

Tripti reached out and squeezed Sneha's hand tightly. "You're not alone in this. We'll figure it out together. I'm here for you."

As Sneha cried, Tripti reached out to hold her hand. Before she could offer comfort, the rattle of keys made both women freeze.

"He's not supposed to be back yet," Sneha whispered, her face going pale.

The lock turned, and Kunal stepped inside, his gaze dark and accusing as he took in the scene. Without a word, he brushed past them and headed upstairs, his movements rigid with anger.

"I didn't know he'd be back," Sneha stammered, her voice shaking.

Tripti's tone was soft but steady. "It's okay. Let's stay calm."

But panic gripped Sneha, and she hurried after Kunal, her heart pounding.

Sneha found Kunal in their bedroom, pacing with his phone in hand. "I just called the Police," he grunted.

"Kunal," she beseeched, "Tripti is my guest. She's done nothing wrong."

Kunal whirled around to face her, his eyes blazing. "Your guest? She's trespassing, Sneha. Interfering in our lives by filling your head with ideas—poisoning you against me."

"No one's poisoning me, Kunal," Sneha replied, trying to stay calm. "I just needed someone to talk to because I can't talk to you … I have never been able to talk to you."

His expression twisted in fury. "Can't talk to me? That's rich, coming from the woman who's been sneaking off to have an affair behind my back. And you sought out Tripti, of all people? Who is too blind to realize that her husband is cheating on her with you?"

"Kunal, stop it," Sneha said, her voice firmer now. "This is about you and me. And if you can't see that, then you're the one who's blind."

For a moment, Kunal seemed stunned by her words, but the anger quickly returned. "You're going to regret this, Sneha," he gritted.

A loud knock on the front door made Sneha jump. She turned around and fled downstairs.

"Good evening, ma'am," Sneha heard an authoritative male voice. "We received a trespassing complaint."

"There must be some mistake, Officer. I was invited here," Tripti sounded nervous but calm.

"Officer, I live here, and Tripti is my guest. This is all a misunderstanding," Sneha stammered, rushing to the front door.

The officer hesitated, his eyes flicking between the women and the house. "Can I see some IDs?"

Both complied, their shaking hands extending their licenses. Sneha rapidly explained the situation. After a tense moment, the officer nodded. "All right. This seems to be a domestic issue. I suggest you resolve it privately. Have a good evening."

After the officer left, Tripti turned to Sneha, her voice shaking in anger. "He called the cops on me? On me? Sneha, this isn't just cruel—it's downright dangerous."

Sneha sank to the floor, face buried in her hands. "I don't know what to do anymore, Tripti."

Sneha's trips to Columbus ceased immediately. Kunal's grip on her life seemed to tighten, but so did her resolve to protect herself and Sahil.

When Tripti called in the following weeks, Sneha couldn't bring herself to answer, letting the calls go to voicemail instead.

*How can I face Tripti now? I need to find a way to fix my life. For myself. And for Sahil.*

One day, summoning her courage, Sneha answered.

"We're trying to sort things out, Tripti," she said tersely. "Please don't call anymore—I'll reach out when the time is right."

Sneha hung up and looked out the window at Sahil playing outside. Deep down, she knew the time for sorting things out was near, and she needed to find the strength to make the change her son deserved.

*The change I deserve.*


# Point of Return

The months deliberated on, each day blurring into the next as Sneha withdrew from polite society and settled into a rhythm dictated by Sahil's Montessori schedule. Her world shrank to the confines of their Dayton apartment and the aisles of Pushpa *Aunty-ji*'s grocery store. Interactions with Reema dwindled drastically—Sneha ignored incoming phone calls and door knocks, or met them with abbreviated responses. Sneha's life became a precarious balancing act: her physical self maintained equilibrium in a house that no longer felt like home while her mind endlessly weighed options for the future.

Kunal had grown completely detached, a rare presence in the apartment marked by curt words and silent actions. When he was not traveling, they shared a bed but slept as strangers, a small separating pillow symbolizing their emotional chasm. They no longer argued. It was as if both were resigned to their fates, unwilling to fight with or for each other.

Late at night, Sneha would lie awake, staring at the ceiling, her mind wandering. She thought of Tripti and Srikant, their partnership flawed but functional. Despite their differences in personality and ambition, they had found a way to move forward together. She thought of Reema and Sanjay, who bickered over the most minor things but with undeniable mutual affection. Even her parents, rooted in tradition, understood the value of mutual respect. These couples weren't perfect, but they tried. They built lives together, navigating differences with care and compromise. Sneha's marriage, in contrast, felt like a cold war—both sides retreating further into themselves with each passing day.

"This isn't the life I want," Sneha whispered to herself one night, her voice breaking the silence. She turned to look at Sahil, who had crawled into bed beside her, his small hand clutching hers. Her heart tightened. She knew then, with absolute clarity, that she couldn't let him grow up in this environment. He deserved better than this—a life filled with warmth and encouragement, not tension and cruelty. For the first time, she allowed herself to confront the truth fully: Kunal was poisoning their son's life.

The realization gave Sneha resolve. She would not let Sahil grow up in a toxic environment. For the first time in years, Sneha felt a small but steady flicker of determination—-to stand on her own feet and be a provider for Sahil. She didn't have all the answers yet, but she knew one thing: she would find a way to ensure Sahil's current and future happiness and well-being.

The thought of separating from Kunal had lingered in the depths of her mind for months.

It had seemed implausible, even impossible.

Not anymore.

There was one place she could go to make a fresh start: her parents' home in Kolkata, where she always felt safe and loved.

At first, Sneha told no one, quietly making arrangements in her head. She began saving the occasional money Pushpa *Aunty-ji* paid her, building a travel fund. She avoided confrontations with Kunal, keeping the peace as she plotted her escape. When the time felt right, she picked up her phone and called Tripti.

"Tripti, I just wanted to say goodbye. I'm leaving for Kolkata."

"Goodbye? Sneha, what are you talking about? What's going on?"

Tripti's shock was palpable.

Sneha sighed but replied in a resolute voice. "This isn't the life I want, Tripti, especially for Sahil. I've tried to make it work, but I can't anymore. I'm taking Sahil and going home to Kolkata. I need to reset our lives."

Tripti's voice softened. "Sneha, are you sure? I'm here for you, whatever you need."

"I know," Sneha said, her voice breaking. "And I'll never forget that. But this is something I have to do on my own."

Tripti's silence was heavy with emotion. Finally, she said, "I want you to be safe, Sneha. And happy."

Sneha blinked back tears. "I'll miss you, Tripti. Again."

Sneha quietly bid goodbye to Reema, Pushpa *Aunty-ji*, and a few other friends in Dayton. They were surprised but sympathetic, offering words of support and encouragement.

"You're doing the right thing," Reema hugged her tightly.

Despite Sneha's protests, Pushpa *Aunty-ji* pressed a roll of bills in her hand. "For the journey. It is not for you. It is for Sahil," she said firmly.

Sneha broached the subject with Kunal over the phone when he was out of town.

"What is it, Sneha? I am meeting a client in a couple of minutes."

She kept her explanation simple.

"Kunal, I've been thinking it might be good for Sahil and me to visit home for a while. It's been so long since I've seen my parents. Sahil is off from kindergarten anyway."

Kunal's irritation sounded amplified. "Home? You mean Kolkata?"

"Yes," Sneha said forcefully. "Just for a few weeks. I think it would be good for … er … all of us. A break."

"Maybe ... maybe ... it would," Kunal replied after a pause. "Things haven't been ... easy. But air tickets are expensive at this time of the year, and I just paid our bills."

"Pushpa *Aunty-ji*'s nephew is a travel agent, and he got us a deal——one of his customers had to cancel at the last minute."

"Oh, that's good. Pushpa *Aunty-ji* is good for something, I guess."

Sneha did not react.

"Why are you calling to tell me this now? Can we talk about this once I get back?"

"We are leaving tonight, Kunal. Reema is giving me a ride to the airport. I just wanted to say bye."

"Oh," Kunal seemed at a loss for words.

"Bye, Kunal. Take care of yourself."

"Uh ... bye, I suppose. Have a safe flight and all that. When are you coming b——," Kunal started to say, but Sneha terminated the call.

*Little does he know, I bought one-way tickets.*

Sneha packed her suitcases that evening, the sounds of Sahil's excitement breaking the tension in the air. She had told him they were going on an adventure back to where he was born and where Mama grew up.

She zipped up the last bag and glanced around the apartment one final time.

*It had never felt like home ... and it never would have.*

With her son's hand in hers, she stepped out of the apartment building and into the cool night air, ready to leave this chapter of her life behind and start a new one.

## Turning Point

Tripti, now a rising star in her company, was being "head-hunted" by recruiting companies and received multiple job offers in the Bay Area.

Meanwhile, Srikant continued to wrestle with his PhD—lost in the minutiae and paralyzed by perfectionism. Tripti, ever the pragmatist, had little patience for his dithering.

"You've been 'almost done' for two years," she said one evening, pacing the floor. "Do you want to spend the rest of your life in a lab, earning peanuts?"

Srikant sighed, massaging his temples. "It's not that simple, Tripti. Writing a dissertation takes time."

"And time is money," she interrupted. "We're moving to the Bay Area. You need to finish your PhD and get a job that pays what you're worth."

Tripti's determination lit a fire under Srikant, and within six months, he defended his thesis and submitted his dissertation. They packed their lives into a U-Haul and moved west.

Life in the Bay Area was everything Tripti had hoped for—fast-paced, lucrative, and full of opportunities for both of them.

However, her relationship with *Amma* remained contentious—their weekly conversations now devolving into arguments about her decision to remain child-free.

"You've been married for years now," *Amma* exasperatedly declared over a video call one evening. "What are you waiting for? Your career is fine, but children are your real legacy. If you wait for too long, you will have complications."

Tripti's jaw clenched. "*Amma*, I've told you before. We're not ready for that. We're building something important here."

"What's more important than family?" *Amma* shot back.

Tripti's frustration boiled over. "You're forgetting, *Amma*, that this is my life. Not yours. Mine."

The screen froze for a moment as her mother's face hardened. "You don't understand now, but one day you will."

Tripti ended the call abruptly, guilt and anger warring within her.

Several months went by.

The news came out of the blue.

*Appa* called late one night, his voice breaking with emotion. "*Amma*'s not well, Tripti *Ma*. She had a brain aneurysm. The doctors do not know how long she will be in a coma. We are unable to locate Rohit."

Tripti's heart sank. She wanted nothing more than to fly immediately to Chennai, but their green card applications were still pending, and traveling outside the U.S. would risk their permanent residency.

"I'll figure something out, *Appa*," she promised, her voice cracking.

Tripti sat frozen, her mind in turmoil. She felt overwhelmed by a sense of helplessness. Guilt incessantly jabbed at her, reminding her of the acrimony of the last conversation with *Amma* and the words she could not take back.

Her sense of pragmatism eventually jolted her out of her stupor, urging action.

But Tripti found no easy options.

In desperation, she called Sneha, with whom she had kept in touch on and off.

Sneha answered on the second ring, her voice warm but cautious.

"Tripti! How are you? It's been a while!"

"Y … yes. How are you, Sneha?"

"I'm well. But … what's wrong?"

"Sneha …," Tripti forced herself to fight back tears and keep her voice steady. "I … I'm sorry to call out of the blue, but it's … *Amma*. She's very, very sick, and I can't leave the U.S. right now because of my immigration status. Rohit is not reachable. Sneha, I … we … need help."

There was a slight pause before Sneha replied calmly. "Tripti, I'm so sorry to hear that. Of course, I'll help. Let me figure something out."

The next few weeks passed in excruciating anxiety, yet each update from Chennai alleviated some. Sneha had taken charge of *Amma*'s care with calm efficiency and pragmatism—even managing to locate and contact Rohit. Tripti's tightly clenched worries began to ease, granting her moments of introspection.

Seated at the work desk in their bedroom one evening, Tripti stared at the Bay Area panorama through her window, her thoughts churning. She had always prided herself on her independence, ability, and drive to live on her terms. However, under the current circumstances, when she was powerless to assist her parents, others she had hitherto taken for granted had stepped in to provide unconditional support.

Tripti's heart ached as she thought of Sneha, who had endured so much yet showed incredible compassion. She had dropped everything to travel across the country to care for *Amma* without hesitation or expectation of gratitude. Even in her trying situation, Sneha had found the capacity to support Tripti and empathize with her struggle.

Then, there was Rohit, her ever-elusive older brother. Tripti smiled faintly, remembering their childhood squabbles. When the family needed him, he did not hesitate to uproot his entire life and reach *Amma*'s bedside.

As for Srikant, her quiet, steadfast husband—how often had she dismissed his opinions and taken him for granted? He had been their bedrock while she charged ahead in her career, enduring her frustrations, impatience, and relentless pursuit of more. His faith in her never faltered. Tripti shuddered to think what her life might have been like with someone like Kunal—domineering, dismissive, pulling her down instead of lifting her. Srikant was her opposite in many ways, but he was the balance she needed, even though she hadn't appreciated it.

Tripti's chest tightened as she realized how fortunate she was to have these people in her life. Despite her flaws, sharp tongue, and sometimes thoughtless ambition, they had all stood by her.

As for *Amma*, whose larger-than-life presence had loomed over Tripti's life for so long—how frail and small she looked in the picture Rohit had sent. How helpless.

A lump rose in Tripti's throat as she recalled how quietly and unconditionally *Amma* had always cared for every need, ensuring there was always food on the table, clean clothes to wear, and comfort during every illness or heartache. She had taken *Amma* for granted, blind to the tireless devotion that nurtured their family, while *Amma* had never asked for her own comfort.

Tripti had resisted, even resented *Amma*'s relentless pushing—but now she understood: it stemmed from *Amma*'s fierce desire to see her daughter succeed and thrive in a world that often underestimated women like her. *Amma*'s high expectations for balancing a career and a family weren't born out of control; they were rooted in love—and in a fierce determination to prepare Tripti for challenges and opportunities that *Amma* herself had never been accorded.

Tripti closed her eyes and let a tear of gratitude slide down her cheek. She resolved to do better, to be better. If they could give her so much, it was time for her to give back.

She turned around, her voice hesitant. "Srikant?"

He looked up from his book, glasses slipping down his nose. "Hmm?"

"I need to talk to you." Her tone was unusually subdued.

Srikant sat up, setting his reading aside. "What's up?"

Tripti hesitated, her hands gripping the back of the chair. Finally, she met his eyes, her voice trembling slightly. "I've been ... awful ... to you. For years."

Srikant's brow furrowed, but he said nothing, waiting for her to continue.

"I pushed you hard, criticized you, dismissed your opinions. I was so focused on what I thought we needed to achieve that I forgot about us—about you, about the people who matter." Her voice broke, and she looked away, unable to meet his gaze.

"Tripti …," Srikant started.

"Please let me finish," she said, her voice firm but shaky. "I was wrong to treat you like that. I thought I was being the practical one, but I was also cruel. You've always been patient with me, always tried to understand me, and I didn't give you the same respect. I'm sorry, Srikant. Truly."

"Tripti," Srikant began, his voice soft. "You've been … intense at times, but I know you've always meant well. You wanted the best for us—for me—even if your delivery could've used some work." He smiled, trying to lighten the mood.

She gave a watery laugh, dabbing at her eyes. "That's putting it kindly."

"But," he continued, "I apologize, too. I didn't always understand your ambition and drive. I thought I was being supportive, but I wasn't as present as I could've been. I let myself get too comfortable with my work-life balance and didn't understand what you were going through."

Tripti looked up at him, her eyes shining. "You've always been my anchor, Srikant. Even when I didn't appreciate it. I want to do better—for you, for us."

"Me too," Srikant smiled, pulling Tripti into a gentle embrace.

Tripti's phone's sharp "ping" broke the silence. She pulled back, wiping her cheeks as she reached for the device to check the message. Her eyes widened. "Our parole visa!" she exclaimed, trembling with excitement. It's been approved. We can go to India!"

# To Be Or Knot   

## Homecoming

Sneha rubbed her eyes, groggily watching the twinkling landscape of Kolkata as her Emirates Air flight accelerated its descent. She glanced at Sahil, deep in the kind of slumber that only visits children, and a sense of irony gripped her. The last time they were 20,000 feet above her city, they were en route to America and in similar states of mind—while he was blissfully untroubled, she had been anxiously hopeful about what lay ahead.

Sneha gently pried the Nintendo console from Sahil's unresisting hands and gathered the rest of their belongings.

Sahil stirred awake, shook his curls, and looked up at her, rubbing his eyes.

"Are we there, Mama?"

"Yes, *beta. Chalo*, use the bathroom quickly."

Sneha leaned back and took a deep breath, steeling herself for the inevitable confrontation with her parents, especially *Baba.* Leaving one's husband was unheard of in their conservative Marwari family circles, multiple generations of whom had made Kolkata their place of business and residence.

The craft landed with a brace of gentle bumps and rolled to a halt. The inevitable swarm of *Desis* crowding the aisles grudgingly parted with some cajoling, allowing Sneha and Sahil to inch their way toward the exit doors and onto the jetway.

As mother and son rolled their luggage cart out of the airport and into the bustling throng of meeters and greeters of international arrivals, a familiar voice rang out.

"Baby *Saheb*! *Chhote Saheb*!"

Jagmit, burly in a familiar red turban, stepped forward with his ageless smile. Holding Sahil's arm, he skillfully maneuvered the cart through the crowd toward a Toyota Innova while maintaining a jovial chatter.

Sneha leaned back in her seat while Sahil bombarded Jagmit with questions about the vehicle's stick shift and right-side driver's seat, both unfamiliar from his experiences riding in his parents' cars in Dayton, Ohio.

"New car?" Sneha idly asked to quell her rising apprehension as familiar landmarks flashed by, signaling the proximity of her childhood home in the Ballygunge area.

"Yes, Baby *Saheb*."

"When will you let me drive it, Jaggu-*da*?" she asked, tongue-in-cheek. It was their mutual secret—Sneha driving the family car under Jagmit's watchful eye—since she was a teenager.

Jagmit roared with laughter. "You don't need anyone's permission now, Baby *Saheb*. And *Ma-ji* tells me you have been driving on American highways."

"That's true," Sneha smiled, recalling her adventures sneaking away from Dayton to visit Tripti in Columbus—all under Kunal's nose.

"And ... how is Kunal *Saheb*?" Jagmit asked, briefly catching her pensive eyes in the rear-view mirror.

"Busy with work," she replied vaguely, wondering how much, if anything, Jagmit knew.

Sneha stepped out of the car, taking in the familiar neighborhood, silent and dark as befitted the hour. *Ma* greeted her tearfully at the door and ushered her inside while Jagmit placed the luggage in her room.

As *Ma* bustled about in the kitchen, Sneha asked tentatively, "*Baba?*".

"Sleeping," came the reply, and Sneha felt a small wave of relief at the postponement of the impending confrontation.

*Ma* served fresh *chapatis*, *rajma*, and *pulao* on a *thali*, and Sneha and Sahil eagerly dug in, even though they had already eaten the airline meal.

Sleep came to Sneha in fits and starts before mercifully settling into a multi-hour stint. Ambient sunlight and the nostalgic scent of sandalwood *agarbatti* awakened her.

*Ma must be adding extra prayers for the coming day*, Sneha reflected wryly … and somewhat guiltily.

Sneha went to the kitchen and poured herself a cup of *chai* from a kettle that kept warm under a familiar quilted tea cozy. She entered the spacious living room, where *Baba* sat at a table with an empty cup in front, face hidden behind the day's edition of *The Telegraph*.

Sneha seated herself across from him, causing *Baba* to lower the newspaper and turn towards her. His black reading glasses rested on his aquiline nose, and his silver mane caught a sunbeam, creating a halo effect. His expression was inscrutable—as if he were about to negotiate a business deal.

"So, you're back," he said, his tone neutral.

Sneha, who hadn't realized she had been holding her breath, took a moment to exhale. "Yes, *Baba.*"

*Baba* folded the newspaper slowly and set it aside, then continued in the same tone, "For how long?"

"I … don't know," Sneha admitted. "I … need time … to sort out things."

"Time? To sort out what? Your mistakes?" *Baba* raised a bushy silver brow.

Sneha's jaw tightened. *Baba*'s demeanor was not unexpected, but his words still stung.

"Leaving Kunal was not a mistake."

Baba's gaze hardened. "You walked out on your marriage. In our culture, a woman's identity comes from the home she creates and the family she nurtures. You had your destiny, your husband's well-being, and your son's future in your hands. And you threw it all away—for what, exactly? Because you got bored? Or because it was hard work?"

Sneha bristled. "No, *Baba*. I left because I couldn't live the way Kunal wanted me to. He didn't respect or trust me."

*Baba* laughed humorlessly, "Marriage isn't about restarting over whenever you feel like it, Sneha. It's about compromise. Commitment. Ask her."

Sneha followed *Baba*'s gaze to *Ma*, standing at the doorway, subconsciously wringing a strand of the beaded curtain.

"Your *Ma*," *Baba* continued, "keeps this household together. She is the ideal *Marwari* wife. It's a pity you didn't learn anything from her."

"*Baba*," Sneha softened her voice. "Times have changed, and women now have more opportunities. In America, we work outside the home, as I did at a *Desi* grocery store and as my friend Tripti does as a professional. Husbands tend to be supportive and equal partners."

Sneha glanced at *Ma*, who offered a slight nod of reassurance. "But I did not leave because it was hard to balance home and work," she continued. "I left because Kunal never appreciated me for who I wanted to be; he wanted me to play a role he had decided for me."

Baba frowned but did not interrupt.

"*Baba*, you just said that *Ma* keeps this household together. You and *Ma* understand and respect each other's roles. All these years, Kunal never once acknowledged my worth as a wife or mother. Is that the life you wanted for me, *Baba*?"

Baba sighed as he removed his glasses and rubbed his temples. "You always want to get your way, Sneha—with words, if not actions. We gave you too much independence for your own good."

Sneha glanced again at *Ma,* drawing courage from the fierce love and loyalty beneath *Ma*'s meek exterior.

"Would you feel the same if I were your son, *Baba*?" Sneha asked, her voice shaking.

A silence descended.

*Ma* stood perfectly still, breathing heavily.

*Baba* pursed his lips and looked away, seemingly at a loss for words.

After a long pause, he spoke. "You've returned after years. That means something to this family. But this isn't your home, Sneha. You can't reset the past and start fresh—not according to our tradition."

"I came back to stand on my own feet, *Baba*. To find a new direction in life—for myself and Sahil," Sneha lifted her chin in defiance.

*Baba* shook his head, muttering under his breath.

"… and this is the only place I can call home anymore," Sneha said, her voice trembling.

*Ma* stepped forward. "She is our *beti, ji*. She needs our support."

*Baba* didn't offer an argument—or even a response. He picked up the newspaper and left the room.

Sneha exhaled in relief. *It could have gone much worse,* she thought.

"You did the right thing, *beta*," *Ma* reached out and squeezed her shoulder. "Now let's go check on Sahil," she added gently.

"Thank you, *Ma*," Sneha nodded, tears of gratitude and relief welling in her eyes.

She had made it through the first battle.

*Of many to come.*

# Bookends

Sahil settled in effortlessly over the next few weeks, charming the household, including *Baba*. *Ma* became his primary caregiver, allowing Sneha to reacquaint herself with the city streets she and Tripti had extensively navigated on her Scooty during their high school days.

"You're an expert now, Baby *Saheb*," Jagmit exclaimed as he rolled down his car window to yell at the hawker whose swerving cart Sneha had reflexively dodged.

"First time you've praised my driving, Jaggu-*da*," Sneha giggled at the colorful insults Jagmit was directing at his target. "You're getting soft in your old age."

Jagmit roared with laughter.

"Why does *Baba* run *Akshar*? He has a capable staff, right?" Sneha asked, passing a tram and effortlessly weaving through the chaotic traffic toward Esplanade.

Jagmit shrugged. "He loves his little bookstore, Baby *Saheb*."

Sneha left the car with Jagmit and entered *Akshar*, which had always been *Baba*'s sanctuary away from home. While *Baba* had experienced managers running his lucrative jewelry and clothing businesses, he personally oversaw the bookstore's operations. *Baba* dedicated long hours tending to an eclectic collection of rare and antique publications, handling each item with care, cataloging it carefully, and loaning it out under strict guidelines to ensure its preservation.

Sneha inhaled deeply—the air rich with the scent of old paper, teak furniture, and nostalgia. The sight of sturdy bookshelves filled with leather-bound tomes and glass cases displaying fragile manuscripts brought back childhood memories.

"*Baba*, it's like this place has escaped time," Sneha observed, "nothing has changed."

*Baba* looked up. While his gaze was frosty, his brief nod conveyed appreciation for her words.

"*Akshar* is my fortress against the fast-paced world," he said with a tight smile. "Despite what you and your generation believe, some traditions are worth preserving."

Sneha chose to ignore the dig and forced a smile. "How's the business doing?"

"It's not a business," Baba corrected. "It's a way of life—a labor of love. And it thrives—like all things nurtured with care and patience."

Wincing inwardly once again, Sneha pressed on, "I have always loved coming here. Can I please work here, *Baba*? It would give me something meaningful to do."

"I suppose," *Baba* conceded somewhat reluctantly.


Sneha began accompanying *Baba* to *Akshar* daily, sometimes giving Jagmit the day off and taking over the driving responsibilities.

For the first few weeks, Sneha was content to observe from behind the counter—watching *Baba* run the store with an old-world charm, relying on handwritten ledgers and verbal membership agreements with long-time patrons.

*Akshar* served as a place for in-depth discussions on various topics, with *Baba* enthusiastically participating. He took care to know each visitor by name, including their preferences, anticipating their needs, and recommending materials that interested them.

*Akshar* was not just a store but an institution, with *Baba* as its sole custodian.

Slowly, Sneha began to assist—organizing books, updating ledgers, and fielding simple inquiries.

*Baba* did not acknowledge her involvement, nor did he obstruct it.


Sneha, noticing inefficiencies in *Akshar*'s operations and the untapped market potential of its contents, cautiously approached *Baba* one day.

"*Baba*, your collection has grown incredibly, yet you only lend to a handful of people. Have you considered expanding membership?"

"It's not a club, Sneha," *Baba* scoffed. "*Akshar* is my way of giving back to the community—by preserving and sharing knowledge with those who value it."

"But, *Baba*," Sneha persisted, "what if we find more such people? Researchers, teachers, scholars, and libraries around the world?"

Sneha's wide-eyed earnestness seemed to soften *Baba*'s demeanor. "And how do you propose we do that?" he asked skeptically.

"Using the internet," Sneha had mentally rehearsed her idea. "We could create an online catalog with digital previews and a secure lending system for pre-screened members. We could offer different subscriptions based on the number of items checked out and the duration."

*Baba* seemed befuddled. "Our family businesses rely on drawing customers into physical stores and selling them products. I cannot grasp the value of what you are suggesting."

"It will work, *Baba*," Sneha said. "Remember my friend Tripti, whom I reconnected with in the US? She told me how she helped small business owners in Columbus, Ohio, using a similar model. We can do this."

"Do what, *beta*?" Baba threw up his hands. "*Akshar* was never meant to be a commercial enterprise."

"But what if *Akshar* becomes self-sustaining? What if it generates profits that help us expand our inventory and reach more people? Wouldn't that ensure that your vision is preserved for the present and future?"

Baba turned away to rearrange books on a shelf nearby. But he seemed to be giving Sneha's words some thought.

"Do what you think is best, *beta*," he muttered.

It wasn't a strong endorsement, but enough.

Sneha spent long days and nights working on her ideas.

Gradually, inquiries about *Akshar* trickled in, followed by membership applications. Within nine months, Sneha transformed the once modest bookstore into a sought-after destination for literary enthusiasts and researchers. *Akshar*'s membership expanded globally, making the store a thriving, sustainable enterprise.

Initially watching the changes with evident skepticism, Baba expressed his reluctant admiration one morning. "I never imagined this place would become what it is now, *beta*," he said, surveying the people and artifacts in the store.

Sneha looked up from her laptop.

"Are you upset?"

"Just … surprised."

"In a good way, hopefully," Sneha smiled tentatively.

"You've done well, *beta*. Better than I ever could," *Baba*'s voice grew tight. "Better than anyone in the family could."

"I learned from the best," she smiled, blinking back tears. A smile played on *Baba*'s lips—the first genuine one she had seen in as long as she could remember.

For a brief moment, the years seemed to fade between father and daughter.


One evening, Sneha approached *Baba* excitedly.

"For you, *Baba*," she said, extending a leather-bound copy of the 1912 edition of Rabindranath Tagore's *Gitanjali* towards him.

*Baba* appeared stunned. He ran his fingers disbelievingly over the gold lettering, voice hushed in reverence, "How … how did you manage to get this?"

"*Akshar* has friends worldwide now, *Baba*," Sneha smiled, unable to hide her pride. "This one is a gift to the store from a collector in London."

*Baba* seemed overwhelmed with emotion. He carefully opened the book, scanning the famous poet's handwritten notes on its delicate pages. Turning to Sneha, he nodded. "*Akshar* is in your hands now, *beta*," he whispered.

"And I'm content to be one of its grateful patrons."

*Baba* turned around, gently tucked the precious volume under his arm, and left the store.

Sneha poured herself into managing *Akshar*'s entire operations, taking over from *Baba*. She shifted her focus to expanding the workforce to keep pace with the store's continued growth. She handpicked new staff who shared *Baba*'s reverence for books—including seasoned librarians experienced in cataloging, archivists skilled in manuscript preservation, and retired educators who served as advisors for sourcing new material. *Akshar* wasn't just a family concern anymore—it belonged to a committed team that implemented and nurtured *Baba*'s vision.

Within a year, Sneha and Kunal reached an agreement to formalize their separation with a divorce. Their conversations were clinical and devoid of emotion, as though they were discussing a business deal rather than the dissolution of a marriage.

Kunal's family welcomed the decision with thinly veiled relief, already murmuring about potential marriage alliances for him. They had long viewed Sneha as the root cause of their son's self-proclaimed miseries. *Baba*'s quiet support and *Ma*'s unwavering loyalty were her pillars of strength during the complex process.

Kunal traveled to India to contest Sahil's custody. The court proceedings were grueling. Kunal made a performative case that Sneha was an unfit mother, questioning her career choices and independence. However, his lack of involvement in Sahil's life and dismissive attitude toward parenting left the court unconvinced.

The judge ruled in Sneha's favor, granting her full custody.

Sneha's lingering disappointment, anger, and self-doubt vanished when the divorce papers were finally signed. She felt liberated—to live on her terms and build a future for herself and Sahil.

# Beginnings

Sneha stood at the reception area of *Akshar*'s new, climate-controlled facility in Kolkata's Salt Lake City, watching the staff work efficiently, and heaved a sigh of contentment. *Akshar* no longer needed her or *Baba* to carry forward its vision; together, they had built something that was not only flourishing but enduring.

Sneha felt she had reached the summit after a long, challenging climb that had filled her with wisdom and purpose.

One afternoon, two men visited *Akshar*—one tall, bespectacled, and clean-shaven, and the other short, stocky, and bearded. Both were scanning the facility with a distinct air of purpose.

Sneha immediately spotted them from her glass-walled manager's cubicle. With the receptionist on break, she stepped out to greet them.

"Welcome to *Akshar*. How can we help you, gentlemen?" she asked, stepping forward with a warm smile.

"Hello. I am Daniel Shaw, a cultural attaché at the US Embassy in Kolkata." The tall man extended his hand affably. "And this is Mark Whitman, an NGO entrepreneur."

"Welcome to *Akshar*," Sneha smiled, shaking their hands and introducing herself.

Daniel adjusted his glasses. "We're looking for a rare publication: 'The Ancient Temple Communities of Bengal.' It's a limited-edition book from the 1960s detailing the region's history. It's essential for a project we're working on, but it's been out of print for decades."

Sneha's brows furrowed in thought. "It's not in our inventory," she acknowledged, "but I'll see what I can do. I assure you, I will personally handle this matter."

Mark offered his business card. "Please get in touch with me if you get any leads. I am leading the project."

Sneha doggedly contacted rare book collectors and scoured online forums. She also contacted researchers at the Asiatic Society of Kolkata, known for its extensive archives of Bengal's cultural and historical heritage.

She learned that a retired professor in Chandernagore owned a pristine copy and was willing to give it away to someone deserving.

Sneha traveled to Chandernagore to collect the book and ensure its safe return.

When Sneha handed Mark the carefully wrapped book, his eyes lit up. "I'm very impressed, Sneha. You tracked this down in less than two weeks. We've had people back in America stumped for months."

Sneha smiled. "It's just about knowing where to look."

They struck up a conversation.

Mark spoke passionately about his NGO's work across South Asia.

"Our organization 'Pathways to Prosperity' does microfinancing projects," he explained. "We empower underserved communities to start small businesses and gain financial independence. Our last project provided electric sewing machines to a socially disadvantaged community in Bihar."

Mark's animated face reflected his passion for social work. "Families who barely scraped by now have steady incomes. Men and women learned to sew and market clothing products, generating household revenue. It's incredible to see the hope and self-reliance that's emerged."

Sneha was captivated.

"Have you ever considered working in this field?" Mark asked, noticing her interest.

Sneha laughed lightly. "I wouldn't even know where to begin."

"Well, would you consider joining our organization as a caseworker? We have a position open."

Sneha blinked. "Me?"

"Absolutely," Mark said. "You've got the right skills for the position—you are empathetic, sharp, organized, and resourceful. Our company is well-funded, and we take excellent care of our employees. Think about it."

As Mark walked away, Sneha stood in silence, her mind racing.

*Stable employment, meaningful work, good pay, and a chance to uplift those in need?*

It felt like a door to a future she hadn't dared to imagine. It wouldn't just be a job, but a lifeline. She could give Sahil the opportunities he deserved and build a life rooted in independence and purpose.

The path ahead felt clear; it felt hers.

A strong referral from Mark, her knowledge and experience with *Baba*'s bookstore operations, and her fluency in English, Bengali, and Hindi made Sneha a new addition to the "Udaan: Wings of Empowerment" project team.

The work was challenging yet rewarding. Sneha traveled across Bangladesh and India, visiting rural villages and urban slums, facilitating loans, and helping start businesses.

Sahil started his second year of kindergarten at the St. Claret School. Though Sneha's job took her away from Sahil during most weekdays, she ensured weekends and holidays were dedicated to spending time together. Their bond grew, filled with laughter, stories, and quiet moments that reminded her why she had made her choices.

## Friend In Deed

One evening, Sneha was preparing for a trip to a village outside Pune when her phone rang. She smiled when she saw Tripti's name on the screen. They had kept in touch, sharing updates about Sneha's new life in India and Tripti's rising career in the U.S.

"Tripti! How are you? It's been a while!"

Tripti's voice was uncharacteristically unsteady. "Y … yes. How are you, Sneha?"

Sneha's concern heightened immediately. She had never heard such vulnerability in Tripti's voice before. "I'm fine. But … what's wrong?"

"Sneha … I'm sorry to call out of the blue, but it's … *Amma*. She's very, very sick, and I can't leave the U.S. right now because of my immigration status. Rohit is not reachable. Sneha, I … we … need help."

Sneha's mind raced to evaluate various courses of action, but she did not hesitate. "Tripti, I'm so sorry to hear that. Of course, I'll help. Let me figure something out."

The next day, Sneha approached her work supervisor with a request.

"I'd like to be added to the Mahabalipuram team," she said, referring to an ongoing project near Chennai that enabled stone artisans to expand the market reach for their sculptures. "I have a personal situation that requires me to be closer to the city."

Within a week, Sneha arrived in Chennai. She was met by Tripti's father, *Appa*, who had been struggling to manage *Amma*'s care—barely balancing hospital visits with the demands of taking care of himself.

"It's a blessing to have you here, Sneha," *Appa* said gratefully. "I don't know how long I could have done this alone."

Sneha took charge, using her organizational skills to assess and address the situation. With *Amma* in a coma, Sneha arranged for her to be moved back to the comfortable and quiet environment of their home. She contacted a reputable agency and coordinated a team of professional nurses for round-the-clock care. She ensured the house was equipped with all the necessary medical supplies—oxygen tanks, a hospital bed, and monitoring devices—transforming *Amma*'s room into a homely medical space.

The days were long, but helping care for *Amma* felt like a full-circle moment for Sneha—a way to repay Tripti's friendship, especially during her darkest days in America, leading up to her decision to leave Kunal.

On weekends, she called Sahil, who was thriving under her parents' care.

Sitting by *Amma*'s bedside one evening, Sneha reflected on how far she had come. From the stifling confines of Dayton to the determined beginnings of Kolkata and now to the resilience of Chennai, Sneha was living life on her terms—with courage, conviction, and self-belief.

*Appa*, visibly less burdened and with eyes brimming with gratitude, constantly thanked Sneha. One day, with a trace of resigned bitterness, he added, "Rohit should be here doing this."

Sneha brought up the topic during a phone call with Tripti.

"It's hopeless, Sneha," Tripti said resignedly. "Srikant and I have tried, but Rohit's globetrotting lifestyle makes him difficult to pin down. He frequently changes phone numbers and is never on social media. Our efforts have hit one dead end after another."

Late one evening, after ensuring *Amma* was comfortable and *Appa* rested, Sneha drafted an email explaining the situation to Mark Whitman.

Mark responded within hours. He had made inquiries leveraging his connections within the U.S. Embassy. Rohit, it turned out, was a U.S. Green Card holder who, like frequent travelers, regularly registered his whereabouts with the U.S. State Department whenever he crossed international borders.

"Through this system, they have been able to pinpoint Rohit's last known location in Southeast Asia," Mark's note said. "He will be contacted and informed of the urgent situation back home."

The phone buzzed in the quiet of *Amma*'s room, breaking Sneha's focus as she adjusted the IV line. She glanced at *Appa*, who was pacing near the window.

Sneha answered. "Rohit," she said, a note of relief in her tone.

"I'll be on the next flight," Rohit said, his voice firm but laced with guilt and concern.

Sneha relayed the update to *Appa*, who nodded curtly. "It's been ages since he's been home," he murmured. "But at least he's decided to show up when it matters."

Two days later, Sneha found herself at the Chennai airport, scanning the crowd for a face she hadn't seen in decades. When she spotted him, her breath caught. Rohit had aged, but his salt-and-pepper hair lent him an air of maturity and authority. His eyes were exactly as she remembered: sharp, thoughtful, and kind.

"Sneha?" he said, stopping in front of her with a small smile.

"Rohit," she replied, unable to suppress her own. "It's been a long time."

On the ride home, they talked, reflecting their shared concern for *Amma* and their unexpected reconnection. Despite the somberness of the situation, there was a surprising ease between them, a nostalgic and comforting familiarity.

Over the next two days, Rohit took charge of *Amma*'s care—coordinating with doctors, managing the nurses, and spending hours sitting by her bedside, talking to her in hopes of eliciting a response.

One evening, as they prepared *Amma*'s room for the night, Rohit turned to Sneha. "I never imagined this is how we'd meet again."

"Neither did I," Sneha admitted. "But I'm glad you're here. Tripti needed you. *Amma* and *Appa* needed you."

Rohit sighed. "I should have been here sooner. I let too many excuses pile up—work, travel, my so-called responsibilities. None justifies being absent when my family needed me the most."

Sneha placed a reassuring hand on his arm. "You're here now, Rohit. That's what matters."

He looked at her with an expression of gratitude. "You've done so much, Sneha. Stepping in where I failed. You didn't have to, but you did. *Amma* couldn't have asked for better care and *Appa*—" He paused, his voice thick with emotion. "You gave him strength when he was running on empty. We'll always be grateful to you for that."

Sneha hesitated, her smile faint and bittersweet. "*Amma* was always kind to me during our school days. Every time I'd drop by to see Tripti, she insisted I stay for lunch or at least have a snack. Her warmth made me feel welcome as part of the family. Being here now, helping care for her—it feels like I'm giving back, in some small way, for all those moments."

Rohit held her gaze for a long moment, then nodded understandingly.

Sneha and Rohit stepped out of *Amma*'s room to join *Appa* at the dinner table.

After they put the dishes away, the three of them sank into the living room furniture, mental and physical exhaustion visible on their faces. Yet, they also unspokenly acknowledged each other's commitment to *Amma*'s care and comfort.

Sneha yawned, "I need to turn in early—we're conducting our final workshop tomorrow."

"Your project is wrapping up?" Rohit asked.

"Yes. I will be able to return home this weekend," Sneha smiled.

"Sneha," Appa spoke up hesitantly. "Can't you stay a few extra days? At least until Tripti gets here?"

Sneha hesitated. She had been away from Sahil, *Ma,* and *Baba* for almost a month. She had rationalized staying on, primarily because *Appa* and *Amma* needed her. But with Rohit's unexpected arrival, she could leave with a clear conscience.

"It's just …," *Appa* cleared his throat, his eyes flickering uncertainly towards Rohit. "It's been good having you here. Your presence … it's made things feel … assuring."

Sneha swallowed, her mind torn asunder. She desperately missed Sahil and longed to be home, but the vulnerability in *Appa*'s eyes and voice moved her.

Then she understood.

*In Appa's eyes, I am Amma's primary caregiver. Rohit hasn't yet earned his trust, especially after being away from home for so long.*

Sneha glanced at Rohit, who shrugged slightly to indicate that the decision was hers.

"Alright, *Appa*. I'll stay a little longer," she smiled.

"Thank you, Sneha," *Appa* gave a nod of gratitude.


## Confrontations and Confessions


A loud series of beeps pierced the air.

Rohit abandoned his cup of coffee and rushed into *Amma*'s room.

"*Appa*, let me help you," Sneha cried, seeing *Appa* struggle to get out of the cane chair in which he had fallen asleep.

Before they got there, Rohit emerged from *Amma*'s room. "Nothing to worry. *Amma*'s blood oxygen level dropped slightly, but it is back up, and she is stable now. Something must be wrong with the sensor. I texted the nurse to look at it as soon as she gets here."

*Appa* was visibly shaking, leaning against the wall for support.

"Hey, hey, *Appa*," Rohit hastened to his side. "Relax. She's fine. I am here."

*Appa*'s relieved expression slowly darkened, and a flood of pent-up emotions burst out of him.

"You are here?" *Appa* spluttered. "Where the hell were you all these years, Rohit?"

"Does it matter, *Appa*?" Rohit looked taken aback by *Appa*'s outburst. "I came as soon as I could ...," his voice faded defensively.

"Sneha had to track you down and summon you like a criminal," *Appa* snapped. "Is that a way for a son to behave?"

Rohit flinched visibly. "*Appa* ... I know I should have been here sooner ...," he stuttered, running his hands through his hair, at a loss for words.

"Years, Rohit," *Appa* thundered. "Years of silence. Your *Amma* kept asking me when you'd call and when you'd visit. I had no answers. Do you have any idea what you put us through?"

Rohit clenched his jaw. "You think I don't feel guilty?"

*Appa* lurched towards him, "Do you? Feelings are nothing, Rohit. Words are something, but actions are everything. Where were you when we needed you?"

"Did you ever stop to think I could have been going through something?" Rohit's chest heaved in agitation. "You and *Amma* never once asked why I was living like this ... running from place to place. You only noticed my absence— you never tried to understand it."

"How would we understand what we did not know?" *Appa* scoffed. "You are our son, Rohit. You could have told us anything."

Rohit's laugh was hollow. "And you would have understood? That I was struggling mentally? That I had no idea what I wanted in life anymore? That I was a shell of a man?"

"Why wouldn't we understand?" *Appa* challenged.

"Because of your conservative *Iyengar* mentality," Rohit muttered bitterly, turning away.

"If that's what stopped you, then maybe you don't know us as well as you think," *Appa* retorted.

"Maybe," Rohit sighed, shoulders sagging, the fight visibly draining out of him.

Without another word, *Appa* turned and walked into *Amma*'s room.

"I need air," Rohit said to no one in particular, shaking his head.

Before Sneha, hovering in the background during the confrontation, could say a word, Rohit slipped his feet into a pair of sandals and walked out of the house.

"Coffee at Brewklyn?" Rohit texted her the following evening as she was returning from work.

"Sure," she texted back and directed the autorickshaw driver to the Elliott's Beach area.

Rohit was waiting, seated at an outdoor high-top table.

Sneha smiled tentatively, alighting from her transport.

As the two sipped, Rohit stared toward the beach, lost in thought.

"Want to talk about it?" Sneha asked gently.

"I felt like a complete villain, arguing with *Appa* while *Amma* was lying helpless in the next room. They say people in comas can still hear ...," Rohit's voice faltered. "And now a part of me feels I shouldn't have come back," he bowed his head, staring into his cup.

"You know that's not true." Sneha marshaled her thoughts, choosing her words carefully. "*Appa* is angry, but it's because he feels hurt. He missed you. *Amma* missed you. They needed to be in contact with you. Even a written or spoken word once in a while would have sufficed."

"I know that, Sneha," Rohit sighed. "I wasn't in touch because I could not be. I just ... couldn't face them ... after what happened."

"Then tell him. And if it helps, tell me," Sneha placed her hand on his forearm.

Rohit turned to look at her, and the vulnerability in his eyes struck her. He placed his other hand on hers, grasping it tightly.

"I have never talked about this," he started hesitantly. "To anyone."

Sneha nodded understandingly.

"I met Leila at a martial arts school in Columbus, Ohio. Not very romantic, I know," a wry smile played on Rohit's lips. "She was from Israel, doing her master's in computer science at the Ohio State University. She was brilliant, ambitious … and relentless. She was extremely knowledgeable about the world—economics, geopolitics, history, you name it. I fell in love with her."

Rohit's expression became distant. "Instead of pursuing a PhD, I joined her at Bechtel, an engineering consulting firm based in the Washington, DC area."

Sneha frowned. "But you wanted to do research."

"I thought I did," Rohit admitted. "But I wanted her more, so I changed my plans—for her … and us. It wasn't a bad career move. Bechtel sent us on the road, and we did cutting-edge infrastructure projects all over America. It was a great professional experience, and I always considered returning to graduate school for a doctorate."

Sneha looked at him intently, "Then … something happened?"

"How did you know?" Rohit chuckled dryly. "Yeah, you could say that. Reality caught up with us. The call came for her to serve in the Israeli military, and her family learned about us. Slowly, a line was drawn between Leila and me."

"Meaning?"

"I had to move to Israel, convert to Judaism, and become a citizen. Her extremely conservative parents convinced her that if I didn't, I'd be treated as a second-class resident, and our children would have it even worse. "

"And you weren't willing?"

"Of course, I considered it," Rohit nodded solemnly. "I truly did. But the more I thought about it, the more I realized I would lose my identity. It wasn't like moving to America, where you can still hold on to your ethnicity and culture while assimilating at your own pace. This meant instantly changing my priorities, values, and my entire way of life."

"But … you loved her."

"I did. But did she truly love me if she asked me to erase myself?" Rohit let out a sigh and gave her a small smile. "We both knew it would not work out. I think she was heartbroken as well, but she also respected my decision. We parted ways, and I decided to bury myself in work as a coping mechanism."

Sneha looked at him thoughtfully. "But that does not explain why you did not set down roots anywhere."

"DC, Columbus … way too many places in America reminded me of the life I once shared with Leila," Rohit said. "I couldn't stay there, Sneha. So, I sought international gigs—traveling to parts of the world no one in Bechtel wanted to. It was sort of what I needed. Somehow, the constant movement subdued and dulled my memories and second-guesses. Exposure to different countries, cultures, languages—they helped me cope—and made the past less … suffocating."

Sneha nodded. She understood Rohit perfectly. Her work with the NGO had shown her how immersing oneself in new experiences could be healing—by letting go of the past.

"I get it," she said. "Being in motion keeps you looking forward, not back."

"Exactly."

"Rohit," Sneha frowned, "I don't mean to be intrusive, but I still don't understand why you cut off all contact with *Amma* and *Appa*," she said, a note of indignation creeping into her voice. "Did you have a fight with them … over Leila?"

"It's complicated," Rohit exhaled slowly. "And reflecting on it after all these years, it's somewhat embarrassing," he shook his head in a gesture of self-reproach.

Sneha stayed silent, feeling she had already said too much.

"The truth is, I never actually told them about Leila. Not specifically, anyway."

"What do you mean?" Sneha frowned.

"I was vague. I wanted to … um … test the waters first," Rohit's face reddened, "… by hinting now and then at the idea of marrying outside the *Iyengar* community. Just to see how they'd react."

"And?" Sneha asked sharply.

"They'd shut me down instantly, going on about how our family doesn't do that, that our traditions matter, etcetera." Rohit chuckled cynically. "The topic usually went nowhere."

"And you took that as rejection?" Sneha stared at him incredulously.

"No," Rohit gestured defensively. "I saw it as discouragement. Their views were clear, and considering the fluid situation with Leila, I felt unable to take a strong stance on something I wasn't even sure would work out."

"I think I see what you are getting at," Sneha said, thinking furiously. "So, when she chose to go with what her parents wanted, you felt—"

"… antagonistic towards my own," Rohit nodded bitterly. "I knew it was unfair, but I couldn't help it. I felt if her parents hadn't broken us up, mine would have."

"Rohit, that's kind of … messed up," Sneha said, her tone gentle yet rebuking.

"It is," Rohit acknowledged wearily. "I was angry, stubborn, and confused. As time went on, I even convinced myself that I was right. I told myself that if they never cared to hear, let alone listen to, and understand what I was trying to say, they wouldn't have accepted my choices. So why bother?"

"So …," Sneha slowly drew out her words. "You blamed them."

"For a confrontation we never had," Rohit murmured, his voice little more than a whisper. "And when the news about *Amma* reached me, it reached deep into my soul … and shook it awake."

They sat in silence for several minutes until Sneha broke it. "You need to talk to *Appa*," she said simply.

Rohit looked at her for a moment, then nodded in agreement. "We should head home now—the doctor is coming to check on *Amma*," he said.

Sneha and Rohit rose from their seats, and Rohit hailed a passing auto rickshaw.

The doctor emerged from *Amma*'s room and assured them her vitals were stable. "She will wake up when she is ready to," he observed. "You all are taking excellent care of her. Just be patient and trust the human body's ability to heal over time."

*Appa* sat silently in his chair, rocking himself gently.

Rohit returned after seeing the doctor off and sat across from *Appa*, who looked up inquiringly.

"Did the doctor have anything else to say?"

"No," Rohit shook his head.

"Do you have something to say, then?"

Rohit hesitated, then nodded. "Yes."

Sneha took a seat away from either's line of sight.

"I was in love, *Appa*." Rohit's voice was quiet but steady. "Her name was Leila. She was an Israeli. We thought we could make it work."

*Appa*'s face was inscrutable.

"She … and her parents … wanted me to move to Israel and to convert," Rohit continued, rubbing the back of his neck. "I couldn't do it, *Appa*. So, I walked away."

*Appa*'s expression softened. "If you had gone through with it, we would have been heartbroken," he admitted. "But … in time, we would have come around."

"What?" Rohit blinked. He was clearly caught off guard.

"You are our flesh and blood, Rohit," *Appa* continued in a quiet voice. "We would not have cut you out of our lives. We would have learned to live with it."

"But," Rohit frowned, "you were always both so rigid. So orthodox in your values and beliefs."

"That's the world we knew," *Appa* said simply. "And we were afraid."

"Afraid of what?"

"Of a world we couldn't comprehend."

"Exactly. That is my point," Rohit cried. "You would not have understood the life I would have embraced."

"But we would have accepted your decision," *Appa* insisted. "And come to understand it … in time."

Rohit fell silent, his expression skeptical.

*Appa* studied him for a few moments. "You're angry that we never asked why you were running," he said gently. "But you never asked what we feared, either."

"I won't deny that," Rohit nodded slowly. "But all my life, I've looked over my shoulder for your approval, whether real or imagined. I never felt like I had the space to make mistakes. My acceptance of your strictness and orthodoxy while growing up was gradually turning into resentment."

"Resentment? Toward us?" The hurt in *Appa*'s face tugged at Sneha's heart, but she desisted from intervening. "Is that why you stopped communicating with us?"

"Yes," Rohit muttered. "You pushed Tripti into an early marriage. I resented you and *Amma* for it. And when I fell in love with Leila, I just couldn't reconcile my two realities. I felt trapped."

"And now?" *Appa*'s voice was hushed. "Do you think any differently of us?"

"I think … I understand now," Rohit continued after a deep breath, "that you and *Amma* weren't trying to control us or our future lives. You were trying to protect us … and position us to succeed … in the manner you thought was best."

*Appa* slowly nodded, looking down at his clasped hands. "Maybe we made a mistake … with Tripti," he sighed. "Maybe we've always put too much pressure on you both. But she has built something for herself. And so have you."

Rohit shook his head vehemently. "I haven't, *Appa*. I have been untethered … just drifting around aimlessly."

*Appa* rose from his seat and stepped forward. Resting his hand on Rohit's shoulder, he said, "The thing about being lost is that one eventually stops to figure out where to turn. Maybe it's time you did that?"

Rohit nodded.

"You should've told us what you were going through, Rohit."

"And if I had?" Rohit's voice trembled, tears in his eyes.

*Appa* met his gaze with misty eyes. "We would've listened, and maybe that would've made all the difference."

Something in Rohit broke. His face contorted, and without another word, he wrapped his arms around *Appa*, sobbing apologetically.

*Appa* held him, gently stroking his son's hair.

Sneha turned away, her own vision clouded with tears.

*For the first time in years, Rohit isn't running.*

*And Appa isn't waiting.*


## Closed Books and Open Chapters

The next evening, the home phone rang.

Rohit answered.

When he hung up, Sneha looked up from *Amma*'s bedside, curiosity etched on her face.

"That was Tripti," Rohit smiled. "Their immigration paperwork finally came through. They'll be flying to Chennai in a week."

Sneha let out a small sigh of relief, her shoulders visibly relaxing. "That's wonderful news. Tripti must be so relieved."

Rohit nodded, his expression softening. "She sounded emotional but mostly excited. She said it feels like a huge weight has been lifted off her shoulders. They're packing already."

Sneha smiled faintly, her voice quiet. "It'll mean so much to *Appa* to have Tripti here. And to *Amma* … even if she can't express it."

For a moment, neither of them spoke.

Sneha felt strangely conflicted.

The promise of Tripti and Srikant's arrival felt like a glimmer of hope amid the uncertainties—a long-awaited reunion to bring strength and comfort to a family that had been holding its breath for far too long.

It meant she could leave Chennai and be reunited with her family in Kolkata.

But it also meant she might never see Rohit again.

The thought lingered—heavier and longer than she had expected.


A miracle happened on the day Tripti and Srikant arrived in Chennai.

As if *Amma* had been holding on, waiting for her family to be whole again, her eyelids fluttered open in the soft glow of the evening light.

Sneha, who had been adjusting the curtains, froze mid-motion, her breath catching in her throat. "Rohit, *Appa*," she called out, her voice trembling with disbelief and hope.

Rohit and *Appa* rushed into the room, their expressions shifting from exhaustion to stunned relief.

*Amma*'s gaze, weak and unfocused, scanned the room.

The doctor arrived shortly and thoroughly examined *Amma* before stepping back with a small smile. "She's responsive—this is a very positive sign. Keep talking to her and maintain her attention."

*Appa*'s shoulders heaved with quiet sobs. Rohit's hands shook as he clasped *Amma*'s frail fingers, blinking rapidly to hold back his tears.

Sneha quelled her rising emotions and left the room to send a text to convey the news to Tripti.


Tripti and Srikant settled down in Chennai, and the atmosphere shifted. Tripti was a whirlwind of energy, coordinating with doctors and efficiently taking over tasks.

Sneha stood back and watched as Tripti and Rohit interacted, the sibling bond evident in their quick banter and shared determination.

One evening, as they all sat around the dining table, Tripti turned to Sneha. "I owe you so much," she said, her voice thick with emotion. "For being here, for helping *Amma*. I don't know what we would've done without you."

Sneha shook her head. "You were there for me in America when I needed you the most, Tripti. This is the least I could do."

The three of them sat on the water tank on the terrace, the warm evening sea breeze whipping around them. A plate of biscuits rested alongside three steaming cups.

"Dang, Tripti," Rohit declared. "You've nailed this Kolkata *chai*. All we are missing are those little clay pots … what do they call them?"

"*Kullad*," said Tripti and Sneha in unison, laughing.

Their conversation had wound through recent matters of *Amma*'s health, Rohit's return, and Tripti's self-realization.

"It took *Amma*'s illness and my inability to help—to appreciate those that I had taken for granted," Tripti confessed. "Especially Srikant, who has been my biggest support."

"I never doubted your marriage for even a moment, Tripti," Sneha said earnestly. "You both were meant to be together."

"You know," Rohit exaggeratedly swirled his *chai*. "We have been laying our deepest, darkest secrets before you. But Sneha … you are an enigma … at least to me. And you're leaving us tomorrow."

Sneha raised her eyebrow, "Me? I have nothing to hide. Tripti knows the story of my divorce."

"Rohit is right, though. You are not saying much," Tripti observed. "Very mysterious."

"Just enjoying the moment, that's all," Sneha smiled.

"Let's start at the beginning, shall we?" Rohit teased. "Do you remember the first time we met?"

Sneha blushed. "Oh God, please no," she groaned.

"You barely spoke to me," Rohit laughed.

"I was barely eighteen," Sneha muttered, blushing deeper.

"Oh, Sneha," Tripti chuckled. "Just admit it."

"Admit what?" Rohit asked.

"Fine," Sneha sighed. "I had a small crush on you, okay?"

"You did?" Rohit grinned. "You masked it well, I must say."

"That was not even the interesting part," Tripti giggled. "She got your hostel address at IITM from me—to write to you."

"Yeah," Sneha grinned mischievously, "I may have sent you anonymous letters."

"Wait," Tripti exclaimed. "You never told me this before!"

Rohit choked on his drink. "Wait—those letters? Those were from you?"

Sneha nodded, giggling.

Tripti rolled on the floor, laughing, "Oh, this is hilarious! I would have paid anything to read them!"

Rohit chuckled, "There wasn't much to them—mostly heart doodles. And no return address. They stopped after a few months. I was convinced that one of my friends was trolling me."

The laughter slowly settled into easy camaraderie as the evening advanced.


Months passed.

Sneha was leaning against her desk in *Akshar*, carefully examining a set of rare manuscripts that had recently arrived, when the front door opened. She glanced up, pen freezing in mid-air.

"Rohit?" she exclaimed, her eyebrows lifting in surprise. "What are you doing here?"

Rohit grinned, hands tucked casually into his pockets. "Well, I am in town for work and called your home. *Ma* picked up and told me you hang out here when you are off work."

"Oh …," Sneha blinked, a flustered smile spreading across her face before she recovered her composure. "And you decided to walk in like you own the place?"

Rohit chuckled, his easy confidence filling the quiet corners of the bookstore. "Can't help it—it's the *Iyengar* charm."

Sneha rolled her eyes, but her smile lingered. "Well, welcome to *Baba*'s kingdom of books and binders."

Rohit glanced around the space—the modern lighting, the scent of old paper, and Sneha standing there with magnifying glasses strapped to her forehead. "Charming place," he said simply.

For a moment, the hum of the air-conditioning was the only sound between them.

Then Rohit cleared his throat, tilting his head slightly. "Coffee?"

Sneha hesitated briefly. "Sure. Let me grab my bag."

They sat across from each other at the small café in a quiet corner, steam curling from their cups.

"So, back to consulting? And globe-trotting?" Sneha asked, stirring sugar in her coffee.

Rohit shrugged lightly, his smile softening. "I quit my old job to help care for *Amma*, but my employer took me back. I'm sticking to projects within India now."

Their conversation meandered through familiar territory—Tripti, *Amma*'s recovery, and individual memories from younger days. Their dialogue was easy, and Sneha found its natural rhythm comforting and disarming.

Rohit drained his cup, and his expression turned serious. "I don't know any details, Sneha. And I don't want to pry. But what was married life like?"

The question, although not unexpected, caught Sneha off guard.

For a moment, she was silent. This wasn't mere curiosity on Rohit's part. He was looking at her not just with interest but with guarded optimism.

*Is he trying to understand what I've been through?*
*And ... perhaps gauge how deeply my past has scarred me?*
*Or ... if I'm ready to dive into a relationship?*
*Am I?*

Sneha decided to address the question at face value. "Life with Kunal was … complicated," she replied measuredly.

"How so?"

"He was very … particular, wanting to control everything. He did not trust me to be an adult and questioned my actions. It was … somewhat suffocating … and demeaning."

Rohit nodded.

Sneha gazed deeply into his warm, brown eyes and decided to be honest and open.

"Like … he tracked my location with a phone app," Sneha started. "… and accused me of having an affair with Srikant when I hacked the app to visit Tripti. The last straw was when Tripti came over to our house because I requested to talk to her, and he called the cops on her for trespassing."

Rohit seemed aghast. "That's not being particular, Sneha. It's several degrees worse."

Sneha shrugged. "I know. I initially thought this was what marriage was. You adjust. You make it work. Especially when you have a child."

Rohit's jaw was tightly clenched. "That's like being trapped. Caged against your will."

Sneha offered a weary smile. "With time, bad memories fade, but good ones remain, Rohit. I cherish my time in America; it taught me self-reliance, brought Tripti back into my life, and opened my eyes to the truth about my marriage. And I have moved forward."

"How can you be so …," Rohit shook his head, "casual about this?"

"Because I have to," Sneha shrugged. "If I dwell on the past, I will remain in the past. I want to live in the present, Rohit, and for the future of my son and me."

Rohit stared at her for a long moment, lost in his thoughts. He finally exhaled, shaking his head, "I still don't get it. How can one just … let go of the past like that?"

"Because holding on to the unhappiness hurts more, and tucking it away only makes it come back at a later time," Sneha said.

Rohit fell silent, gazing into nothingness.

"Perhaps … that's the difference between us, Rohit," Sneha said gently. "I've let go of my past."

"And … what do you think I am holding on to?" Rohit focused his eyes on her.

"I think you need to figure that out for yourself," Sneha replied. "You have stopped running in circles, Rohit. Maybe you need to move forward."

Rohit looked at her intensely, "Maybe I do."

The evening light filtering through the window started to fade as they finished their coffees, each deep in their thoughts.

"Sneha," Rohit interrupted hers, his tone hesitant. "I am grateful to you … for so many things. You have made our family whole. *Amma*'s recovery is on track thanks to you, as is my relationship with my parents."

Rohit stopped, seemingly searching for the right words. "You've also given me a lot to think about. I want to ask you a question but hesitate only because I don't want to complicate things for you."

He paused to see if she understood what he was getting at.

Sneha nodded in acknowledgment and looked down at her cup. "Rohit … I haven't even allowed myself space to think beyond my work and Sahil."

Rohit nodded slowly, his eyes warm and understanding. "I understand. You've been through so much and have worked hard to build an incredible life for yourself and Sahil."

She looked up at him, her gaze steady.

"I … I'd like to stay in touch, Sneha. If that's okay with you."

Sneha smiled softly, her eyes glistening. "I'd like that, Rohit."

They stepped out and exchanged goodbyes, dusk settling around them. In that fleeting moment, there was no rush, no pressure—just two people standing at a crossroads, choosing to stay connected despite the paths ahead.

Over the following months, Sneha's and Rohit's lives crossed repeatedly. Their work took them across the country, and by design, they connected in the same city. Their meetings were usually abbreviated—a quick coffee break squeezed between their busy schedules. Other times, they would explore unfamiliar corners of familiar towns, revisiting places they had loved in their youth or simply sitting in companionable silence over shared meals.

Through these encounters, they shared pieces of themselves—their triumphs, their regrets, their quiet hopes for the future. Rohit listened to Sneha's stories with undivided attention, his thoughtful gaze never wavering. Sneha, in turn, found herself opening up in ways she hadn't allowed herself to in years.

What started as a tentative friendship gradually deepened into something steady, warm, and full of quiet understanding. Neither felt the need to rush forward or define what they shared. For Sneha, it was enough to feel seen and valued— something she had never experienced with Kunal.

Sneha received a message from Tripti: "I'm in the Bay Area now, and we have a new home. Come visit us!"

Sneha decided to take Sahil on a trip to California, which would combine a reunion with her old friend and a chance to show her son a new part of the world.

When they met, Tripti greeted her with a tight hug. "You look amazing, Sneha," she said, stepping back to take her in.

"Thank you," Sneha said, smiling. "Life has been … unexpectedly good."

They sat in Tripti's kitchen overlooking the Golden Gate Bridge. Sneha shared her story about her work and growing relationship with Rohit.

"Wait—Rohit?" Tripti said with a sly grin. "Your teenage crush?"

Sneha smiled shyly, cheeks coloring. "The same. But … it's different now."

"Honestly, what's taking you guys so long?" Tripti's eyes twinkled. "I was picking up on romantic vibes between you two in Chennai."

"That," Sneha laughed, shaking her head exaggeratedly, "was all in your head."

"In all seriousness, better late than never, I'd say," Tripti said, her sincere smile widening as she extended her hand across the table to squeeze Sneha's. "You deserve all the happiness in the world, Sneha."

As she gazed at the sun sinking into the horizon, Sneha felt a deep sense of peace.

Although her journey had been painful, it had also been transformative.

She had found her strength, independence, and, perhaps, a chance at love.

*And I'm ready.*

Sneha stood on the balcony of her modest Kolkata apartment, the air humming with the anticipation of *Diwali*. The streets below bustled with vendors setting up their wares—garlands of marigolds, colorful *rangoli* powders, and boxes of firecrackers. Children darted between stalls, their laughter enhancing the festive chatter. The faint aroma of freshly fried *samosas* wafted, blending with the distant hum of devotional songs from a nearby *Mandir*.

Sneha sipped her *chai*, savoring its warmth, and her thoughts drifted to Rohit. Over the past year, their meetings had deepened their bond. It was no longer just friendship—it felt more profound.

When he wasn't traveling for work, Rohit made it a point to visit. He and Sahil had developed a close connection, spending hours building LEGO sets and planning mischief. Watching them together brought Sneha a joy she hadn't known she was missing.

Her phone buzzed as she gazed at the flickering lights in the street below. *"Free for dinner tomorrow? Pick you up at 7."*

Sneha smiled, the anticipation of seeing Rohit lighting up her face. She typed back quickly, "*See you then … and Happy Diwali in advance!*"

The eve of *Diwali* dawned bright and lively. Sneha spent the morning cleaning and decorating her home. Sahil assisted her in arranging *diyas* on the balcony and stringing fairy lights, filling the apartment with a warm glow.

By afternoon, the neighborhood buzzed with celebration. A bouquet of fresh sweets and fried snacks filled the air, and neighbors exchanged festive greetings. Sahil ran off to play with his friends, leaving Sneha with her thoughts.

That evening, Rohit arrived punctually, dressed in a crisp white kurta and a traditional silk vest. His smile was as warm as the lamps lining the street.

"Ready?" he asked, holding out his hand.

Sneha nodded, adjusting her *dupatta*. "Where are we going?"

"You'll see," he replied with a playful glint in his eyes.

They arrived at a riverside restaurant.

The soft glow of lanterns rippled and shimmered on the Hooghly River beside their table. In the distance, crackling bursts of color lit up the city skyline.

As they dined, Rohit leaned back, his gaze pensive.

"You've changed me, Sneha," he said, his voice quiet but clear amidst the festive noise.

"Changed you?" she asked, tilting her head.

"In a good way," he replied, smiling.

Sneha raised her eyebrows, but Rohit did not elaborate.

After dinner, they walked along the riverbank, with the painted sky and city lights reflecting on the water, blending with the soft glow of *diyas* drifting down the current.

Rohit reached for Sneha's hand, his grip warm and steady. They came to a halt and stood facing each other.

"Sneha," Rohit began, his tone soft but resolute, "I've been thinking about us."

Sneha's heart fluttered, but she stayed silent, letting Rohit continue.

"Sneha, this past year, I have come to know you truly—your compassion, your strength, and your quiet grace in the face of everything life throws your way. I've also come to understand something about myself."

Rohit paused to gaze into her eyes, his lips curved into a small smile of certainty. "I love you, Sneha. With my heart and soul. I'd very much like to spend my life with you."

Sneha's breath caught, her chest tightening with emotion as the world seemed to pause.

"I want us to build a future together, Sneha," Rohit continued earnestly. "Not just for Sahil or convenience, but because I can't imagine my life without you. Will you marry me?"

Tears welled up in Sneha's eyes, reflecting the flickering lights around them. "Rohit," she whispered, "I … I never thought I'd find this … this kind of love."

"Me neither," he said gently.

A tear slid down her cheek, and she nodded, her voice steady despite the overwhelming emotion. "I love you, Rohit. The answer is yes."

Rohit pulled her into his arms just as a fresh volley of fireworks brilliantly illuminated the sky, celebrating their love and new beginnings.

# Glossary

**ABCD** (*ey-bee-see-dee*) — Short for "American-Born Confused Desi," a somewhat pejorative reference to **Desi** kids born in the US (or Canada, for that matter).

**Abbe** (*ub-bay*) — Informal greeting, popular on college campuses in India.

**Adda** (*uh-duh*) — A casual hangout spot.

**Agarbatti** (*uh-gur-buh-tee*) — Incense stick.

**Aiyyo** (*eye-yoh*) — A South Indian exclamation expressing dismay, surprise, or concern. Like "uh oh".

**Anna** (*un-nah*) — Way of addressing or referring to an elder brother. [in Tamil]

**Aunty** (*aan-tee*) — Colloquial **Desi** term for a housewife (all ages).

**Aunty-ji** (*aan-tee-jee*) — Respectful version of **Aunty**.

**Avunaa / Avunnu** (*ah-voo-naa, ah-voo-noo*) — "Is that so?" "That is so." [Telugu phrases]

**Baadshaah** (*baahd-shah*) — Emperor.

**Baba** (*baa-baa*) — Father, grandfather, spiritual leader, or a boy child.

**Bachcha** (*buhch-chaa*) — Child.

**Badi** (*buh-dee*) — Elder.

**Bahu** *(buh-hoo)* — Daughter-in-law.

**Baraat** *(buh-raat)* — Wedding procession heralding the groom.

**Basmati** *(baas-muh-tee)* — Aromatic **Desi** rice.

**Beta** (bey-taa) — Son. Also, a term of endearment for a younger male or female.

**Beti** (bey-taa) — Daughter. Also, a term of endearment for a younger female.

**Bhajan** *(bhuh-jun)* — Devotional song.

**Bhangra** *(bhang-raa)* — **Desi** dance.

**Brahmin** *(braa-min)* — Name of a Hindu caste.

**Carnatic** *(kar-naa-tik)* — Classical South Indian music.

**Chachi** *(chaa-chee)* — Aunt.

**Chai** *(chai)* — Tea brewed with milk and spices, often ginger and/or cardamom.

**Chalo** *(chuh-loh)* — "Let's go!"

**Chapati** *(chuh-paa-tee)* — Soft, round, thin flatbread.

**Chennai** *(chen-nai)* — Indian city. Formerly Madras.

**Chhote** *(cho-tay)* —Junior.

**Dal / Daal** *(daal)* — Lentil preparation.

**Desi** *(they-see)* — Pertaining to the Indian subcontinent.

**Didi** *(dee-dee)* — Way of addressing or referring to an elder sister.

**Diwali** *(dih-vaa-lee)* — Hindu festival of lights.

**Diya** *(dee-ya)* — Earthen oil lamp, popular during **Diwali**.

**Dupatta** *(doo-put-tuh)* — Long scarf worn with certain **Desi** outfits.

**FOB** *(eff-oh-bee)* — "Fresh Off the Boat" — a pejorative term for a recent immigrant.

**Garam Masala** *(guh-rum muh-saa-lah)* — Blend of **Desi** spices.

**Haldi** *(hul-dee)* — Turmeric; also a wedding ritual.

**Hyderabadi** *(high-druh-baa-dee)* — From Hyderabad, a city in South India.

**Idli** *(id-lee)* — Steamed rice cakes.

**Iyengar** *(eye-yung-gahr)* — A Tamil **Brahmin** sect.

**Jijaji** *(jee-ja-jee)* — Brother-in-law (sister's husband).

**-ji / Ji** *(jee)* — Honorific suffix, indicating respect.

**Kali** *(kaa-lee)* — Hindu Goddess.

**Kanjeevaram** *(kun-jee-vuh-rum)* — Place in South India famed for its silk **saree**s.

**Kullad** *(kul-ludh)* — Clay cup for serving **chai**.

**Kurta** *(koor-taa)* — Long sleeve, unisex **Desi** shirt.

**Ma** *(maa)* — Mother; also a term of affection.

**Machi** *(muh-chee)* — Slang for friend or buddy in Tamil; literally "brother-in-law."

**Mama / Mami** *(maa-maa / maa-mee)* — Uncle and aunt.

**Mandir** *(mun-deer)* — Hindu temple.

**Marwari** *(maar-waa-ree)* — Business community in India.

**Masala** *(muh-saa-lah)* — Mix of **Desi** spices.

**Mausi** *(mow-see)* — Mother's sister; maternal aunt.

**Naan** *(nawn)* — Oven-baked flatbread.

**Namaste** *(nuh-muh-stay)* — Traditional greeting.

**Navratri** *(nuv-raa-three)* — "Nine Nights", a Hindu festival.

**Nukkad** *(nook-kud)* — A street corner.

**Paagal** *(paa-guhl)* — Crazy person.

**Paan** *(paan)* — Betel leaf chew, usually combined with spices, nuts, and sometimes tobacco.

**Paneer** *(puh-neer)* — Indian cottage cheese.

**Papa** *(paa-paa)* — Father.

**Pooja** *(poo-jah)* — Worship ritual.

**Prasadam** *(pruh-saa-dum)* — Blessed food offered after a **Pooja**.

**Pulao** *(poo-lao)* — Spiced **Desi** rice dish with vegetables or meat.

**Rajma** *(raaj-maa)* — Kidney bean curry.

**Rangoli** *(run-go-lee)* — Colorful floor art made with powdered colors.

**Rasam** *(ruh-sum)* — Spiced South Indian soup made with tamarind stock.

**Rasgulla** *(rus-goo-laa)* — Soft cheese balls soaked in scented sugar syrup.

**Ras Malai** *(rus muh-lye)* — **Rasgullas** in sweetened milk.

**Salwar Kameez** *(sul-waar kuh-meez)* — Traditional outfit: pants (**salwar**) and tunic (**kameez**).

**Saheb** *(saa-heb)* — Formal or respectful address for a man, sometimes used to address a woman.

**Sambar** *(saam-baar)* — Spicy lentil, tamarind, and vegetable stew.

**Samosa** *(suh-moh-saa)* — Pyramid-shaped deep-fried pastry typically stuffed with spicy potatoes.

**Saree / Sari** *(saa-ree)* — Traditional draped garment worn by **Desi** women.

**Shaadi** *(shaa-dee)* — Wedding.

**Shemma Kadi** *(shem-mah kuh-dee)* — "What a pain!" [**Chennai** slang]

**Sherwani** *(sher-vaa-nee)* — Long, formal coat worn by men at weddings.

**Sindoor** *(sin-door)* — Red powder worn in the hair parting by married Hindu women.

**Sitar** *(si-taar)* — Stringed instrument.

**Tadka** *(tuhd-kah)* — Tempering of spices in oil or ghee.

**Thali** *(thaa-lee)* — A plate or meal platter.

**Thanjavur** *(thun-juh-voor)* — A region in South India famous for its musical tradition, temples, bronze sculptures, and silk **sarees**.

**Uncle** *(un-kul)* — Colloquial term for the husband of an **Aunty**.

# Author's Note

*Knots* is my second collection of short stories (after *Bonds*), and it would not have taken its current shape without the able guidance of its editor, Meera Srikant. I love writing, and Meera made the editing process equally—if not more—enjoyable. Thank you, Meera. I learned so much while working with you and am deeply grateful for your role in not only reshaping *Czech, Please,* but also bringing *To Be or Knot* into existence.

My immense gratitude goes to all my beta readers—Aditi, Ananth, Aryan, Chandrasekhar, Dinesh, Manisha, Padma, Rajesh, Satish, and Shalini—for your thoughtful feedback and support.

Special thanks to Tulsi for her beautiful calligraphy and artwork that bring the book title and each chapter title to life. Thanks also to Aditi for her creative contributions throughout the writing, editing, and production processes and to Paat for providing the final professional touches to the book cover.

Finally, thank you, dear reader, for your time and support. Please do connect with me via:

Email: snkashyap@kashyapcreative.com
FB/IG: @s.n.kashyap.writer
Web: snkashyap.com

Warmly,
S. N. Kashyap

# About the Editor

Meera Srikant is a freelance writer, author, editor, and translator. She has published romance novels and loves writing about complex human emotions and relationships. She has also published biographical works based on interviews. Meera Srikant has been a mentor for aspiring authors in workshops conducted by Katha, and blogs regularly (www.meera-lastingimpressions.blogspot.com).

9 781967 629008